Missing and Presumed Dead

Other books by Andy Van Loenen...
Justice for Amy
What in the World is God up To?

Missing and Presumed Dead

Andy Van Loenen

Iroquois Point Publishing
Grand Rapids, Michigan

Published by Iroquois Point Publishing
Grand Rapids, Michigan USA

Printed in the United States of America

ISBN: 978-0-9835759-1-7

Library of Congress Control Number: 2012922832

Cover design by Amanda Ball

The wicked flee when no man pursueth:
but the righteous are bold as a lion.
                                    —Proverbs 28:1

Chapter 1

U.S. Coast Guard Station—Grand Haven, Michigan
Saturday, October 14th. 7:54 a.m.

SEAMAN APPRENTICE, ANGELA CRUZ knocked sharply once and stuck her head in the door of Lieutenant Commander Roger Estes' office. "Sir, they're asking for you over in radio. There's a mayday coming in."

Estes immediately dropped his pen, pushed his chair back from his desk, and stood. "Notify air operations to have a hee-lo standby," he said as he hurried past her, heading with purposeful speed to the Comm-Room.

Even before he entered he could hear the edge of panic in the voice crackling over the radio speaker. "Mayday, mayday, mayday! This is the cabin cruiser, *Marti Celeste*. I think I'm somewhere near the south buoy. I have a strong smell of gas and my engine's acting up! Mayday, mayday! I'm in trouble! Please help me!"

Several of the enlisted personnel were huddled around the radio operator. "You people have jobs to do?" Estes snapped as he approached from behind them. "Yes sir," they said in near unison as they broke away and headed for their desks.

"What's going on here, Mason?" Estes put his right hand on the back of the radio operator's chair as he leaned over, placing his left hand on the desk.

Petty Officer Second Class, Ed Mason kept his intent focused on his work. "Sir, I'm getting a mayday. This is the fifth or sixth time it's come in, and I think the guy's in a panic 'cause he's holding his mike keyed and I can't talk to him."

The panicked message came in again as Estes stood and turned. "Parsons, contact Milwaukee and Calumet Harbor.

See if they're picking this up. Let's try to triangulate a fix on this guy."

"Mayday, mayday, mayday! This is the cabin cruiser, *Marti Celeste*. Please help me! The gasoline smell is getting—"

The *whump* sound of the beginning of an explosion ended the radio transmission.

"*Cruz!*" Estes yelled out into the main office area. "Get that hee-lo in the air! Head them toward the south buoy! See if you can get another one from Milwaukee while you're at it!" He turned back to the radio operator. "Mason, sound general quarters. I'm heading for the boat. We're going out."

Grand Rapids, Michigan
Sunday, October 15th

MARTI FORRESTER ROLLED OVER and looked at the clock in the headboard of the bed she'd shared with her husband, Greg, for five years. It was 1:47 a.m.—seven minutes later than the last time she'd looked. It had been Sunday for almost two hours now. The horrible day had past, but the horrible feeling in the pit of her stomach remained.

Saturday had started out much like any other Saturday. No rush to get up and get going; the warm blankets wrapped around her felt good in the chilly house. It was her favorite time of the year: too cool for the air conditioning and too warm for the furnace. Greg had wanted to make love, but she'd put him off. Now he was gone, and the words of the newscaster played over and over in her mind:

> Tonight's top story: The Coast Guard, this afternoon, is reporting the wreckage of the cabin cruiser, *Marti Celeste* in the chilly waters of Lake Michigan about ten miles northeast of the south buoy. Missing and presumed dead tonight is prominent commercial real estate developer, Gregory Forrester.
>
> The Coast Guard is reporting that the older,

wooden hulled vessel exploded and burned sometime during the early morning hours today. This from a non-specific mayday call that ended abruptly and prompted an air and sea search. Wreckage spotted by a Coast Guard helicopter was later confirmed to be from the *Marti Celeste* when a search vessel picked up a piece of the wreckage that bore the boat's name. We go now to our lakeshore reporter, Keith Grimm, for more details:

"Thanks Rick. Standing with me is Coast Guard Lieutenant Commander, Roger Estes. Commander Estes, have you found anything else or any sign of Gregory Forrester?"

"No, not much, I'm afraid. We've picked up five life belts, and two life jackets floating in the vicinity. That number leads us to speculate that perhaps Mr. Forrester was not wearing a life preserver. Two Coast Guard helicopters have grid searched the immediate area from the air, but so far have not spotted any sign of Mr. Forrester."

"What are the chances he might have survived the explosion?"

"I would say, slim. The boat was completely destroyed. However, assuming he was blown clear, the water temperature at the south buoy is about 57 degrees, Fahrenheit. The chances for survival beyond about three hours in that kind of cold, and without a life preserver are virtually nil."

"How long do you plan to continue searching?"

"We'll continue searching the surface until dark, and if we don't find anything, we'll resume again tomorrow. That's all I can say for now. Unfortunately, the lake is well over 500-feet deep in the search area, making it impossible to do much more than a surface search."

"Thank you Commander. That's all for now from the lakeshore, Rick. This is Keith Grimm, reporting live from the Grand Haven Coast Guard Station. Back to you."

Thanks, Keith. Gregory Forrester's wife, Martha,

spoke briefly with reporters today and confirmed that her husband had taken the boat out. However, now she is said to be in seclusion and unavailable for comment. We'll have more on this developing story as more facts become known.

In other news tonight, the Vice President, on the campaign trail in Florida, announced today that, if elected...

She got up and went into the kitchen for a glass of water, stepping lightly so as not to awaken Jenny. Dear Jenny. She'd dropped what she was doing and immediately rushed to her side, bringing Liz with her, practically before the phone was cold. They'd spent the entire day with her on the lakeshore waiting for news that never came. Now she was asleep in the next room and Liz down the hall, while their husbands slept alone at home. They were true friends, true sisters—both of them.

Marti took her water and walked out onto the three-season porch. She set it down on the glass-topped table and pulled a blanket around herself before sitting on the white wicker sofa. She brought her feet up onto the flower print cushions and adjusted the blanket to cover them as she leaned against the wicker side and stared into the inky sky. She was dead tired, but would not be sleeping this night.

She closed her eyes to thoughts of Greg; sorry for what happened, sorry she had put off his advances yesterday, but unable to cry.

Chapter 2

Sunday, October 30—Five Years Later

Gunshots! There goes the perp! Mitch is down! I've got to get to him! Run!
"No! Harry, get down! There's somebody behind—"
Muzzle flash! Ohhhh! More gunshots! Falling...
"Harry!...Harry! Hang in there, man! Help is on the way!"
Where am I? Who is that laying on the ground?
"Mulvaney, help me get his jacket off!"
It's meee!
"Give me your handkerchief...I've got to stop this bleeding."
Linda? Linda, don't go!
"It's not time yet, Harry. You have to go back."

HARRY BRANNAN WOKE UP in a cold sweat; another nightmare, and his right shoulder hurt like a bad toothache. He looked at the clock on the nightstand next to his bed. 5:37 a.m. *Close enough,* he thought, as he got up to take more painkillers. He didn't know why they called them painkillers. They didn't really kill the pain and they made his stomach hurt if he didn't eat something with them.

He limped into the kitchen, got a glass of water, and ate four small soda cracker squares. Then he went into the bathroom and took the pills. They did help—some. And anything was better than nothing. If only they'd keep the nightmare away he'd buy stock in the company.

What to do? There was no sense in going back to bed. The adrenaline rush from the dream pretty much guaranteed he'd not be getting any more sleep for a while. He pulled open his top dresser drawer. He could get dressed and go see if the Sunday paper was in the press tube, out at the curb. He looked at his watch. *It would be a miracle,* he thought, *if that stupid girl who delivers it could get off her cell phone long enough to get it here much before eight.* He'd never seen anything like it. How could you drive a truck, talk on a cell phone, and deliver papers, all at the same time? Who was there to talk to at that time of the morning on a Sunday?

Old Mr. Humboldt had always had the paper there before six a.m. He was a good old guy; had one of those old Post Office Jeeps, with right-hand drive, that he used to deliver newspapers. Actually, it was his only vehicle. The thing was rusty as all get out, but it always started, no matter how cold it got; and old Mister Humboldt had never failed to have that paper in the tube by six a.m. on Sunday mornings. Sometimes, if the pain or the nightmare had awakened him early, Harry would see him coming down the road from his window and go out in time to talk with him for a few minutes.

He worried about the old guy and went over to Radio Shack one day and bought him an amber strobe light for the roof of the Jeep. Best 25 bucks he'd ever spent. He could have sworn he'd seen tears in the old man's eyes when he gave it to him early one Sunday morning—and again when he'd helped him install it in the driveway of the little two-bedroom house where he lived alone, out in Plainfield Township.

Then one day the paper didn't come. It was a Monday, and the paper was always in the tube by 3:30 on weekdays. Finally, at five p.m. Harry had driven out and found the Jeep, still parked in the gravel driveway. He knocked on the back door. When nobody answered he tried the knob, and finding the door unlocked, walked in.

A heart attack had claimed the life of 74-year-old John Humboldt. Harry found him laying dead on the kitchen floor, a broken coffee mug lying next to him, its contents spilled out in a puddle that had collected in front of the refrigerator; the Sunday paper lying in a disheveled heap nearby. For the first time in his recent memory, Harry cried.

HIS FOREARMS WERE RESTING on the top edge of the open dresser drawer when his thoughts returned to the current day. His service pistol was in his hand. He didn't realize he'd picked it up. He pulled it out of its belt-clip holster and hefted it in his right hand. A Glock 27, one of the finest semi-automatics made. The so-called subcompact pistol fit his hand perfectly. At just under half an inch in diameter, the .40 caliber bore was big for a small gun. Unlike the .38 police special he'd carried in the early days, the 155-grain Ranger hollow-points in this thing had considerable stopping power—although he'd never fired it at another human being. He hadn't even fired it at a target in over a year.

He ejected the clip. Eleven shots—twelve if you kept one in the chamber. He turned the clip over in his hand a few times and then reinserted it into the handle of the gun. He could feel oil residue from the clip on his hand as he pulled back the hammer. *It would be so easy,* he thought. *Just press the thing up against my temple and pull the trigger— one big boom, and no more pain, no more nightmares.*

He lingered there for a moment. Old John lay dead in his kitchen for a day and a half before he'd found him. He may have been the old guy's only living friend—at least he was the only person aside from a brother and his wife who attended the funeral.

Harry wondered how long it would be until somebody found him. After all, if the paper hadn't been late he never would have driven over to old John's house. *And,* he thought, *nobody is depending on me for anything these days.* He was just a 51-year-old former cop with a shot-up shoulder and titanium alloy knee. *I haven't had a personal phone call in, what, a month? Who knows how long I'd lay there?* On the other hand, why should he care? After all, when you're dead it just doesn't matter any more.

But it did matter—at least to him. He'd walked into crime scenes before where the victim was in an advanced state of decomposition. He'd had to put the Vicks Vapo-Rub under his nose—not that anything could mask that awful smell. He didn't want to be found in that condition. Besides, it's not like he had no friends at all.

Mitch is a friend—among all the people I know maybe my only real friend. He'd groomed that southern boy, preparing him to one day take over his job. It's just that he'd never thought the day would come so soon. Mitch would care. And so would his pretty wife, Liz—the lady with the hugs. The thought of Mitch finding him in that condition made him shudder. The thought of disappointing him made him ease the hammer back down, holster the gun, and put it back in the top dresser drawer. *It's not that bad...yet.*

Harry dressed, walked out to the kitchen, and washed the oil off his hands at the sink. Then he got a gel ice pack out of the freezer above the refrigerator. He held it against his shoulder as he walked out to the living room of his small apartment and lay down on his back on the sofa, the ice pack trapped between his shoulder and the seat back. He closed his eyes. The cold felt good. In concert with the pain killers it would relieve the inflammation in his shoulder.

He awoke to the phone ringing and quickly sat up, making his head swim a little. He picked up the cordless phone from the coffee table and pressed the talk button. "Hello," he said in a sleepy voice. He looked at the clock in the DVD player. It was 8:27 a.m.

"Harry? It's Mitch—Mitch Ferguson. Did I wake you up?"

He rubbed his face with his left hand. "Umm, that's okay. It was time for me to get up anyway. What can I do for you?"

"Well, it's more what I can do for you. Remember we talked a few months ago about you maybe going out on your own. Well, I have something you might be interested in."

"Yeah, what's that?"

"It's a woman, a friend of Liz's—"

"You're not trying to set me up, are you," he interrupted.

"No, nothing like that. Her husband died five years ago—killed in a boat explosion out on Lake Michigan. They never found his body. Well, somebody thinks they saw him up north last week."

"Yeah, right! You know how common that is. And it never pans out."

"I know. And that's why the brass won't let me investigate it."

"I'm surprised you even asked."

"Yeah, well, ordinarily I wouldn't have, but she's a good friend of Liz's, and she's had a hard way to go these past five years. She pretty much lost everything after her husband died, and not having a body to bury, she's never had any closure."

"Look Mitch, I'm not even licensed. You know that. There's no way I could do it—at least I couldn't do it and charge for it."

"Well, she couldn't afford to pay you anyway—at least not much.

"You want me to go traipsing all over...wherever it is, for free?"

"Look, I just thought it would be a chance for you to see if you were interested in going out on your own. Clay, Clay Ramsey, you remember him. He and I have agreed that we'll cover all your expenses, whatever they might be."

"You must really like this woman."

"Yeah, she's a good friend. Look, I'd do it myself if I could, and I'll give you whatever help I can, unofficially of course."

"Yeah, well, I'll think about it."

"Why don't you come over for lunch today and talk to her? I didn't make any promises on your behalf. I only told her that I'd run it by you, that you're not a licensed investigator, and whether you did anything or not is strictly up to you. What harm will it do to talk with her? Besides, it's a free lunch."

"Yeah, what are we having?"

"It's just hamburgers on the grill, but it's going to be a nice day. We'll eat out on the deck. Who knows how many more opportunities we'll have to eat outside this year?"

Harry gave a heavy sigh. "Yeah, okay. What time do you want me?"

"Well, we'll eat between 1:30 and two, but why don't you come over at one so we can spend some time catching up. What's it been, a month or two?"

"Yeah, something like that. Okay, I'll be there. See you about one."

Harry rang off, put on his shoes, and dropped the ice pack back in the freezer, as he went out to get the Sunday paper. Then, throwing the paper in the car, he set out for André's Grill to enjoy their big sausage and cheese omelet; a cholesterol laden extravagance he allowed himself once a week while he sat and read the Sunday paper. It was also nice just to be around people, to hear the chatter—even if it meant putting up with Nancy-nice-waitress, who always called him, "honey."

Chapter 3

IT WAS 12:55 P.M. WHEN LIZ opened the front door and greeted Harry with a hug. "Harry! It's so good to see you. We don't see near enough of you anymore." She put her hands on his shoulders and pushed him back a little while she scanned him with her eyes. "You're looking good. Looks like you've taken off a few pounds."

"Yeah, I guess," he said as she took his hand. "Once I healed from the surgeries I've been able to be more active."

She led him toward the back of the house. "Come on through. Mitch is out on the deck getting the charcoal going." She led him first into the kitchen, where two other women were busy preparing food. "Harry, this is Jo Ramsey and Marti Forrester. Ladies, this is Harry Brannan, Mitch's old boss."

Harry shook their hands and exchanged pleasantries with them. Both women, like Liz, were in their mid-forties. Dark-haired, Jo was obviously Clay Ramsey's wife. That meant the auburn-haired, Marti Forrester was the woman with whom he was to meet.

He took her in with his eyes. She was about 5-foot-4 with a good figure and a pretty face. Very feminine.

An uncomfortable silence was beginning to develop as he turned to Liz. "Where did you say Mitch is?"

"Out back on the deck. Clay's out there with him. They're waiting for you."

"Well, uh...I guess I'd better get out there, then," he said, as he turned and walked off. He thought he heard them giggling as he stepped out through the sliding glass door, and wondered if it had anything to do with him. He chastised himself for being paranoid.

At lunch he was given one of the "seats of honor" at the end of the rectangular table. Mitch was seated at the other end with Liz on his left and Marti next to her. Jo sat on Mitch's right with Clay next to her. That put Marti on Harry's right.

An outsider, looking on, might have imagined a scene of domestic bliss: three couples enjoying lunch together on a Sunday afternoon. But Harry was uncomfortable, feeling he'd been "paired" with Marti as they all held hands while Mitch prayed for the meal. He wondered if she felt the same. *Maybe they arranged the seating this way so she and I can talk.* On the other hand, Mitch, of all people, knew that you can't carry out an effective interview as part of the general conversation around a picnic table.

After lunch, they all took their plates and other items back into the kitchen. Marti stayed and helped Liz and Jo with the clean-up. When she eventually returned, she took a seat in a padded chaise lounge on the deck.

Harry pulled up a chair and turned it so he was sitting at her left hand, facing her at an angle. He bent down, putting his elbows on his knees and folding his hands. "So, Mitch tells me you think you might need the services of a detective. Can you tell me a little bit about why?"

Marti scootched around in her chair a little so she could face him better. "Yeah, I guess. My husband died, or at least I thought he did (they never found his body), in a boat explosion a little over five years ago. Well, one of the sales guys where I work thought he saw him up in the U.P. a couple of weeks ago."

"Ms. Forrester—"

"Please call me Marti," she interrupted.

"Marti," he continued. "I have to tell you that this kind of sighting is a fairly common occurrence. But in thirty years of police work, I don't know that I've ever heard of it panning out. Truth is, unless the person is wanted for a serious crime, police agencies won't touch something like this. The problem is, even if it turns out to be true, you can't force an adult to come back against his will. I'm telling you this up front because you need to know that, even if it turns out to be him, you'll most likely be wasting your money."

"Yeah, I know. That's what Mitch told me, too. Thing is, Gary was so sure it was Greg. And I just haven't had a moment's peace since then."

"Gary? Gary who?"

"Gary Hammond, one of our sales guys. See, Greg was a partner in a commercial real estate company, and Gary sold them their health coverage, so he knew him."

"Greg was your husband?"

"Yes, Gregory Baines Forrester."

"Where do you work?"

"I'm an administrative assistant in the sales department at Choice Care HMO, here in Grand Rapids. We've recently been licensed to provide coverage in the Upper Peninsula. Anyway, Gary Hammond was up there, calling on the Waishkey Bay Casino, when he saw, or thought he saw Greg. He went over and talked to him, but the man denied he was Greg. Said his name was Alan something. I don't remember. I have it written down at home."

"Okay, Marti, the fact that Gary Hammond had more than a passing acquaintance with Greg adds some weight to the idea that it might indeed be him. If you're sure you want to go ahead with this, I'd be willing to check into it for you. But you need to understand up front that I'm not a licensed investigator. I guess Mitch told you that."

"Yes, he did. And I do want to go ahead with this—assuming I could afford whatever you'd charge me."

"Not being licensed, I couldn't charge you. But I would need to have my expenses covered. Maybe we can meet at a restaurant or something, and sit down and talk about this at length. I'm going to need as much background information as you can give me to help me get my head around what might be going on here. I'm also going to need to talk to this Gary Hammond fellow. Can you arrange that?"

"I think so, but it would have to be after working hours. I'd be uncomfortable about him taking off on company time for my personal business"

Ah, a woman with integrity. "Sure, that would be okay. Something early in the week?"

"I'll see what I can do. And if you don't mind, how about we have dinner at my house, seeing as I'm covering expenses; say...Monday or Tuesday? I have prayer meeting on Wednesday night, and I'd like to get going on this as soon as we can."

"Sure, either will be fine."

"Okay, how about Monday? I'll try to set up a time with Gary for you on Tuesday."

"Sounds like a plan. What time do you want me?"

"Would six be okay? We'll probably eat around 6:30."

"Six it is. Where do you live?"

Chapter 4

HARRY PULLED INTO MARTI'S driveway at 5:45 on Monday afternoon. He shut off the engine and looked around. Her house was small by today's standards—maybe 24 by 32 feet. The lot, also small, had a split-rail fence around its perimeter and a mature tree, sans most of its leaves, in the front yard. The concrete driveway, to the left of the house, led to a detached one-stall garage that was tucked partially into the back yard.

He got out of his car, walked to the side door and knocked.

"Harry. Hi, come on in. Thank you for coming over." Marti pulled open the inside door for him and stepped back, allowing him to enter. She was dressed modestly, in jeans and a dusty pink pullover of some sort with a matching corduroy shirt, which she wore open and untucked, over it.

"Thank you for inviting me. It smells good in here."

"We're having meatloaf and baked potatoes. Liz told me you're a big fan of her meatloaf and I have her recipe. It's nothing fancy. I hope you don't mind."

"Not at all. I'm a meatloaf kind of guy so it sounds great to me. Is there anything I can do to help you?"

"No, we're just waiting on things to finish up. Why don't you sit down?" She pointed in the direction of the living room. "The paper's on the coffee table, if you're interested."

Having already read the evening paper, Harry sat politely in an easy chair while Marti busied herself with the final preparations for the meal.

Her house was neat. That impressed him. The small kitchen morphed into a dining area which morphed into the living room in which he sat.

He watched her while she worked and found himself intrigued. Did she have children? Why had she not remarried? Was she seeing anyone?

Where did that come from? Objectivity is what was called for here; and objective is what I will be.

When they sat down to eat, Marti bowed her head and prayed silently. Raising her head, she spoke. "I'm assuming you checked me out today; and I guess the fact that you're here means you're still interested in helping me."

Harry was surprised at her forthrightness and he smiled. "Well, I didn't run you through NCIC or anything like that, but I did call Mitch and ask him about you. He thinks you're a pretty shady character, and told me to be careful around you. But, I figured, what the heck, I've got nothing better to do..."

Her unanticipated smile was big, and she put her hand in front of her mouth as a blush rose in her cheeks. "I guess I deserved that."

"He said you're a nice lady, very level-headed, not given to flights of fancy, and that I needn't have any misgivings about taking your case. Does it bother you that I asked? By the way, this meatloaf is delicious."

"Thank you. No, it doesn't bother me. I still want you to help me...if you're willing."

"Yes, I am. Why don't we clear these dishes away and get down to business?"

He helped her clear the table, and she came back with biscotti and mugs of coffee as they resumed their previous places.

Marti sipped her coffee as Harry took a spiral notebook out of his inside jacket pocket. She set her cup down. "So, where would you like me to begin?"

"Well, Mitch said that Greg turned out to be not a very nice guy. So I suppose it would be helpful to know how you managed to get involved with him in the first place."

"Greg worked for my uncle—my father's brother, Ray Stafford, with whom I was very close. See, my father died in Viet Nam when I was five-years-old. And my mother...resented me, I guess. She took off the day after I graduated from high school and I've not seen her since.

"As you might imagine, I was in pretty tough financial straits. But I was a wiz at typing and shorthand, and with Uncle Ray's help, I managed to land a job as a secretary at a commercial real estate company he did business with, here in town. That's what he did, commercial real estate." She got up, refilled Harry's coffee mug and returned the carafe to the coffee maker.

"Uncle Ray died...let's see...eleven years ago," she said as she sat back down. "He left me half a million dollars and his old cabin cruiser, the *Marti Celeste,* which he'd named after me. Aunt Helen had been dead for a couple of years by then, but he had two kids of his own, my cousins, Jeanie and Ken, so I was really surprised.

"Greg brought the boat up, and he just...stayed around. Well, actually, he sought me out and, I have to admit, he was...charming. He was three years younger than me. I was 35 and he was 32, but it didn't seem to matter. He took me out to dinner, made excuses to see me, bought me flowers and little gifts, took me places—things like that.

"I had never, in my life, gotten flowers from a man before. To tell you the truth, he was only the second man I had ever gone out with. But he was a perfect gentleman; looked out for my needs, helped my daughter, Camille, get setup in nursing school, told me he loved me, but never once pressured or even asked me to sleep with him. So, a year later, when he asked me to marry him, I said 'yes.'"

"Who is Camille? Were you married before?"

Marti shook her head.

"Sorry. None of my business," Harry said. "So you got married."

"Yes. We were married in the fall. And things went really well, at first. But by the next spring he seemed to have lost interest in me. To be fair, he was trying to set himself up in the commercial real estate business here and it took a lot of his time. But I thought it was something *we* were doing rather than just him; after all, it was *my* inheritance that was financing everything.

"Anyway, he wasn't having much luck and I was still working at my job at Bryson Commercial Properties when I met Clay and Jenny Ramsey. They had just gone into the medical equipment business and were looking to lease building space. Did you know Jenny?"

"I met her once or twice, but I really didn't know her."

"Well, we found them a building and that made Greg angry. He thought I should have hijacked them away from Bryson and sent them to him. But I couldn't do that. Our business wasn't off the ground, and we were in no position to do something like that yet. Besides, I didn't feel right about doing that kind of thing. So I ended up quitting, after eighteen years, and going to work for Choice Care."

"What happened?"

"Greg spent a lot of money, but he never did get the business off the ground. Instead he bought in with a guy he knew from college, Scott Jacoby, and they formed Jacofor Properties."

"I think I've heard the name."

"Yeah, you might have. Anyway, things went pretty well, or so I thought. Scott was already established, so we didn't have that long lean period while waiting for the business to become profitable. Good thing, too, because he pretty much used up my inheritance. Although we did have enough left for a good down payment on a house, plus what I had set aside to complete Cam's education. But things were not going well. I hadn't been at Choice Care very long and I didn't know very many people there and my job wasn't challenging and I was just miserable. That's when I got a call from Jenny Ramsey. She'd found out where I was from George Bryson and called me from the lobby of the building one day. She'd come to take me out to lunch."

"What did she want?"

"Just to be friends. God sent her to me—I am absolutely convinced of it. He knew I needed a friend, and with his usual generosity, he gave me two of them: Jenny and Liz. We three became best friends—sisters really, in more ways than one. You see, it was through them that I came to the Lord. But, if anything, that made things worse between Greg and me. He didn't want anything to do with God, or Church, or praying together, or anything of the sort.

"I, uh...didn't have a lot of experience with men. I guess you could say I was naïve. I needed to love somebody and be loved in return. I loved Cam and she loved me back. But I also needed to love a man and have him love me back. I loved Greg and I married him because I loved him. And I continued to try to love him, right up until the end. But, hindsight being what it is, I can see now that he never really loved me. That's why he ignored me most of the time. I mean, he wasn't even particularly interested in sex. That should have been a giveaway, I guess, but I didn't see it at the time."

"So you think he married you for the money?"

"I'm sure of it, because by the time of the accident, it was all gone. Even then, though, I wouldn't have thought much of it except that he had borrowed heavily: snowmobiles, an SUV, unsecured signature loans; he even borrowed fifty thousand dollars from Scott. I ended up having to sell the house and everything else, just to pay everybody back. Then there were the women. I had a couple of twenty-somethings show up at the door, at different times, thinking they should be entitled to a piece of his estate." She gave a mordant laugh. "As if there were one. The nerve of those women! I invited them to help pay his debts, but they, *surprise,* weren't interested. I guess I know now why he wasn't interested in sex."

"He sounds like a real sterling fellow."

She gave a mirthless chuckle. "The reason I told you this whole, big, long story is to say that I have, admittedly, been naïve—too willing to trust. But, I'm not naïve anymore! And if Greg really is alive, I want him found and I want him to answer for what he did. And I want a divorce from that adulterer, and I want to be free of him, forever!"

"Well, that's why I'm here. May I ask you some questions?"

"Yes, of course."

"You said that Greg worked for your uncle down in Chicago. Do you know if he was from Chicago?"

"No, he was from Elgin—Elgin, Illinois. Or so he said."

"Okay. This man that Gary saw, Alan. You were going to look up his last name?"

"Yes, I did. It's Coombs, C-o-o-m-b-s."

Harry wrote the name in his book "Good. Now let's move on to the accident. Did you know he was taking the boat out that day?"

"Yes. It was late in the year, October 14th. He said it had a full tank of gas and that he was going to run most of the gas out of it because he had an appointment to take it in for storage."

"Okay. *When* did he tell you?"

"I'm not sure—a few days—maybe as much as a week before. Is that important?"

"It could be. If he really is alive, it probably means he was planning it all along. What time of the day did he go out?"

"I don't know. It was early, still dark when he left home. I went back to sleep."

"Did he ask you to go with him?"

"No, but then, he never asked me anyway. I used to like to go out in the summer with Uncle Ray and Aunt Helen, but it never was much fun with Greg. He was too careless and it frightened me."

"Did the Coast Guard get involved with the search?"

"Yes. They found the wreckage out by the south buoy in Lake Michigan."

"Did they put forth any theories as to the cause?"

"They thought it was a gas leak—that the fumes built up and exploded. The boat was totally destroyed; they only recovered pieces of it. Plus, they had a mayday call from Greg that he smelled gasoline, and they actually heard what they thought sounded like the beginning of the explosion on the tape of the call."

"Do you know if there was a life raft or anything like that on board?"

"There were life jackets and life belts, but no raft that I know of. There was a little rowboat that came with it that Uncle Ray used to tow behind it on a rope. But Greg never used it and it was still in the marina after the accident."

"Okay, do you know the name of the marina where the boat was kept?"

"Not off the top of my head. Someplace in Holland. I could dig back through some old billing statements or canceled checks and find it for you."

"That would be fine. Do you know if Greg was ever bonded or fingerprinted for any reason, and by whom?"

"I don't know. Scott might know, you could ask him. Why would that matter now?"

"Well, if I can get a set of prints, I'll have a basis for comparison when I find this guy."

"Do you think he's just going to give you his fingerprints?"

"Well, there's more than one way to get fingerprints. On the other hand, if the guy is not Greg, he may just be willing to offer a sample—you never know."

"I suppose."

"If you can remember, can you tell me what was going through your mind at the time? I mean, I'm assuming you had a waiting period while the search was going on, and I'm wondering if there were any little clues that he might have inadvertently dropped that led you to believe at the time that he might have faked the whole thing."

She closed her eyes and thought for several minutes before she spoke again. "No. Nothing comes to mind. But then that was the worst week of my life. I was in pretty bad shape, and Jenny and Liz were staying with me over that weekend. But on Monday, Jenny had to go to work, so she left my house early in the morning to go home to Clay. On her way home she was hit by some guy who had been up drinking all night and was killed."

"Oh, I remember that. Clay was just devastated. Mitch and I had to keep him back from killing the guy with his bare hands."

"I...we...all were...dev..." She began to cry.

Marti stood and began to rush off, but Harry quickly stood and caught her in his arms. She struggled briefly, but then allowed him to hold her. "I'm sorry," she choked out.

"Shhh, don't be sorry." He patted her back. "You loved your friend. I can only imagine how much it must have hurt you, and how much it hurt you now to relive it."

She clung to him for several minutes while she cried it out. When she began to regain her composure, Harry let her go, pulled a couple of tissues from the box on the table and gave them to her.

"Thank you," she said as she dried her eyes. Then she blew her nose.

"You okay?" he said gently.

"Yes. I'm sorry. I didn't know I had any tears left."

"It's okay." He laid his hand on her shoulder as she stood there. "Maybe you could see if you can find the name of that marina."

She nodded her head. "Okay," she said, and stuck the wadded up tissues in her pocket as she began to walk toward the hallway.

He called after her. "And your most recent picture of Greg, too, if you have one."

Harry sat back down at the table and reviewed the notes he had taken while Marti searched for the requested items. When she returned she resumed her seat at the table.

She pushed a picture of two men standing together in his direction. "The name of the marina is Schneider's, and this is a picture of Greg and Scott. Greg is the one on the left."

He wrote down the name of the marina and looked at the picture. It provided a fairly decent head shot of Greg. "When was this taken?"

"A few months before the accident. I don't remember the exact date, but it was just before Scott's wife left him.

Harry's eyebrows went up. "Any chance the two of them may have run off together?"

"I doubt it. She was gone a good three, maybe four months before the accident. Plus, I seriously doubt she would have been Greg's type. She was kind of a shrew, and he just could not abide that in a woman."

"No, given what you've told me about him, I'd guess not."

Marti got up and got her purse. Then returning to the table, she removed a card from it and handed it to Harry. "This is Gary Hammond's card. I wrote his home address on the back. He can see you there at seven p.m. tomorrow, or you can call him directly and setup another time."

"Thanks. Is there anything else you can think of that you think I should know?"

She thought for a moment and shook her head. "No, nothing that I can think of at the moment."

Harry wrote on a blank page of his spiral book, tore it out and handed it to her. "I'm sorry I don't have a card or anything to give you, but here are my phone numbers. If you think of anything else, or if you just want to talk about this, give me a call." He stood and pushed his chair back under the table. She did the same.

He put his spiral book in his inside jacket pocket and then picked the picture off the table. "I'll make a copy of this and return it to you unharmed."

"Would it sound callous of me if I said I didn't want it back?"

"No, I understand."

They walked to the door and her face took on a seriousness he had not previously seen. "If Greg's alive, I want you to get him. He is as responsible for Jenny's death as if he'd been driving the car that killed her."

Harry opened the inside door and she extended her hand. He took it, but instead of shaking hands with her, he stepped forward and laid his left hand on her shoulder. He spoke gently to her. "I'm so sorry to have made you relive all that unpleasantness. Would you like me to call Liz for you? Knowing her, I'm sure she'd be happy come over and keep you company."

Marti shook her head. "You're very kind, but I'll be all right."

"Okay then," he said, releasing her hand, "I'll be in touch."

Chapter 5

IT WAS JUST AFTER EIGHT P.M. when Harry arrived home. The first thing he did was place a call to the Ferguson's. Liz answered.

"Liz? Harry Brannan."

"Oh, hi, Harry. Hold on, I'll get Mitch for you."

"No, it's you I want to talk to."

"Oh, okay. How'd things go at Marti's tonight?"

"That's why I called. I'm afraid I made her relive some pretty painful memories. I made her cry. I felt bad about it and asked her if I could call you for her, but she said she'd be all right. Even so—"

"Yeah," Liz interrupted. "I'll bet it was about Jenny Ramsey. She's always felt responsible for her death, and she was just beside herself with grief over it. She's never been able to talk about it without breaking down."

"I figured it was something like that. Listen, could you give her a call, or if it's not too late or too much trouble, maybe even stop over? I think she could use a friend right about now."

"Why Harry...!" She hesitated, but then continued. "Sure, I can hop in the car and be there in a few minutes."

"Thanks. Listen, do me a favor, will you, and don't tell her I called you. Maybe you could just happen to drop in?"

"Why Harry Brannan, you old softie."

"Yeah, well, don't let it get out, okay?"

"My lips are sealed."

Harry hung up the phone, walked into the little bedroom he used as an office, and turned on his computer. When the machine finished booting, he scanned in the photo Marti had given him and opened it in his image editing program. He cropped the picture to remove Scott, and saved it under a different file name before printing four 3 by 5 copies of it on a single sheet of paper. He cut the pictures out and left them on the dining room table to dry overnight.

THE NEXT DAY, HARRY got up early and drove out to the Coast Guard station in Grand Haven. He arrived just after eight a.m. and spoke to the petty officer behind the desk.

"Hi. I'm researching a boat explosion that took place in Lake Michigan five years ago." He opened his spiral book. "The boat was a cabin cruiser, the *Marti Celeste,* and the date was—"

"Just a minute sir," the woman interrupted, holding up her hand. "I need to have my commanding officer speak with you about that."

The woman disappeared into an office and came out a few seconds later behind a full commander. He walked up and extended his hand. "Roger Estes. And you are?"

Harry shook the man's hand. "Harry Brannan. I'm trying to get some information about any investigation the Coast Guard might have undertaken into a boat explosion and sinking that took place about five years ago." He released the man's hand. "It was a cabin cruiser—the *Marti Celeste.*"

"Oh yeah, I remember that. Just what is your interest in this?"

"I'm a detective, and I've been retained by the woman who owned the boat. Her husband was apparently killed in the explosion, but the body was never found. Somebody thinks they saw him up north recently."

"*Really?* Wow! We did an air and sea search, but never did find a body out there. We all just assumed he died in the explosion. I mean, that thing was blown to smithereens. All we found were pieces.

"Did you run any tests on the debris to check for the presence of an explosive or accelerant?"

"No. As I recall, we got a mayday call from him reporting a strong smell of gasoline." He scrunched his eyes shut for a moment. "In fact, as I recall, we heard the explosion while he was still on the radio." He scrunched his eyes again. "Yeah, I'm sure we did...look, uh...far be it from me to tell you your business, but there was no way anybody could have lived through that blast."

That was a bust, Harry thought as he left the Coast Guard station and set out for Holland. And, given that the boating season had already been over for a few weeks, he didn't expect to do much better at the marina.

Once he was underway, he opened his cell phone and called Mitch's office number.

"Lieutenant Ferguson."

"Hey, it's Harry."

"Hey, yourself. What's up? Liz told me you called last night."

"Yeah, I managed to reduce Marti to tears with my questions, and I thought maybe Liz could cheer her up a little." He sighed. "You know, I think if I live long enough, I'll have the entire female population of Kent County convinced I'm an insensitive lout. They'll form a society against me, and Lisa will be its president, and they'll hang me in effigy every Mother's Day at high noon."

"She's not worth it, Harry."

"Yeah, I guess," he said flatly. "Listen, I'd like to round-up a set of prints on Greg Forrester. He's from Elgin, Illinois, but he also lived in Chicago before he came up here. I'm not aware that he committed any crimes, so I don't know if there's a rap-sheet on him, but I was hoping you could see if there's anything out there. I'd like to have some prints to compare if I find this guy up in the U.P."

"Yeah, I'll see what I can do. And, by the way, Liz doesn't think you're insensitive. You really impressed her last night."

Yeah, well, don't let it get out. I wouldn't want to lose my standing. Catch you later."

"Yeah, see ya."

Schneider's Marina was set in a natural cove about midway down the southern shore of Lake Macatawa, a large inland lake with a channel accessing Lake Michigan. Harry turned right off South Shore Drive and parked next to the only other car in the parking lot.

The door to the office was locked, but hearing the noise of machinery running, he walked toward a building nearer the shore. As he passed the corner of the office he saw a large movable crane transporting a boat to a prepared berthing place to the west of the building. He caught the operator's attention and waited for him the set the boat down and climb out of the machine before he approached and introduced himself.

"Herm Dykstra. What can I do for ya?"

Harry released the man's hand. "I'm researching a boating accident that occurred about five years ago out in Lake Michigan. It was a cabin cruiser, the *Marti Celeste,* and it was—"

"Oh yeah, I remember that boat," he interrupted. "Old wood Chris-Craft, about 30, 32 feet long; inboard—beautiful thing. Guy kept it there, slip fourteen." He pointed in the direction of the slips.

Harry removed one of pictures he'd made of Greg Forrester from his inside jacket pocket and handed it to the man. "Is this the guy?"

Herm studied the photo for a moment before handing it back. "Yep, that's him. Been a while, but that's him, I'm sure of it."

"Did you know him well?"

"No, not really—no more than to say, 'hello.' And to be honest, I didn't say that too often. I didn't like the guy."

Harry's eyebrows went up. "Really? How come?"

"Well, he had a wife—pretty thing, too. She'd come out here with him once in a while. Most of the time, though, he'd come out here with some young floozy or other, wearing a bikini about the size of a postage stamp, and they'd spend all day out there somewhere on that boat, doin' heaven knows what." He gestured with his arm toward Lake Michigan. "I tell you what: I don't hold with that kind of folderol. Been married to one woman for forty and two years, never once even thought about doing that kind of thing. Just ain't right. Him a married man and all. Ask me, he got what was comin' to 'em."

"Did you see him go out on the day of the accident?"

"No, I didn't. As I recall it was early, real early, when he went out—still dark. But that was just what I heard. I wasn't here, myself."

"Do you have a night security guard or something?"

"No, it was one of the other boaters saw him. Umm, think his name was, uh...Kevin...Kevin somebody or other. Don't remember his last name. He's not with us anymore,"

"Do you remember any of the details?"

"Yeah, sure. Seems he was on the outs with his wife and livin' on his boat. We don't allow that 'cause our insurance don't cover folks livin' on their boats here in the marina. He ended up gettin' a divorce I guess, and he must a sold the boat 'cause I ain't seen it around in...oh, number a years now."

"No, I mean about the *Marti Celeste*."

"Yeah, uh...I was gettin' to that. Uh...Kevin's boat was in thirteen, so they shared a walkway in between the two slips. Apparently this guy; it was Greg or somethin' wasn't it?"

"Yeah, that's right; Greg Forrester."

"Thought so. Anyway, this Greg made four or five trips up and down the walkway and woke Kevin up. Guess he was loadin' stuff up for a trip or somethin'.

"Then he started the boat and let it warm up a while before he backed out and headed for the channel. Kevin got up to see what all the commotion was about, but he stepped on deck just about in time to wave to the guy."

"So he was sure it was Greg Forrester?"

"About as sure as he could be, it bein' about dawn and all, and the light not bein' so good. 'Course we was all sure later. Never did find his body ya know."

"Yeah, I know. Listen, before he came out here, he said something to his wife about having an appointment for later in the day to have the boat pulled out for the winter. Do you remember anything about that?"

"Naw. We don't do that anyways. If you want us to pull it out and store it, you make that deal up front and, dependin' on the weather, we automatically do it about the last week in October—like I'm doin' now."

As Harry drove back to Grand Rapids, he mentally reviewed what he had learned. It was precious little: Kevin, the eye witness, would probably not have had a reason to lie about seeing Greg Forrester take the boat out on the day in question. However, given the less than ideal lighting conditions, the possibility existed that it could have been someone else. Thirty years of police work had taught Harry that eyewitnesses often see what their minds think should be there rather than what is actually there. It's not that they're intending to lie; it's that most people are not particularly observant. Still, the fact that he apparently had no trouble starting the engine and that he let it sit and idle while it warmed up, heavily favored it being Greg. A thief would likely get out of there as soon as he got the thing started to avoid being noticed.

Another interesting thing was that he had made several trips back and forth to the boat. *I wonder what he was loading? It must have been big or heavy items, or there must have been a lot if it. Otherwise, why all the trips?*

Then there was the apparent lie about the appointment to have the boat pulled out. Of course, maybe he was so accustomed to lying to Marti that this lie had no particular meaning beyond being an excuse to get away and do whatever he had planned for that day.

So far, Harry's quest to learn more about Greg Forrester had turned up little. On the other hand, he had more information than when he started out this morning. But the question was whether it had any meaning beyond the apparent fact that Greg actually had taken the boat out into Lake Michigan on the day it exploded.

IT WAS 6:58 P.M. on Harry's watch when he shut off his car engine in Gary Hammond's driveway. He stepped up onto the stoop, and as he was ringing the bell, the door opened.

"You must be Harry Brannan." The man opened the storm door and proffered his hand. "Gary Hammond."

Harry shook his hand. "That's right. Thank you for seeing me Mr. Hammond."

"Call me Gary," he said as he stepped back. "Please come in."

Harry followed him into the living room. "Have a seat." He gestured toward an easy chair. "Can I get you anything?"

"No thanks," Harry said as he sat down.

Gary sat on the sofa opposite him, a concerned look was on his face. "I'm not sure what I can tell you. I guess I opened a can of worms when I told Marti I thought I saw Greg up in the Yoop. I didn't know she'd be upset enough to hire somebody to check it out. I half feel like it would have been better if I'd kept my mouth shut."

"Are you having second thoughts about what you saw up there?"

"No, it's not that. It's just that she's a nice lady and I...well...I don't know. He looked like Greg, but Greg's dead, right? Look, I know she doesn't make much money, and it makes me feel kind of bad to think I made her spend a lot on what will most likely turn out to be a wild goose chase."

"So you like her, then?"

"Yeah, I like her. I mean, she's a lot older than me, and I think she's religious. She brown bags; always has her lunch in her cube, and prays before she eats. I don't know; there's something different about her. She's nice to everybody. Doesn't get involved in office politics or gossip, stuff like that. She's just a nice lady, that's all. And I don't want to cause her trouble."

Harry removed the picture of Greg from his inside jacket pocket and half stood as he reached across the coffee table and handed it to Gary. "Is this the man you saw?"

Gary studied the picture very carefully, turning it slightly one way, then another before he responded. "Yeah, that's him. I'm sure of it. He's a little older than in the picture and he has darker hair and a beard, but that's him."

Harry's eyebrows went up. "A beard? What kind of beard?"

Gary made a face and shook his head. "I don't know. I mean, I know beards have names, but I don't know what they are." He put his fingers above his upper lip and pulled them down to his chin. "It was a moustache that turned into a small beard."

Harry pulled a ballpoint pen out of his pocket. "Do you think you could draw it on the picture?"

"Sure, if you don't mind me ruining it."

"That's okay, I have extras."

Gary drew a moustache and what amounted to a goatee on the picture before handing it back to Harry."

Harry looked at the picture. "You said his hair was darker; in what way?"

"Well, it's not black. I guess dark brown would probably be the best description."

"Any gray? Or do you think he's covering gray?"

"Oh, that could be, I never thought of that. I don't think there was any gray."

"Okay, thanks. Now, how well did you know Greg?"

"Actually, I knew him fairly well. Scott too, Scott Jacoby. I sold them their health coverage for their company. You ask me, they're a couple of ruthless ba...well, let's just say they're not very nice guys. It's hard for me to imagine what Marti had in common with Greg, unless he was a completely different guy at home."

"How do you mean?"

"Well, first of all, they think that because Marti works at Choice Care, they should get a discount. That's a joke. Even employees don't get discounts. Then they end up buying the absolute best plan we have for themselves and the absolute cheapest, most stripped down plan we have for their employees. They've got, or at least had, a couple of secretaries and a couple of sales guys working for them. I don't know, I don't call on them any more."

"I see. Tell me the name of that casino where you think you saw him?"

"Waishkey Bay Casino. Wa-ish-key, that's actually the name of the bay on Lake Superior. It's simple to get to. Just stay on 75 after you get across the Mackinaw Bridge. Then go west on 28 to 221, it's the road to Brimley. When you get to Brimley, turn right at the blinker and go past the state park. It's on the left, you can't miss it."

"Okay, I'm sure I'll be able to find it. Now, tell me about this guy; and I want you to give me the first thing that pops into your head: When you saw him there, did he look comfortable with the place, or did you get the impression it may have been his first time there?"

"Oh no, he carried on like he owned the place. My guess is that he's a regular there. People seemed to know him."

"Okay. What do you know about Scott?"

"Not much really. But then I really don't *know* much about Greg either, past what he looks like and that he didn't treat his employees very well. I do know Scott's wife took off on him a few months before Greg's boat blew up."

"Did you know her at all?"

"No, it's just something I heard. I never met her."

Harry stood to leave. "If I am able to find this guy and get a picture of him, would you be willing to identify it before I go to Marti with it?"

"Yeah, sure, no problem."

Harry held out his hand. "Thanks, Gary; I appreciate your help."

Chapter 6

HARRY DROVE BACK TO his apartment. The place was chilly and he adjusted the thermostat up a little as he walked into the kitchen.

He put a TV dinner into the microwave; the old familiar sense of loneliness creeping over him as he set the timer and pressed the start button. He watched through the oven window as his supper turned slow pirouettes, and his mind turned once again to Marti. Was she seeing anyone? Was she home alone, like him? Was she lonely?

Why was he thinking these things? Surely he'd learned his lesson. Women are fickle—like cats. They want what they want, when they want it, and when they decide they don't want you anymore, they throw you away. The last thing he needed was some woman—any woman.

The microwave beeped its five short beeps, and he took out his meal; carefully removing the cellophane covering so as not to be burned by the escaping steam. He sat at his small dining room table and ate in silence. If you're resourceful, he'd discovered, the only utensil you really need to eat a TV dinner is a spoon. And when he finished, he carefully washed his spoon with hand soap and, after drying it, put it back in the drawer.

He threw away the empty meal container and picked up the cordless phone on his way to the sofa. He sat there thinking, turning the phone over and over in his hands for a long time before he dialed. A woman answered and he tried to make his voice sound upbeat. "Lisa. Hi, it's Harry."

"What do you want, Harry?" Her voice was flat.

"I was, uh...hoping to speak with Curt."

"He's not here right now."

"Ah. Well, uh...when do you think—"

"Harry, it's over between us and there's no—"

"Yeah, well, I didn't call to talk to you. I just wanted to see how Curt's doing."

"Well, he's not here. Look, don't call anymore. Okay?"

The click-sound in his ear indicated the connection had broken and Harry pressed the button to hang up his end before returning the phone to its charging stand on the end table.

He tried to watch television, but after surfing through all the channels several times he finally gave up and went to bed.

GUNSHOTS! THERE GOES THE PERP! Mitch is down! I've got to get to him! Run!

"No! Harry, get down! There's somebody behind—"

Muzzle flash! Ohhhh! More gunshots! Falling...

"Harry!...Harry! Hang in there, man! Help is on the way!"

Where am I? Who is that laying on the ground?

"Mulvaney, help me get his jacket off!"

It's meee!

As if apart from his body, Harry saw himself lying on the concrete apron below the loading dock, the circle of blood getting larger and larger on the concrete beneath his shoulder, his right leg bent at an impossible angle beneath him. Now in his body, he saw Lisa standing over him, a smile on her face, as she held his Glock in both hands and pointed it at his face. He could see the glee in his eyes, and suddenly he was awake.

Chapter 7

HARRY WASN'T ABLE TO get an appointment with Scott Jacoby until two p.m. on Thursday. He arrived at Jacofor Properties at 1:55 and, upon entering, spoke with the receptionist.

"I'm sorry sir, Mr. Jacoby has not returned from lunch yet. He should be back any minute. Please have a seat."

Harry sat in one of the nicely upholstered chairs and looked around. The place gave the impression of opulence. Apparently Jacoby was doing well, or at least giving a real good impression of it. He perused a copy of *Architectural Digest* while he waited.

At 2:20 p.m. Jacoby arrived. He spotted Harry waiting and walked over to him. "You must be my two o'clock. Sorry to keep you waiting."

Harry stood and extended his hand. "Harry Brannan."

"Scott Jacoby," the man said as they shook hands. "Come on back."

Harry followed him into his office and sat in an identically upholstered chair in front of his desk as Scott sat in the plush leather executive chair behind it. His face was flushed and Harry guessed he had drunk at least a portion of his lunch.

"What can I do for you, Harry? I understand you're a detective and that you want to talk about Greg Forrester."

"That's right."

"Well, what's this about? You know, Greg's been dead for...," he gestured, his arms bent at the elbows, his palms up, "five years now."

"Yes, I know. Somebody thinks they saw him recently in the U.P."

"You're kidding! Does his wife...uh—"

"Marti."

"Marti. Does Marti know about this?"

"Yes, she's the one who hired me."

His face took on a serious look. "Son of a gun!" He shook his head. "That's hard to believe. Are you sure?"

"No, I'm not. And frankly, these kinds of sightings are more common than you might think. That's why I'm here. I'd like to ask you some questions about Greg, and about your business together, if I may.

"Sure, go ahead."

"Thank you. How is it that you knew Greg?"

"We were roommates in college—Northwestern. He's...he was, from the Chicago area, you know."

"Yes, I knew that. So you guys decided to go into business together while you were roommates in college?"

"No. He had a job lined up down there and I had one up here. But I realized I was never going to make any real money working for somebody else, so I went out on my own. Greg joined me a few years later. He bought in and we became partners."

"How did that go?"

"Fine. It was a plus for both of us. The business was at a point where we could actually make more money as partners than as individuals. We've grown beyond that now, and have a sales and secretarial staff, but at the time it was a big plus for both of us."

"I see. If you don't mind me asking, what was your partnership agreement? It appears that Mrs. Forrester is not at all involved in the business."

"That's right. Our agreement was that everything reverted to the surviving...Say, you're not suggesting that I had something to do with Greg's—"

"No, no, nothing like that," Harry interrupted, holding up his hands. "I'm just trying to get as full a picture as possible, that's all."

"You know, he died owing me money. Fifty thousand."

"I understood that Mrs. Forrester paid that back."

"Yes, she did, but the point is that I had every reason to want him alive and no reason to want him dead."

"Believe me, I understand. And I'm not making any accusations. Now, if we could move on. I understand that your wife left you. Is that correct?

"It's news to me. Unless she left sometime after breakfast this morning."

"So you're saying she came back?"

"I'm saying that these are personal questions—none of your business. I don't see how they apply to any discussion about Greg."

"Look, here's the deal: I was given to understand that your wife left you just a few months before Greg's accident. Given the shortness of time between the two incidents, I was wondering if there was a connection. To be blunt, I was wondering if Greg may have run off with your wife. Please understand if he's dead, this is obviously a non-issue. But if he really is alive, there has to be a reason why he wanted everybody to believe he's dead."

"I'm sorry. I didn't see where you were going." He sighed. "It's a good question, and one I guess I can't answer. As far as I know, they didn't know each other all that well. Plus, I doubt that she would have been Greg's type. She was pretty feisty and Greg preferred his women to be more the compliant type. He liked to be in complete charge."

"So you're saying your wife did leave you."

"Yes."

"Have you heard from her since that time?"

"No."

"I take it that you've married again."

"No, not really. I was just reacting to what I thought was too personal a question."

"I see. From your statement a minute ago, I got the impression that Greg was not being faithful to his wife. Is that the impression you intended to give?

"Well, he liked the ladies, I know that. He talked a lot, but I can't say I know of a specific instance where he was unfaithful to his wife. I will say that I suspected that he had something going with his secretary, but it was just a suspicion, nothing I could prove or even tried to prove. She left the company shortly after the accident."

"What was her name?"

"Vicki. Vicki Thomas."

"Do you have any data on her—address, that kind of thing?"

"Maybe. It would be five years old, but I could have Krista check for you before you go."

"Thanks. You said that Greg owed you money. How about the company? Did you have any big monetary surprises after the accident?"

"No. Greg liked to live large, but the way the business works, we each essentially pulled down a salary. On the other hand, Greg's wife came into a fairly large inheritance. I'm not sure how much it was, but I know he used her money to buy into the business. I assumed that was his money source; although why she put up with it I wouldn't know."

"Did you know her well?"

"Not really. She was darn good looking, and nicely put together. He gestured an hourglass with his hands. "I always wondered what she'd be like in the sack, you know. But I never could get comfortable around her. I think she was religious or something." He paused. "How's she doing, anyway?"

Harry frowned. "Okay, I guess. He pretty much cleaned her out."

"Humph, sorry to hear that. I guess I understand now why she hired you. You going after him, then?"

"I'm not sure. I'll get back with her and let her know what I've found out. After that, it'll be up to her if she wants me to proceed."

Scott stood and extended his hand. "Yeah, well, good luck. Let me know if you find him. If he's alive I wouldn't mind punching him in the nose myself."

Harry shook the man's hand and accompanied him to the receptionist's station, where he obtained a photocopy of the information he'd requested on Vicki Thomas.

When he got into his car he opened the folder and checked her address. She lived in an apartment complex about ten minute's drive from his current location. He checked his watch. It was 3:35 p.m. when he set out for home.

Had Vicki Thomas been Greg's mistress? Scott Jacoby' suspicions were little to go on. However, Marti's certain knowledge of Greg's philandering added sufficient credence to the idea to make it at least worth checking out.

When he got home, Harry rushed in and picked up his digital camera. Then he set out for Vicki's apartment complex, stopping at a convenience store on the way to pick up a small bag of dry roasted peanuts and a cold Diet Pepsi.

He stopped at the main entrance of the complex and checked again for the address of her building before continuing on; following the signs that led to the one he sought. Each of the buildings contained four units. Two up, two down. Her building number was 1541.

The layout was such that there were parking spaces in front of each building. Cars parked with wheels butted against a curb. These parking spaces were obviously for visitors. Across the roadway, and in front of each building, were carports labeled with the building numbers and A through D where the tenants parked. Beyond the curb was a sidewalk and about a thirty-foot grassy strip that constituted the front yards. Another sidewalk led up to the centered front doors of each building.

According to his information, Vicki lived in apartment A. There was no car parked in that space in the carport so Harry backed into a visitor space of the building next door that afforded him a good view without being obvious. He exited his car and entered the building.

The mailboxes were just inside the door and he checked A. The name read, Thomas. He was in luck. Before going back out he looked around the entryway. Apartment A was on the lower level—the door on the left. Harry returned to his car. His watch read 4:50 p.m. when he opened his peanuts and drink.

By 5:35 p.m. his snack had been gone for fifteen minutes. Having missed his lunch, all it had done was whet his appetite for something more substantial. Also, a delivery van had pulled in next to him half an hour ago, and it was still there, partially blocking his view of the parking space he was observing.

Suddenly a red Miata pulled in to space A in the carport. Harry quickly grabbed his camera, turning it on as he exited his car. He hurried around the car, not bothering to close the door, and leaned up against the back right side of the van at about the time the woman exited. She was about thirty, 5-foot-7 or 8, with long blonde hair and a knockout figure.

She stood while putting the strap of her purse over her shoulder, and Harry got a good shot of her head and upper body before she leaned back in and removed her laptop computer from the floor behind the driver's seat. As she stood and straightened out, he got a close up of her face and head, with the lens extended.

HARRY CUT OUT THE two 5 by 7 pictures he'd made of Vicki Thomas and left them to dry on the table as he sat down to a meatloaf and red potatoes TV dinner. As he ate, his mind went back to the meal and meeting he'd had with Marti on Monday, and he wondered if she would want him to go on with the investigation. He guessed he'd find out when he dropped in later, but the thought sent a feeling of exhilaration through him. It was a feeling he hadn't had in a long time, and it suddenly dawned on him that the woman had gotten to him: She was good, and decent, and she had been wronged, and he felt the need to help her. But even as the thought made its way through his mind he realized it was more a male thing, maybe even a generational male thing, than a cop thing. Still, he had to admit, it also felt good to be on a case again. And in spite of the less-than-convincing evidence, he hoped she'd want him to proceed.

He threw away his meal container and washed his spoon before he went into the bathroom and brushed his teeth. He didn't know why, but he checked himself out in the mirror on the back of the bathroom door and decided to tuck his shirt in better. Then he placed the pictures in the folder he'd received from Jacofor Properties, and collected it with his notes as he set out for Marti's house.

As he turned into her driveway he spotted a green Toyota Tacoma pickup parked next to her door and his feeling of exhilaration disappeared. He seriously doubted she would drive a truck, so, obviously, she had company. *Well, I'm here on business,* he thought as he exited his car and walked to her door. He was about to knock when the inside door opened, startling him.

"Oh! Harry! You startled me," Jo Ramsey exclaimed, stepping back before she pushed the storm door half open.

Harry put his hand over his heart. "Yeah, you startled me too. You drive a truck?"

"No, its Clay's. It just happened to be the last thing in the driveway." She looked out at his car. "Would you mind letting me out?"

"Oh. Sure."

Harry went for his car as Jo turned around and shouted into the house. "Marti, Harry's here!"

By the time he returned to the door, Marti was waiting for him. "Harry! What a surprise. Come on in." She held open the storm door allowing him to enter. "So, what brings you over tonight? I wish you had called, I would have made you something to eat."

"Oh. Well, I'll definitely call next time then," he smiled. "I just wanted to spend a little time with you, going over the information I've gathered the last couple of days." They walked into the dining area and sat down.

He opened the file folder and slid the pictures of Vicki Thomas in front of her. "Do you recognize this woman?"

"Umm, I don't know—maybe. Who is she?"

"She's Greg's former secretary. I was wondering if she may have been one of the women who showed up on your doorstep after the accident."

Marti shook her head. "I don't know. She looks somewhat familiar, but I'd hate to say and be wrong. It's been a while, and it's not something I've tried to remember."

"That's okay. Did you know that he was seen taking the boat out of the marina on the day of the accident?"

"No, I didn't know that."

"Apparently the guy in the slip next door saw him leave and waved to him. According to one of the employees out there, the guy also noted that Greg made several trips out to the boat before he took off. Do you know if he may have been loading anything on the boat before he left?"

"No, I'm sorry, I don't know. I hate to sound so stupid about this, but there never was any kind of serious investigation done. The Coast Guard had the tapes of the mayday call, and everyone just assumed that gasoline fumes exploded."

Harry put his hand over hers. "You don't sound stupid. I pretty much gathered the same thing from talking to the Coast Guard. I just wondered if he might have said something, that's all."

"So where does that leave us?"

"Well, it's up to you. The fact that he was actually seen leaving the marina on the boat lends credence to the idea he was on it when it blew up. On the other hand, according to the guy who works at the marina, he lied to you about having an appointment to have the boat taken out of the water. They don't do appointments. That, plus him apparently loading something on the boat, plus Gary Hammond being sure it was Greg he saw, argue in favor of him being up to something. I'm still willing to go up north if you want me to."

She removed her hand from under his and placed it over his. "I still want you to find out for sure." She squeezed his hand lightly. "I hope you understand that I need closure on this."

Harry smiled at her. "Of course I understand." He pushed his chair out and stood. "I'll leave for the U.P. tomorrow morning."

"How long do you think it will take?"

"I don't know. I've already done an Internet search on Alan Coombs and several other name variations in the 9-0-6 area code, but I didn't come up with anything. Of course, he may not have a phone. Those things are not much more than glorified phone books anyway. Maybe he's got a cell phone. My guess is, though, that there probably aren't a whole bunch of cell towers up there. He may well have given Gary a phony name just to get him off his back." Harry walked to the door. "I'm going to start by hanging out at the Waishkey Bay Casino. I figure that's my best bet for tracking him down. If things go well, I'll try to be back on Saturday or Sunday. I'll call you...and I'll try to make it around a meal time."

She laughed. "You do that."

Her face took on a somber look as she stepped toward him. Then, apparently thinking better of whatever she was going to do, she stepped back and tentatively laid her hand on his upper arm. She took a shaky breath. "Be careful, Harry."

He smiled. "I will."

Chapter 8

WHEN HE ARRIVED AT HOME, Harry brought in a Michigan map from his car and opened it on his dining table. It had been a few years since he'd been to the Upper Peninsula and he folded the map so only the northern part of the state was showing. Where to stay? He didn't know if the Waishkey Bay casino offered any lodging accommodations, and he didn't particularly want to stay there even if they did.

He thought of his conversation with Gary Hammond as he scanned east and west of Brimley along M-28. The thing about the U.P. is that there are not a lot of choices. It is largely a wilderness, broken up by mostly small towns every ten or fifteen miles. And some of the towns are so small that if you blink as you're passing through, you'll miss them. That pretty much limited his choices to larger towns: Newberry on the west or Sault Sainte Marie on the east. Sault Sainte Marie, or 'The Soo,' was a lot closer, so he did an Internet search for lodging and made a reservation at the Essex Hotel. Then he packed a bag and went to bed.

By 3:30 on Friday afternoon he had checked in and deposited his luggage in his room. The place didn't have a restaurant, so Harry drove around and searched for something close that looked like it might be good. Then he drove over to Brimley and found the casino. Despite the early hour, there were a significant number of cars and motor homes already in the parking lot. He wondered if the motor home drivers actually slept on site. He wondered, too, if the man he sought was already inside, but, figuring he'd probably end up having to follow the guy home, decided to use the remaining daylight to drive around and get a feel for the area. When he later returned to the parking lot he needed his headlights.

A bitingly cold wind blew in off Lake Superior. *The gales of November are early again this year,* he thought as he stepped out of his car. He shivered as he buttoned his topcoat, fluffy flakes of lake-effect snow blowing sideways past him as he set out for the building. He wondered if the snow signaled the beginning of an early winter as he stepped inside.

Harry transferred his digital camera to his pants pocket before hanging his coat. Then he, once again, checked the picture of Greg Forrester and returned it to his inside jacket pocket before stepping into the casino proper.

Immediately inside the entrance were banks of slot machines, and video-poker machines. To the right were gaming tables: craps, roulette, etc. toward the front of the building; blackjack and other card games toward the rear. He tried to appear inconspicuous as he walked among the machines, eying the players. This wasn't difficult as most of them were too intent on what they were doing to take notice of him.

Not finding his man, Harry walked among the gaming tables and card games; but in spite of being careful to get a look at every face, he didn't find him there either.

As he walked back toward the slot machines he wondered if Gary Hammond had managed to be in the right place at the right time—that he'd had a random sighting. Still, Gary conveyed the distinct impression that the man he saw, Greg, had seemed familiar with the place, and seemed to know people there. Of course that could merely mean that the guy was gregarious. Maybe he didn't live in the area and had just been visiting. Or, maybe he was one of those people whose day never really begins until after ten p.m. *I should have asked Gary what time he saw the man.* On the other hand, maybe he didn't frequent the place. Maybe he had other plans this week or maybe he'd dropped a bundle gambling and couldn't afford to come back for a while. Harry realized, however, that he really didn't know enough to know, and it's a mistake to theorize ahead of your data.

To the left of the slot machines, Harry entered a walled off area that turned out to be a lounge with a floor show.

He stood in the entryway taking the place in. To his left, in the front of the building, was a long bar that ran parallel to the front wall. Round tables that could easily seat 4 people took up the area between the bar and a good sized stage at the rear of the room, on his right. It was a large area; he estimated it contained at least 125 tables.

In the wall directly opposite where he stood, double doors led to what he surmised to be a kitchen. Booths occupied the wall space on both walls of the bar side of the room.

Fortunately, the floor show had not yet begun, so fewer people were sitting on that side. A perfunctory scan of that area yielded no fruit. However, the bar side was quite well attended. All of the tables and booths had occupants, and cocktail waitresses, who appeared to have been chosen for their impressive cleavages, were busily scurrying back and forth, carrying drinks to the patrons.

Harry walked to the bar and, after waiting for an empty stool, sat down. He waited several more minutes for the bartender to appear.

"What'll you have?" the man asked.

"Just a ginger ale will do."

While the man was getting his drink, he took several bills out of his wallet and relocated them to a side pocket of his sport coat. He gave the man a ten dollar bill when he set the ginger ale before him. "Keep the change."

"Hey, thanks!"

Harry slid a picture of Greg Forrester toward him. "Ever see this guy?"

The bartender looked at the picture on the bar and then picked it up for a better look. "No, doesn't ring a bell with me. Sorry," he said as he set the picture back on the bar.

"He may be wearing a beard—a goatee, these days." Harry slid forward the picture upon which Gary Hammond had drawn.

The man looked at the new picture. "No, sorry, I don't recognize him. Maybe Melissa would know; she's been here longer than me." He looked to his left. "She's busy down at the other end right now but I'll have her stop over when she gets a chance."

Harry thanked the man and nursed his drink while he waited for Melissa. It was a good ten minutes before she appeared in front of him. "Jimmy said you wanted to see me?"

"Yeah, I'd like to have you look at a couple of pictures— see if you can identify them. But first, how about a refill? Ginger ale," he said, holding his glass up.

She took his glass. "Sure, I'll be right back," she said as she walked off.

While she was gone, Harry arranged the pictures with the drawn-on one underneath. Then he extricated another ten dollar bill from his pocket for Melissa.

As she returned, she set his refilled glass before him. "There you go."

He gave her the ten dollar bill. "Keep it."

"Thanks. Now, what do you want me to look at?"

He gave her the pictures. "Ever seen this guy? He may be wearing a beard like on the picture underneath the one you're looking at. Sorry, the drawing's a little crude."

She separated the pictures and held them side-by-side as she studied them; looking back and forth between them. "Does he have to have blonde hair?"

"No, not at all. In fact, I'm given to understand that it's dark brown now. Sorry, I forgot to mention that."

She nodded. "Yeah. Yeah, I'm pretty sure I've seen him. If it's who I think it is, he comes in here a lot."

"Have you seen him tonight?"

"No, not yet. But I wouldn't be surprised if he shows up. Seems like he's usually here on the weekends."

"You wouldn't happen to know his name, would you?"

"No, I'm afraid not. I'm not even a hundred percent sure it's him. But it looks like a guy who sits at the bar once in a while. Always seems like he's on the make; looking for some woman to pick up. Tried to pick me up once, but I told him that I'm married." She set the pictures back on the bar.

"Are you?"

"No."

Harry chuckled. "Well, thanks, Melissa. I really appreciate your help."

"Yeah, no problem. Check back with me later. If he comes in I'll point him out to you."

"Thanks," he said as she walked off.

Harry turned so that he could face the room. Leaning against the bar, he sipped at his drink while he scanned the area. He sat there for a long time watching people come and go from the lounge. Shortly after his forth drink, he himself left the lounge to use the restroom. He was not accustomed to drinking so much, but a man with a drink in his hand is far less conspicuous than a man just wandering around looking at faces.

When he returned, he got another ginger ale from the bar. However, not knowing who might have come in while he was gone, he decided not to sit. Instead, he wandered about the room to get a better look at the patrons.

That's what he was doing when he saw the man he was looking for seated in a booth on the kitchen side of the room. He was with a dark-haired woman who appeared to be in her early thirties. They were holding hands across the table.

He made his way back to the bar. This time he went to the side where Melissa was working; the same side of the room that the booth was on. He leaned back against the bar and sipped his drink; doing his best to appear nonchalant as he watched the booth.

The man was facing away from him and the seat backs of the booths were high enough so that all he could see of the man was the top of his head. However, he had a fairly good view of the woman's face. It was a pretty face with a nice smile, and he wondered if she had allowed herself to be picked up by the man. He wondered too how long they'd been sitting there. He was pretty sure they had not been there when he arrived.

A cocktail waitress was walking in the aisle between the tables and the booths, heading in his direction when he saw the man's hand go up and wave to get her attention. She stopped and bent slightly, listening to something the man was saying, then picked up the glasses from the table before resuming her trip to the bar. She walked past him and he turned and followed her to the waitress station. As she set her tray down she turned toward him with an inquiring look.

"Excuse me," Harry said softly. "Do you know the man in the booth where you just picked up those glasses?"

She shook her head. "No. You a cop or something?"

"Or something," he replied. "Which glass was his?"

"The Old-fashioned glass," she said, pointing at the shorter one. "Scotch and soda. The tall one belongs to the woman—Tom Collins."

"I'll give you ten bucks for the Old-fashioned glass and another ten bucks to keep your mouth shut about it."

"What's this all about?"

"It's safer for you if you don't know too much," he said, hoping to frighten her into not mentioning the incident to the man. "Let's just say that, if he's who I think he is, he has a wife. And it's *not* the woman he's sitting with. Somebody is very angry about that and I've been hired to track him down. I need the glass for a fingerprint comparison." He pulled a twenty dollar bill out of his jacket pocket and held it out to her.

She looked at it for a few seconds, then took it and stuffed it in one of the pockets of her apron. "I've got to go to the ladies' room. I'll be right back."

As she walked off, Harry removed a brown paper lunch sack from his side jacket pocket and, using his handkerchief, carefully picked up the glass and gently placed it inside. Then he folded over the top and discreetly carried the bag out to his car; depositing it on the floor behind the passenger seat.

Several artificial trees occupied the area just inside the entrance to the lounge. Harry stopped behind the ones on the bar side when he returned, and removed his digital camera from his pocket. He turned it on and extended the lens; pushing it through the greenery as he looked through the view finder at the man's face. The lighting was far from ideal and the red warning light came on as he pressed part-way down on the shutter release, indicating he should use the flash. But when the man turned his way, he snapped the picture anyway, hoping for the best. Then he retracted the lens, shut the camera off, and placed it back in his pocket.

He returned to the bar for another drink and nonchalantly wandered into the floor show side of the room, where he sat at a table in good view of the booth where the man and woman were sitting, not caring if he was observed as he nursed his drink.

When he finished it he got up, glass in hand, and set out for the bar using the aisle way between the tables and the row of booths on the kitchen side of the room. When he reached the one where they were sitting he stopped and pasted on his, 'I can't believe this' face as he stared intently at the man for several seconds, acting a little tipsy.

"Greg...Greg *Forrester. How the heck are you!* Man, I hardly recognized you with that beard." He set his glass down on the table, slid in next to the man and put his arm around him. "What's it been, ten, eleven years? Son of a gun. I mean, what are the odds of meeting somebody else from Chicago—much less somebody you know? So, *how you been?"* he said, pulling him in close a couple of times before relaxing his grip.

"Look, I'm sorry, but you've got me confus—"

"You don't recognize me do you? Harry quickly interrupted, not giving him a chance to finish. "Harry. Harry Kimble. City of Chicago, D-CAP." He turned to the woman. "Department of Construction and Permits." Then he turned back to the man. "You worked for Ray Stafford back in the '90s. After he died, you married his...uhhh..." He lifted his right arm and moved his hand around. "Daughter..." He looked at the woman. "You must be...I can't remem..." He looked closely at her. "No, you'd be too young.

The man wriggled out from under his arm. "Look, you've made a mis—"

"So what have you been doing with yourself?" Harry quickly interrupted again. "Man, that kid of Ray's...what the heck is his name?" He briefly put his fingers against his temples as he waited, hoping the man would slip and say the name. "Ken. Ken, that's it." He looked at the woman. "And you'd be Jeanie," he said, pointing a moving left index finger at her. "No...no, you're too young to be Jeanie...she'd be in her mid-forties by now."

He looked back at the man. "Anyway, he's run the business into the ground. I mean, I don't even recall how long it's been since we issued a permit for any work for them."

"*Listen,*" the man interrupted; clearly becoming agitated. "I. am. *not—*"

"Good thing you're not with them anymore," Harry kept on. "I always told Ray that he wasn't the man for the job. And he knew it, too, but Helen," he looked at the woman, "his wife," he looked back at the man. "She just had her heart set on her Kenny taking over the business. Me, I always thought you were the best guy for the job. He never had the gift—the head for business. You did. Man, I miss that guy. So, what are you doing these days, Greg? It's really good to see you. Don't see many guys from the old days anymore."

"Stop. Just *stop* a minute." The man held up his right hand as if stopping traffic. "I am *not* your friend, Greg...whatever. My name is Alan Chambers, and I have never even *been* to Chicago, much less lived there."

"You're pulling my leg, right?" Harry looked at the woman. "He's kidding me, right?" He looked back at the man. "Look Greg, I know we didn't know each other all that well, but I don't want anything from you. It's just nice to see you again after all these years. You don't have to try to snow me. I mean, my lips are sealed." He ran his right index finger quickly across his lips. "I haven't seen Jeanie in...humph, years. And I'm sure as heck not going to look her up when I get back tomorrow, and tell her I saw you up here with...this young lady, here."

"Look, I just told you, I am *not* Greg...Forrester," the man rejoined.

"Yeah, well, if you're not him, you sure look enough like him to be his twin brother."

"Look, my name is Alan Chambers, and I'm from Bay City, Michigan. I've never been to Chicago, I've never been to Illinois, and I've never been *here* before tonight. Obviously I look something like this man you knew, but you've made a mistake, I am *not* him. This lady is my wife."

The woman's almost imperceptible flinch put the lie to the man's words. "And we're just here to have a few drinks, stick a few quarters in the slot machines, and see the floor show. Now, we would appreciate it if you would go away and leave us alone." The woman was nodding in agreement.

Harry looked intently at the man. "Look, there's no need to be unpleasant. Running into old friends again should be a happy thing, Greg. Really, you've got *nothing* to fear from me." He slid out of the booth and, bending down, picked up all their glasses. "Now, let me go get us some more drinks, and then we can talk about old times. What are you drinking?" His gaze went back and forth between them.

A light went on in the man's eyes. "Scotch and soda."

The woman gave him an importunate glance and then looked at Harry. "Tom Collins."

"Great! That's more like it," he said happily. "I'll be back in a few minutes." He looked at the busy bar. "Well, however long it takes," he said as he walked off, carefully balancing all of their glasses in his hands.

Harry forced himself not to look back until he had reached the bar and set the glasses down. When he did turn to look, he glimpsed the man and saw the woman, her arm extended, as he rapidly led her out of the lounge by the hand. This was what he had hoped would happen. He hurried to the lounge entrance and observed what he had also hoped would happen: they were leaving the casino.

He walked slowly to the entry hall so as not to arrive while they were putting on their coats. When he got there, he peeked around the corner in time to see the man hold the door open for the woman and then step out of it himself.

He quickly put on his topcoat, and looked carefully out through the glass door before exiting. Once outside, he saw them getting into a red Jeep, Grand Cherokee. They were parked in the same row his car was in, but between him and his car. Not wishing to run the risk of being seen following them, Harry hunkered down behind the nearest car to stay mostly out of sight.

A small amount of snow clung to the horizontal and non-smooth surfaces of the vehicles parked in the lot, and the man ran his front and rear windshield wipers before quickly leaving the lot, a trail of exhaust vapor teeming out of his tailpipe in the cold and snowy air. Harry waited until he had turned right before rushing to his own car and getting it started.

He threw his car in gear and pressed hard on the accelerator, screeching his tires slightly as he followed with his headlights off. Once out of the casino area there was no street lighting, and going was difficult until his eyes became accustomed to the dark. He could see the Jeep's taillights in the distance and he sped up a little so as not to loose sight of it.

As they neared the junction with M-221, just north of Brimley, Harry could see street lighting in the distance and he slowed some, almost losing sight of the Jeep as it went trough the intersection and continued westbound on Lakeshore Drive. He had expected the man to turn left on 221 as it was the most direct route to the main drag, M-28, and was surprised when he went straight. Of course, there were at least two more casinos down this road. He'd past them on his drive-around earlier in the day, but turned back when he'd gotten to the Point Iroquois Historic Lighthouse, so he didn't know for sure what lay beyond there. He looked at the clock in the car radio. 9:17 p.m. *I'm going to freeze my butt off if I have to wait while they visit another casino.*

The curvy road mostly followed the Lake Superior beach; some places being just a stone's throw from the water. But there was also a housing area in a stretch of road that turned inland; he'd driven through that, too, earlier in the day. However, as far as he could tell, it was part of a Native American Reservation. So he doubted the man was headed there.

Back in the dark again, he sped up until he caught sight of the Jeep and was close enough not to loose him if he turned off. Fortunately, his car was a very dark gray. It would be quite difficult for the guy to spot in his mirror.

Harry dropped back as they neared the lights of first casino and had to deal with an oncoming car, the driver of which was flashing his lights and blowing his horn at him. Then the road curved sharply left into the housing area, and he lost the Jeep. The area was not particularly well lit, but it was bright enough so he could be seen. He had no choice but to keep back.

The second casino was near the other end of the housing area, and Harry drove slowly past it, looking for the Jeep in the parking lot. He didn't see it, but he didn't get a good look either. *If I have to, I can go back later and drive through the parking lot.*

Once he was in the dark again he went as fast as he dared and was well past the Point Iroquois Light before he spotted taillights in the distance. This was a section of road upon which he had never traveled, but he kept his speed up until he was sure of his quarry.

The Jeep eventually reached M-28 by way of Ranger Road, and Harry followed it in a right turn that led them to M-123, where it turned left. He hung back at the corner until the taillights were well in the distance before he too turned south, but hadn't much more than got the Jeep nicely in his view when the lights suddenly disappeared in another left turn.

He followed by turning left on Strongs Road, but didn't spot the taillights again until he rounded a sweeping left curve that pointed him back north. The area was open there, but became dense woods as it came within a couple of miles of M-28. Thinking back to his drive-around earlier that day, he wondered why the guy had not just turned south on Strongs off M-28 rather than going out of his way to go around a long block. Then he saw the Jeep turn right into a driveway that disappeared among the trees and he knew. The guy was taking the woman to his house and he wanted to confuse her about where it was. The trip down Lakeshore was longer, slower and much more confusing than a straight shot down 221 to 28 to Strongs.

Harry didn't dare drive into the driveway, so he drove past and parked in an open area on the other side of the road, several hundred feet away. He exited his car and closed the door softly before proceeding on foot to the rural mailbox near the entrance to the driveway. He was glad it was not snowing this far inland because the darkness would make it difficult to see him from the house.

It was too dark to see detail, so he removed a small flashlight from the side pocket of his topcoat and covered the lens with his hand as he turned it on. Then, allowing only enough light to escape to be able to see, he read the house number off the mailbox: 11643 Strongs Road. He said the number over and over to himself as he went back to his car and, taking advantage of the dome light, wrote it down in his spiral notebook. Unfortunately, no name had been painted on the box.

Harry left his car again and set out for the house. The ascending, serpentine driveway was at least a quarter mile long and turned sharply left after a short distance. Then it hair pinned back to the right for a way and then left again, before it straightened out in front of the garage.

The place sat quite a bit higher than the surrounding terrain, but was well secluded from the road; the driveway having been built to go among rather than through a stand of mature spruce trees. A light next to the front door and another one over the garage door provided a moderate level of illumination to the clearing wherein the Cape Cod style house had been built. However, the trees were so dense that you had to be more than half way up the driveway before you could begin to see the glow.

From his vantage point, mostly hidden within the boughs of a tree, Harry had a good view of the front yard. The garage door was down and the Jeep was apparently inside, as it was nowhere to be seen. His intention had been to get the license plate number, but that wasn't going to happen tonight. *Too bad,* he thought; considering whether just the house number would be sufficient, or if he should stay an extra day to get the plate number.

He looked at the house. The drapes were open, and in the brightly lit living room he could clearly see the woman standing in the picture window, looking out into the yard. A sense of foreboding came over him. *Where is the man?*

It was time to leave this place and Harry knew it. The hairs on the back of his neck were standing up as he began to turn and simultaneously heard the snapping of a twig behind him.

Chapter 9

HER PHONE TRILLED THE familiar double ring of an outside call and Marti looked at the number on the display, not recognizing it.

"Choice Care Sales and Marketing, Marti Forrester speaking."

"Marti. Scott Jacoby. I'm glad I caught you still at work."

"Well, Scott! What a surprise! I haven't heard from you in ages. How are you?"

"I'm fine. Just great. How 'bout you?"

"Yeah, I guess so. What can I do for you?"

"Did I catch you on your way out?"

The clock on her computer display read 4:34 p.m. "No, I've got a few minutes yet."

"Listen, uh...I was wondering if you'd be interested in having dinner with me tonight? I know it's short notice. And what with it being Friday and all, maybe you already have a date. But I've been thinking about you ever since talking to that detective you hired; thinking it would be nice to see you again, maybe catch up a little. What's it been, four years?

Marti pulled the handset away from her ear and briefly looked at it, wide eyed, before putting it back against her ear. "Yeah, something like that. Closer to five, I think."

"Listen, I hope you don't think I'm taking too much for granted here, but I've made seven o'clock reservations at The Signet, and I was hoping I could pick you up between a quarter after six and 6:30."

Marti looked at the handset again. *The Signet? Wow!* "Uh...sure. Boy, you don't give a girl much time. Why don't you make it closer to 6:30?"

"Okay, it's a date. I'll see you then."

She quickly shut down her computer and hurried to punch out. *A date?* she thought as she hurried home in her car. *Oh-my-goodness, I've just agreed to go out on a date with Scott Jacoby. I've got to hurry. I've barely enough time to get dressed. Does he even know where I live now? He must or he would have asked.* She shook her head. *A date? Me?*

MARTI CHECKED HER HAIR in the mirror, and then leaned in to check her teeth and apply her lipstick. She rubbed her lips together to level it before blotting the excess on a tissue. Then, turning to the full length mirror on the back of the bathroom door, she took herself in. Her one black dress, a classic A-line pullover, still fit her after, what had it been, five or six years? It was conservative, even modest, by current standards; coming just below the knees and showing only the barest hint of cleavage, but it suited her. She couldn't imagine herself in one of those low-cut things that seemed so popular nowadays. Nor could she imagine why the women who did wear them would be willing to show so much of themselves to anyone who cared to look. And men did look. How could they help it? Of course, that was the point. They were advertising—showing their wares. *Loneliness can change your perspective, I guess.*

She was suddenly struck with the depth of her own loneliness. But even as familiar tears began to form in her eyes she knew she would never try to get a man by deliberately causing him to lust after her. Besides, who would want a man gotten on the strength of such shameless advertising; a man you had to bare yourself to get? She quickly blotted her eyes with a couple of tissues before her mascara had a chance to run.

It was 6:20 p.m. when she stepped into the living room and turned the ceiling fan on full-blast. She stood in the air current, letting it cool her down while she waited for Scott to arrive—which he did at 6:25. She shut off the fan and grabbed her coat, putting it on as she headed for the side door where he was knocking.

Marti had never been to The Signet. The place was elegant and everyone was dressed elegantly—almost like an old movie from the forties. Scott politely waited for the Matrie'de to seat her before taking his own seat across from her.

She bent to lay her clutch on the vacant chair to her right. When she sat back up, Scott was looking at her intently—drinking her in with his eyes. It made her mildly uncomfortable and she gave him a wan smile while tilting her head.

"The years have been kind to you, Marti. You look good."

She could feel her cheeks getting warm. "Thank you," she said looking down and spying her menu. She quickly picked it up and opened it.

The waiter came and took their orders, and, after he left, Scott kept her laughing, with his jokes and funny stories, until their meals arrived. They made small talk while they ate, and then split a seriously decadent large chocolate brownie with caramel sauce for desert.

A dribble of caramel got on her chin and he took his napkin, and dipping it in his water, wiped it off. "You got a little of the sauce on you."

"Umm, thank you," she said, dabbing the spot dry with her own napkin. "I didn't mean to make a pig of myself." She looked down and scanned the front of her dress to be sure none of it had fallen there.

He smiled as he leaned back in his chair. "I think we got it all."

"Thanks."

"So, tell me how the search for Greg is going."

Marti folded her napkin and laid it next to her plate. "Well, I know my detective friend, Harry, talked to you, but I really don't know how much he told you."

"Just that somebody thought they spotted him up in the U.P."

"Yeah, it was Gary Hammond—you know him."

"Oh, sure."

"Anyway, Gary saw him, or at least he was pretty sure it was him, in a casino up there. I wouldn't have paid much attention to it except that he knew Greg fairly well."

Scott nodded.

"I mean, if it had just been a passing acquaintance that would have been one thing—"

"Yeah, we both knew Gary pretty well; spent quite a while hammering out our policies with him. So I can see where you're coming from."

"Yeah, and that's what makes it hard to ignore. Harry's up there now trying to find him."

"And if he does find him?"

"I don't know. This whole thing is so hard for me to believe. I guess, if it turns out to really be him, I'll go up there and confront him. At the very least I'll be divorcing him. But I don't know past that. I guess I'll just have to—"

"Listen, uh...if you want me to go up there with you, just say the word. Assuming it really is him, of course."

"Humph, that just the point. Harry says that these kinds of sightings are fairly common, so," she gestured with her hands. "I don't know. I guess we'll just have to wait and see. But thanks for the offer."

"My pleasure."

"You ever hear anything from Jan?"

Scott shook his head. "No, not a thing. Been over five years now. It's like she dropped off the face of the earth."

"I'm sorry."

"Well, the truth is we weren't getting along all that great toward the end anyway. I don't know what happened: she changed, I changed, we both changed." He sighed. "I don't know. She wasn't very pleasant to live with, I know that. Your detective friend wondered if she ran off with Greg, but I can't see that."

"Yeah, he raised that issue with me too, but I can't see it either. Jan was just too strident for..." She suddenly made a face. "I'm sorry."

Scott waved it off. "Don't be. She *was* strident—down right hard to get along with. That doesn't mean I didn't miss her; at least at first. But it's in the past now, and I've moved on. I'm not sure what it was that I saw in her in the first place."

"So, you never married again?"

"No. I've not known what to do. I mean, whether she's alive or dead—not that I have any reason to suspect that. But it's just the not knowing—"

"Yeah, believe me, I understand."

Scott nodded. "Yeah, I guess you would understand."

MARTI WAITED ON THE stoop as Scott shut the car door and turned to face him as he approached. "Thank you for the wonderful dinner. I had a very nice time."

"Yeah, me, too. We'll have to do it again."

An uncomfortable silence built between them, and Scott raised his eyebrows, a self-conscience look on his face, and threw open his arms. Marti stepped into his embrace.

He held her for a moment, and then kissed her cheek before letting her go. "Goodbye, Marti," he said as he walked to his car. "I have to go out of town next week, but I'll call you when I get back."

He gave a couple of short beeps on his horn and Marti waved as he drove away.

She stepped into her house, and shut the door, simultaneously locking it and turning off the outside lights. Then she prepared for bed, carefully hanging her dress in the closet while she tried to examine her feelings about the evening.

This was the first time she'd been out with a man since Greg had...gone missing. Well, she'd had dinner with Clay once, a year or so before he met and married Jo. But that had been as friends, and neither of them had had any expectation that it was more than that.

Is that what this was? Was it merely a friendly gesture on Scott's part? Somehow she doubted it. A friendly gesture might have been to take her to the local Applebee's. The Signet was the finest, most expensive restaurant in the city. He had tried to wow her. And he'd succeeded. But what did it mean?

Does he suddenly, after not seeing or speaking to me for five years, discover that he has some kind of feelings for me? Not likely. Maybe it was just what he said: talking to Harry had brought me to his mind. But why the full court press and the promise to call me? Is he really interested in me? Could I ever be interested in him?

And what about Harry? I have a feeling...

Harry. Suddenly she was moved with the overwhelming impression that she should pray for Harry, and she fell on her knees beside her bed.

"Father. I don't know why, but I feel as though I should pray for Harry. I don't know where he is or what he's doing at this moment, but I pray that you will be with him to keep him safe; that you will protect him from any danger, and extend to him your grace for whatever he may be going through right now. Please be a comfort to him, and give him your peace. Thank you for this day and for bringing me safely through it. In Jesus' name, amen."

Marti climbed into bed and pulled the covers up over herself. It was 10:31 p.m. when she shut off the light and tried to settle down for sleep. But sleep eluded her as her mind turned over and over why she'd had the sudden impulse to pray for Harry.

Chapter 10

HARRY QUICKLY TURNED, AND in the dim light saw the man coming slowly toward him, wielding a knife...or something in his upraised left hand. Now found out, he rushed at Harry, causing him to jump back out of the cover of the tree.

In the improved light of the yard Harry could see that the man was not carrying a knife, but a syringe. And he was about to plunge it into his shoulder. Instinctively, Harry grabbed the man's wrist with his right hand and stumbled backward with the man's momentum, falling to the ground.

The man was on top of him now as they wrestled; Harry trying desperately to keep the syringe at bay, the man trying desperately to plunge it into him.

He got both of his hands on the man's left wrist and pushed as hard as he could, causing the man to go off balance. Taking advantage of the situation, he kept pushing and managed to roll the man off and get on top of him.

Energized by his disadvantage, the man fought harder, using his right fist to pummel Harry in the face and head as he writhed underneath him, trying to throw him off.

The pain was excruciating, and Harry held his head as far to the right as he could, trying to lessen the impact, but it didn't help. The man's fist connected with his left jaw, almost knocking him off and causing him to see spots before his eyes.

Harry's right shoulder was on fire. He could feel it giving way. He shifted forward and to his right to add the weight of his upper body to the man's left arm and further decrease the effects of the man's fist. But it was no good. He was the one off balance now, and the man was quickly on top of him again.

His strength slipped away as the younger, stronger man pressed against his grip. Seconds later, a stroke of lightening went from his neck to his fingertips as he felt the shoulder give way.

He cried out in pain, struggling to hold off the syringe with his left arm alone. But the needle penetrated his flesh above his collar bone.

Harry screamed with pain again, trying to dislodge the diabolical device. The man, with cold malevolence in his eyes, fought to get the plunger down.

Now struggling for his life, Harry grabbed the man's throat with his left hand and squeezed as hard as he could, using his thumb to try to collapse the man's windpipe. The man let go of the syringe, but only long enough to use both of his hands to dislodge Harry's hand from his neck and then give him a sharp blow to the side of the head with his left fist.

The blow left Harry dazed as the man went for the syringe again, using his left hand to make a fist around it and his thumb to depress the plunger.

Terror filled him with renewed strength and he powerfully writhed under the man, causing the syringe to dislodge as the loathsome concoction began to inject; sending most of it into the lining of his sport coat.

Harry's left hand instinctively went for the injection site as the man pulled the syringe back. He raised the syringe in the air like a knife. But as he brought it down, Harry sharply raised his left hand, intercepting the man's intended plunge with his forearm and knocking the syringe out of his hand into the yard somewhere.

The man's eyes went in search of his weapon. Spying it, he leaned to his right, but it was out of his reach and Harry managed to scramble out from underneath him and get on his feet, causing the man to abandon his attempt and rise to his feet as well.

He charged at Harry in a blind rage. But Harry, injured and beginning to feel ill, gave the man a sharp kick to the groin; knowing it was his only chance of escape.

The man careened into him and they both fell to the ground, but Harry got back up, leaving the man to writhe in pain as he took off through the trees, heading for the road.

He was shaking badly when he reached his car. The pain in his shoulder had largely immobilized his right arm, and he had to grip the sleeve of his coat with his left hand to help raise it so he could retrieve his keys from his pocket. He opened the door with his left hand and got in, transferring the keys to his left hand so he could put them in the ignition.

Fear gripped him. He'd spent a long time struggling with the keys before he finally got the engine started, and he kept looking back in the direction of the driveway, expecting the man to appear at any second. Finally, after a struggle to get the car in drive, he sped north on Strongs to the junction of M-28 and turned right; heading east toward the Soo.

All of Harry's senses were piqued as he drove on the deserted road. He felt a strange excitement, a nervousness inside and he was trembling. He didn't know if it was the adrenaline wearing off or the effects of the substance the man had injected into him. Whatever that stuff was it smelled awful. The smell alone made him feel sick at his stomach.

The clock read 10:51 p.m. and he'd long given up looking in his rearview mirror for the man to be following him. He didn't know for sure how long he'd been on the road; only that he'd not seen another car and wasn't sure where he was. It was almost like driving in dense fog. Nothing looked familiar, and he had a level of background anxiety that he might have missed his turn.

But then, little or no traffic at night was not an uncommon thing in the U.P. He remembered driving to Newberry with Mitch several years ago to interview an inmate at the prison there. They left for home at five the following morning and didn't see a single car the whole seventy miles back to St. Ignace.

He spied a blinker light in the distance and was filled with elation when he discovered that it marked the junction with M-221, the road to Brimley. That meant his turn-off at I-75 was only six or seven miles ahead. But by the time he got there, he felt cold all over and was having trouble staying on the road. As he turned onto the northbound ramp, his elation and general level of excitement had given way to a deepening depression. Things were getting blurry and felt the right front tire drop onto the shoulder. He jerked the steering wheel back to the left as he fought to get enough air into his lungs. *What's happening to me?* He thought as he struggled to stay on the road.

Harry stumbled out of the car in the hotel parking lot, hurting his shoulder again as he hit the asphalt. He pulled himself up on the open door and tottered from car to car until he reached the building entrance. The door opened and he stumbled in, blinking rapidly, trying to see, but someone had put fog in the lobby.

A voice came from somewhere: "Sir, are you all right? Sir?"

He tried to turn toward the sound, but his knees buckled and he hit the floor.

HARRY FELT A STINGING sensation. He opened his eyes and saw a young, blonde-headed woman withdrawing a syringe from his right arm. Wide awake now, he jerked back and winced at the pain in his shoulder. *"What are you doing? Who are you?"* He looked around the room, his panic subsiding. "Where am I?"

She pressed a square of gauze at the point where she'd withdrawn the needle and taped it down with a plastic bandage. "You're in the hospital, Mr. Brannan. My name is Alicia and I just drew some blood from your arm."

"Am I okay?"

"Well, you seem okay to me, but then I'm a phlebotomist, my job is to draw blood," she said as she picked up her kit. She spoke over her shoulder as she headed for the door. "I'll stop at the nurse's station and tell them you're awake."

The nurse came and took his temperature. She noted his blood pressure, pulse and respiration rates from the monitor and listened to his heart with her stethoscope before promising to call the doctor. She also told him that he was in Memorial Hospital and that it was ten minutes after eleven on Saturday morning.

It was well after lunch when the doctor came in. He walked over to Harry's bed and extended his hand. "I'm Dr. Parker, David Parker."

Harry winced as he gingerly shook the man's hand. "Harry Brannan."

"How's that shoulder feeling?"

"Well, it's still pretty sore, but at least I can move my arm without help."

"You be sure to keep that ice pack on it, and when the swelling goes down, you can try some heat and see if it helps. We X-Rayed it last night, and nothing is broken, but there's a lot of swelling in there and it looks like you messed it up pretty good at some point in the past."

"Yeah, somebody shot me." Harry paused and then quickly spoke again. "I used to be a cop, but I'm retired now, thanks to that...and my knee."

"Yeah, we saw the scar on your knee when we admitted you last night. What happened to you, anyway? They picked you up off the floor over at the Essex Hotel. You remember anything about it?"

"No not much," Harry lied. "I got mugged over at the Waishkey Bay Casino. A big guy with a ski mask knocked me around, and injected something into me, but I moved and most of it went into my coat."

"Really?" the man exclaimed. "There's another good reason to stay away from those places. Did you win a lot of money or something?"

"No, not at all. I don't know what to say except that in my line of work, you make enemies. It's something I've learned to live with."

"Well, he really nailed you—left a big bruise on your upper shoulder. That's what initially put us on to the idea that you had been injected with something."

"What the heck was it, anyway? It smelled awful."

"That's what we wondered too," he said as he flipped open Harry's chart. He studied it for a moment before speaking again. "The specific substance we found in your blood was coniine."

"What?"

"Co-knee-een," the man replied. "It's an alkaloid, a poison—a basic constituent of the plant, Conium Maculatum, or Poison Hemlock."

"Hemlock? You mean, like the stuff that killed Socrates?"

"Yep, same stuff. You're lucky you moved when you did or it would have killed you too. But, as it stands, he didn't get enough of it in to you to do any real damage. Probably killed your coat though."

"Yeah," Harry chuckled, but then he became serious. "Where would he get something like that? Can you just go out and buy it?"

"I'll be honest with you, this is the first case I've ever seen, so I had to read up on it. There is a synthetic version, but it's not something you can go out and buy. On the other hand, you wouldn't have to because it grows wild all over the place, and if you knew what you were looking for, it would be a fairly simple matter to make it yourself."

Harry shook his head. "Wow. Why doesn't somebody do something about that?"

"Yeah, good question. I guess the answer is, because humans are rarely affected by it. Most of the available literature comes out of veterinary medicine. Animals tend to avoid it, but they may eat it if they don't have enough forage or regular pasture grass. When the do, they get sick and sometimes die. It's also been known to cause birth defects when eaten by a pregnant animal, assuming she survives."

"What about me—am I going to be okay?"

The doctor studied the chart again before speaking. "The level of coniine in your blood has decreased significantly since last night and your serum globulin levels have returned to near normal. So I'd say that you're a lucky man, Mr. Brannan."

"So, can I go home, then?"

"I'd really like to keep you overnight. We'll discontinue the catheter, but keep the IV going. And I'll have your nurse come in and take you for a walk. The IV and the exercise should get the stuff out of your system altogether.

Then, if your blood looks good in the morning, you can go home. I'll be here for early rounds before church and I'll sign you out."

Harry gratefully, but gingerly shook the man's hand. "Thank you, Dr. Parker."

"My pleasure," he said as he turned to leave.

"Oh!" Harry spoke-up. "Can I get something to eat? All I had for lunch was clear broth and a cup of tea. I didn't have any supper last night and I'm hungry."

Dr. Parker turned in the doorway. "Sure. I'll have your nurse bring you something from the nourishment room and we'll be sure you get a tray for supper tonight."

"Thanks," Harry called out as the man disappeared down the corridor.

When he returned from his walk, he found two police officers waiting for him in his room. He felt bad about giving them the same story he'd given the doctor. But the truth was that he was not a licensed investigator, he'd arguably provoked the man, followed him home, and trespassed on his property to spy on him. That did not excuse the man trying to kill him—especially in the *way* he tried, but it was more trouble than he needed at the moment.

Chapter 11

HARRY WAS ON THE road by nine a.m. on Sunday morning. His blood tests had come back in the normal range, and he'd had a good breakfast. All things considered, apart from a very sore shoulder, he felt pretty good. *Interesting,* he thought, *how your perspective changes.* A week ago he'd been leaning against his top dresser drawer ready to press the barrel of his pistol against his temple; today he was glad to be alive.

What's the difference? Even as the thought went through his head he knew: Today he had a purpose. Today he wasn't just taking up space. There was a reason for his existence. Today somebody needed him. And it felt good.

It was just past 1:30 p.m. when he arrived at home. He'd turned down the thermostat in his apartment before he left and the place was chilly, so he adjusted it up to a more comfortable temperature. Then he put a pan of water on the stove to make some tea.

While he waited for the water to boil, he turned on his computer and checked his e-mail. He had fourteen messages; all spam. He highlighted them all and deleted them, en-masse, without reading them, before he went out to the kitchen and made his tea. When he returned, he inserted the memory card from his digital camera into a slot on the front of his computer and opened the picture he'd taken of the man in the casino.

The hot tea warmed him as he drank it and worked on the picture in his image editing program. It was a good head shot, in reasonably sharp focus, but seriously under exposed because he'd been afraid to use the flash. He lightened it as best he could while still preserving a decent measure of contrast in the man's face. Then he printed two

4 by 6-inch copies on a single sheet of glossy photo paper and cut them out. He blew on them as he took them to the dining table and set them down to dry.

After that, he went out to his car and retrieved his luggage, and the bag containing the glass with the man's fingerprints. He called Gary Hammond and arranged to be at his house at 3:30 p.m. to have him view the photo. He was back at his apartment by 4:15 with the assurance that he and Gary had seen the same man.

He unpacked his bag, setting aside his sport coat and topcoat to go to the cleaners and putting the rest of his dirty clothes in the laundry basket. Then he picked up the phone and dialed Marti's number. It was ringing as he sat down on the sofa.

"Marti? Hi, it's Harry."

"Oh, you're back! How did it go?"

"Pretty good," he said impassively. "Can we get together? I've got a picture I'd like you to take a look at."

"Uhhh..."

Harry didn't know why, but he felt her hesitation in the pit of his stomach. "Uh...look," he interrupted. "I, uh...shouldn't have called, shouldn't have expected you to drop—"

"No no no no no!" she interrupted in rapid-fire. "I want to see...the picture. It's just that I was going to leave for church in about fifteen minutes. Jo and Liz and I are doing the special music tonight and we were going to practice one last time."

"Oh, I see."

"Listen, why don't you come? When church is over, we can get a bite to eat and talk about what you've found out. I'd really like to see that picture."

It had been a number of years since Harry had been in church, and he wasn't sure if now was the time to go back. On the other hand, he really wouldn't be going back; he was just meeting Marti there.

"Uh...sure, I guess so. Where do you go?"

"Calvary Community Church. Do you know where it is?"

"Yeah, I've driven by it before."

"Great. I'll keep an eye out for you. The service starts at six."

Harry decided to shave and take a shower. Then he went to his bedroom to get dressed. Never having been to her church, he wasn't sure how people dressed for the evening service. *I should have asked,* he thought. He looked at the clock. *Too late now.* So he put on a charcoal suit with muted pinstripes and a red silk tie over a crisp white shirt. *Can't go wrong with a suit.*

The service had already begun when he arrived, so he slipped into a back pew and sat down next to the center aisle. There were a lot of people there. That impressed him. In his experience, evening services were not that well attended. He looked around in the crowd, trying to spot Marti, but he didn't see her until the ladies trio went forward to sing.

When they finished, it was time for the offering. He bowed his head while the pastor prayed and then took some money out of his wallet as he watched the ushers moving down the aisle in his direction.

He'd lost track of Marti during the prayer and was startled when she slid in next to him, on his right. "Hi," she whispered.

"Hi," he whispered back.

She was beautiful in a soft pink cardigan sweater that really brought out the red in her hair, and a pair of dressy, ivory-colored slacks. He averted his eyes lest she think ill of him.

The ushers left with the offering plates and the worship leader went up to the pulpit. "Number 323 in your hymnals. 3-2-3, *O Love That Wilt Not Let Me Go.* Please stand as we worship the Lord together." He lifted his arms, inviting the congregation to stand.

Harry put his hand out to get a hymnal, but there were none in the rack directly in front of him. So Marti reached over to the next rack and picked one up, opening it to the correct page.

This was uncomfortable. He wished she'd picked up two, but resigned himself to sharing as he reached out and held the left side of the book.

He did all right on verses one and two. But by verse three, even though his mouth was moving, no words were coming out. Then, about half way through verse four, the tears came and he beat a hasty exit into the foyer.

The ushers, coming back from wherever they'd taken the offering, were between him and the exit. So, to avoid them, he veered left and went down the first hallway he saw. Finding a men's room, he entered and locked himself in.

This is so embarrassing. He splashed cold water on his face. Such a thing had never happened to him before. Why now; and in front of a woman for Pete's sake? It was the words, something about words; they had unexpectedly found their way into his heart.

He dried his face and stood there for a few minutes, breathing deeply while he regained his composure and contemplated his escape. *Go up this hallway to the main hall, turn left and head for the door. She'll have to get somebody else. I'll never be able to face her after this.*

He opened the door of the men's room and stepped out. Marti was leaning against the opposite wall, waiting for him. *Oh great. This is all I need,* he thought as she stepped toward him. But there were tears in her eyes, and compassion on her face as she opened her arms and captured him in her embrace.

"I'm sorry," she whispered hoarsely as he stood stiffly upright in her arms. "I heard the hesitation in your voice on the phone and I should have suggested something else."

He relaxed some and allowed his arms to go around her loosely in lackluster response. "That never happened to me before." He exhaled through pursed lips. "It caught me by surprise. I'm sorry to have embarrassed you."

She stepped back from him, compassion still on her face, her hands catching his as he let her go. "I'm not embarrassed, but I can see you're in pain. You want to talk about it?"

He shook his head.

She let go of his hands. "Well, why don't we leave, then? If you want to follow me home, I'll make us something to eat, and we can talk about what you've found out."

Harry followed Marti to her house and parked in her driveway as she continued on into the garage. He was waiting for her and held open the storm door as she unlocked the side entry door to let them in. She was wearing a medium-weight leather car coat, and he helped her take it off; holding it as she retrieved a hanger from the closet.

She hung up her coat. "Thank you. Now, let's see what I have to eat around here," she said as she closed the closet door and headed for the kitchen, Harry following. "I usually just have leftover's after church on Sunday evenings," she spoke over her shoulder. "But I was thinking I could make—"

"Leftover's are fine with me," he interrupted. "Or, we could order out; I'd be happy to spring for a pizza or something, if you'd like."

"Yum. That sounds a whole lot better than chicken breasts and broccoli. Plus, I think I have a coupon."

Marti ordered the pizza and then went upstairs to her bedroom to change her clothes. When she returned, Harry was standing in front of her fireplace looking at the pictures on the mantel. She approached quietly on his right and he was startled when she spoke. "I hope you don't mind me wearing jeans and a sweatshirt. I feel kind of funny; you wearing a suit and all. But I didn't want to risk spilling pizza sauce on that sweater."

"I don't mind at all. You look great in jeans and a sweatshirt...not that you didn't look great in what you were wearing—"

"Well, thank you, sir." She blushed slightly as she interrupted. "You clean-up pretty good yourself." She ran her fingertips lightly behind his lapels and blushed again as she dropped her hands. "Liz thinks you look like Jeff Daniels."

Harry laughed out loud. "The actor? Oh, brother, is that what you three were giggling about last Sunday when I first met you?"

"Oh you heard that, huh? Yeah. Sorry." She smiled sheepishly.

Harry laughed again. "Well...I'm flattered...I guess. He didn't appear naked in anything, did he?"

Marti put her head down and blushed deeply.

Harry, seeing her predicament, picked up a picture from her mantel and held in front of them. "Is this you and your daughter, when she was little?"

She held the right side of the frame. "No. That's my daughter, Camille, and her daughter, Callie—my grand-daughter."

"She's very beautiful. They both are."

"Thank you. I think so too, but then I'm prejudiced." She walked to the other side of the fireplace and picked up another picture as Harry set the one he'd been holding back in its place. "Here's a more recent one of the whole family."

He held the left side of the frame as she pointed out the people. "This little guy, here, is Ben. He's three now, and Callie's five. And this is Cam's husband, Roger. They live in Fort Collins, Colorado. He's an engineer with the National Institute of Standards and Technology and she's a nurse at Poudre Valley Hospital, there."

"Nice looking family."

"Yeah," she said wistfully. "I miss them."

She set the picture back on the mantel, and Harry followed her into the kitchen. "How about some cola? All I have is diet."

"Sounds good."

"You want to get some glasses down? They're in the cupboard right in front of you."

Harry set the glasses on the counter and she filled them from a two-liter bottle. Then she returned the bottle to the refrigerator door, and closed it before turning once again to Harry.

She was reaching for her drink when she saw his face in the bright light and stopped short. "What *happened* to you?"

"Hmm?"

She abandoned reaching for her cola and stepped toward him, lightly touching his left jaw with her fingertips. "Your *face*. What happened to your face? It's all bruised."

"Oh," he said impassively, reaching into his inside jacket pocket. He produced the picture he'd taken of the man and handed it to her. "He did. I found him in that casino, and I was bugging him a little bit—trying to get him to slip up and admit he's Greg. Then I followed him home. Somehow, though, he got wise to my presence in his yard and snuck up on me as I was hiding among some trees."

She looked briefly at the photo then set it on the counter and gently caressed his cheek with the fingertips of her right hand as she spoke. "Does it hurt?"

He shook his head in small movements. "Not as much as it did on Friday night."

Tears began to form in her eyes. "Oh Harry, I'm *so* sorry." She gently laid her open hand against the side of his face before removing it. "This is all my fault. If I hadn't asked—"

"Shhh," he interrupted. "It's not your fault. It never once entered my mind to blame you for this and you shouldn't blame yourself. You have no control over what other people do, and I've been in this business long enough to know the dangers."

Her face showed that she was genuinely hurt by what had happened to him, and in that instant he knew he couldn't tell her about the syringe and the poison hemlock. However, he didn't know if it was because he didn't want her to feel sorry for him or he didn't want to hurt her further. What he did know was that his heart felt warm for the first time in his recent memory.

He heard a car drive into the driveway and seconds later the doorbell ring. As Marti went for a tissue, he picked up her coupon from the countertop and removed his wallet, banishing his feelings as he walked to the door. *She's a nice lady being nice, but this is business. Don't get drawn in. Don't even think about getting involved with her. Getting involved with a woman, especially a client, is the surest road to more heartache.*

Harry paid for the pizza and set it on the countertop while Marti brought their drinks to the table. Then she put a couple of slices of pizza on each of two paper plates she'd removed from a cupboard and brought them to the table.

They sat down. "Would you mind praying?" she said as she simultaneously grasped his hand and bowed her head.

He froze for a second, his heart beating so hard he could feel it, but then he spoke. "Father, thank you for this food. We ask your blessing on it that it will be to our good and that you will strengthen us that we might serve you. In Jesus' name, amen."

She gave his hand a light squeeze before letting it go. "Thank you."

She happily set about eating her pizza as if the most natural thing in the world had just occurred. And try as he might, he couldn't make himself hold it against her as he choked his past the lump in his throat.

They each had another slice before Marti got up from the table and threw her plate away. "You want another piece?" she said, lifting the lid on the box.

"No, I'd better not. I like the stuff, but it's not good for my figure."

She laughed and closed the lid. Then she washed her hands and picked up the picture before sitting back down to look at it.

She studied the photo carefully for several minutes. "This sure looks a lot like him, but I can't be certain." She ran her finger over the cheek bones of the image. "His facial features are...remarkably like Greg's, but his hair is too dark and I never saw Greg with a beard. Plus it's been five years."

"He told me his name is Alan Chambers, but I met with Gary Hammond earlier this afternoon and it definitely is the man he saw—the man who said his name was Alan Coombs. Plus, he's in the right age range; early to mid-forties."

"So he was lying to one of you."

"My guess is that he was lying to both of us, and that his real name is Greg Forrester. He said he was from Bay City. That's a lie. He lives in a little town named, Strongs, near the junction of M-28 and M-123. Whoever he is, he has something to hide—something big. Otherwise, why would he try to...why be so violent with me? Why not just call the sheriff? Let me ask you this: 'was Greg right or left handed?'"

"Left. He was left handed."

"I'm pretty sure this guy is left handed."

Her eyebrows went up. "So where does that leave us?"

"Well, I bribed a cocktail waitress to let me have the glass he was drinking from. So I guess my next step is to process it for fingerprints. Mitch is checking to see if he has a record, and if he does, there should be prints on file somewhere. Otherwise, we can just take a chance and run the prints through AFIS and see what comes back."

"AFIS?"

"Automated Fingerprint Identification System—it's a national database of fingerprints. If someone has committed a crime near any population center and been fingerprinted, it's most likely in AFIS."

"And you have access to that?"

"Not anymore, but Mitch does. I'm sure it won't be a problem. He's offered to help me in any way he can."

"I don't know if this makes a difference, but I can tell you he was never in any trouble that I know of as long as we were together."

"Well, let's see what turns up. AFIS is fairly new in the grand scheme of things, but a lot of jurisdictions have entered older fingerprints as well as current ones. You never know, we may get a hit."

Marti nodded.

"I also know his address," Harry continued. "So if he owns that house where he lives, or if he pays his own power bill, I should be able to trace his real name."

"What is his address?"

Harry consulted his spiral book. "11643 Strongs Road."

"I can just go up there and confront him face-to-face. Then I'll know for sure if it's him," she interjected.

Harry shuddered internally at the thought. "Well, let's just see what turns up. Then, if we have to, we can go up there together." *And I'll make sure I have my gun with me.*

"Can I ask you something?" Her face took on a tentative look.

"Of course."

"When you saw him up there, was he alone?"

Harry shook his head and answered with compassion. "No. He was with a dark-haired woman. I didn't get her name, but I'd make her age to be somewhere around thirty.

She was maybe five-foot-six, 130 pounds, large breasts. Ring any bells?"

She shook her head.

"Does it matter?" he said as he stood.

"No, I guess not," she replied as she got up, too. "Time to leave?"

"Yeah, I'd better be going. It's been a long day for me, and I'm dead tired." He walked to the door and then stopped and turned toward her. "As soon as I know anything, I'll call you."

"Thank you." She made a tentative step toward him. "If you don't mind, I'm going to pull a Liz on you," she said as she embraced him. "Thank you, Harry, for helping me. I'm sorry you had to take a beating for it. I'm also sorry to have hurt you by inviting you to church tonight. If you ever want to talk about it, I'll be here for you."

He suddenly found himself trying to swallow past the lump in his throat again as he allowed himself to briefly embrace her. "I'll be in touch," he said more hoarsely than he would have liked. Then he left, trying to be as nonchalant as possible, but not wasting any time lest he further embarrass himself with another display of emotion.

Chapter 12

IT WAS JUST AFTER NINE p.m. when Harry arrived at his apartment. He went straight to his room, emptied the pockets of his suit and hung it in the closet. Exhaustion had overtaken him earlier in the evening and he realized that he'd overdone it. The doctor had told him to rest for a couple of days and he could tell when he'd left the hospital that his stamina was nowhere near normal. Now, as he walked from the bathroom back to his bedroom, it seemed a chore just to put one foot in front of another.

He fell into bed, pulled the covers over himself and, in the same movement of his arm, reached up and switched off the lamp.

It was 9:50 when he was awakened by the ringing of the telephone.

"Hello?" he said, his voice full of sleep.

"Harry? It's Marti. Did I wake you?"

"Yeah...just a minute." He set the handset down and reached up and turned on the light, squinting against the brightness as he brought himself to the sitting position on the edge of the bed. He rubbed his eyes before picking up the handset again. "Okay, I'm back."

"I'm really sorry I woke you up. It didn't occur to me you'd be in bed."

"Well, usually I'm not," he said in an attempt to let her off the hook. "It's just that I've had a tough few days and I...just couldn't go on anymore. Anyway, you've got me now, so what can I do for you?"

"Well, I remembered something about Greg. He was a real gadget nut. When we had our big house, he installed sensors so that if you walked or drove up the driveway they would detect you and beep and turn on a camera. I'll bet that's how he knew you were in his yard! Plus, that's more evidence that it's really him!"

Her voice had excitement in it and Harry couldn't help but smile as he considered her words. "That would certainly explain how he knew I was there. I hadn't thought about that. Thank you for telling me."

"But it was nothing that couldn't have waited until tomorrow. I'm really sorry I woke you, Harry."

"That's okay. I can tell you're excited about remembering, so I'm glad you called."

"I hope you can get back to sleep."

"As tired as I am, an act of congress wouldn't keep me awake."

"Bye," she said plaintively.

"Goodbye, Marti."

Harry hung up the phone, switched off the light and pulled the covers over himself as he laid back down. But, in spite of his confident assertion, sleep did not come easily.

Passive infrared sensors! Good night! I should have thought of that before I so blithely walked up that driveway! It's not like they're new or anything. Man, that little bit of sloppiness darn near cost me my life! I must be getting careless in my old age.

Of course that doesn't prove it's Greg—lots of people have sensors installed in their yards. But she's right; it's more evidence that it really is him. Taken with everything else, it's got to be him. Maybe I'm being too objective not to just acknowledge the obvious, but I'm still going to dot all my I's and cross all my T's on this—just to be sure. And the next time I go up there it will be with the Chippewa County Sheriff.

She sure was excited. He shuddered as he thought of their discussion earlier in the evening. *I can't have her going up there on her own to face him. There's no telling what he'd do to her. I don't want her seeing him at all until he's in handcuffs. Maybe I can get her to just stay here and let me handle it.*

He rolled onto his side and scrunched the pillow under his head, realizing that his protective instincts were working overtime and wondering why.

She's a different kind of woman—different from any I've ever known, anyway. A little touchy-feely for my taste (humph, she even had me doing it), but nice—very nice, and pretty, too.

Aw...who am I trying to kid? I liked it when she touched me and I liked touching her. I like talking with her and I liked it when she hugged me—both times.

Man, that was embarrassing—crying in front of her. What is going on with me, anyway? Must be the exhaustion. Maybe I'm not fully recovered from that hemlock stuff he shot into me. I should have told her about it. No. She's obviously befriended me and I could see I hurt her just telling her how I got the bruises. I can't hurt her.

What's with this, "I can't hurt her," business? He remonstrated with himself. *It's time to back-off, mate. Of course I don't want to hurt her. I don't want to hurt anybody else either. And I especially don't want to hurt myself. And that's where getting involved with her will inevitably lead. Of course, that assumes she'd even want to get involved with me in the first place.*

Stop, already! Go to sleep, for Pete's sake!

IT WAS JUST PAST NINE a.m. when Harry got up on Monday morning. Once he'd gotten back to sleep he slept like a log until he moved wrong and the pain in his shoulder awakened him. He was surprised it had taken so long to happen as he got up and took some pain killers before shaving and getting cleaned up. Then he set out in his car, stopping at McDonalds for a large, black coffee and a breakfast burrito; which he ate on the way to dropping off his dry cleaning. From there he drove directly to the sheriff's department. It was 10:25 a.m. when, bag in hand, he appeared at the open door of Mitch's office and knocked lightly on the door frame.

Mitch looked up from his work. "Harry! Come on in! You don't have to knock." He walked around his desk to where Harry stood and extended his right hand. "Have a seat."

Harry shook his hand before sitting in one of the two chairs in front of what had once been his desk and placing the bag with the glass in it on the floor next to him. "Thanks."

Mitch closed the door and walked back to his desk. But, instead of sitting in his own chair, he came back and sat in the chair next to Harry, turning slightly to face him. "Now, what can I do for...*Man,* what happened to your *face?*"

Harry's left hand involuntarily went up and touched the side of his face. "Oh...I found the guy up in the Yoop. And I guess you could say, he found me too. He took rather violent exception to my meddling in his life."

"Well, I haven't seen *him,* but it looks like you got the worst of it."

"Oh, I did—for sure. He attacked me out in his yard— tried to inject me with poison hemlock, of all things. I was lucky to get away from him. And I wouldn't have if I hadn't kicked him in the groin and run for all I was worth. But before that, my shoulder gave out as I fought with him, and he managed to get a little of that junk injected into me. It made me sick—put me in the hospital from Friday night to yesterday morning."

"Wow. Are you okay?"

"Well, the doctor says I'm lucky to be alive, but yeah, I'm fine now; except for being tired and having a very sore shoulder."

"Man, I'm sorry about that. If I hadn't gotten you into this—"

"Don't worry about it," Harry interrupted. "Hazard of the job; and you and I both know it."

"Yeah, well, I'm still sorry you got hurt. What did Marti say? Liz mentioned you two got together last night after church."

"I didn't tell her the whole story. I couldn't avoid telling her about the bruises because she saw them, but I didn't mention the rest of it because just that made her cry."

"I think she likes you."

"Yeah, she seems to have befriended me."

"No, I think it's more than that—"

Harry held up his hand as he interrupted. "Yeah, well, the last thing I need is—"

"Listen to me, Harry. Not all women are like Lisa. Next to my salvation, Liz is the best thing that ever happened to me. She's—"

"Yeah, well, you hit the jackpot with Liz, but she's the exception."

"Not true! I know that Clay and Jo feel the same way about each other. And there's not a nickel's worth of difference between Liz, Jo or Marti when it comes to that. They don't have a disloyal or uncaring bone in their bodies."

Harry took a deep breath and exhaled it. "Anyway," he said, changing the subject as he picked up the bag from off the floor. "I managed to get the guy's prints on a glass and I was wondering if you could clear the way for me with Darlene to process the thing. I'm hoping she'll be willing to do it for me on her own time. I'll find a way to pay for the powder and stuff."

"Not a problem. You know she'd do practically anything for you since you saved her bacon on that Internal Affairs beef."

"Yeah, I know, but it just seems...proper I guess, to run it through you first. By the way, did you get any hits when you ran his name?"

"No. No wants, no warrants, no prints, no nothing. I even checked with the FBI. The guy's squeaky clean. I also ran a credit check on him, but there's been no activity since about the time he went missing. Social Security hasn't seen any activity on him either. If he didn't die in that explosion, he's living under a different name. Of course that assumes Greg Forrester really is his name; maybe it isn't—hard to say based on what we know at the moment. I will say though, that his Michigan driver's license photo is the same guy as in his Illinois license photo. It's definitely the guy we knew as Greg."

"Hmm, good point about the name. I wondered about that myself. I tell you Mitch, I've got a bad feeling about this. I managed to snap a picture of him and it is, for sure, the same guy that Hammond saw. And Marti is fairly sure it's him based on his facial structure. But with a difference in hair color and the fact that he wears a beard where Greg didn't, she doesn't want to say for certain until she can see him face-to-face and hear his voice.

"Thing is, if he's not Forrester, why try to kill me? I mean, slug me maybe—even beat me up, but injecting that stuff into me goes way beyond the pale. If it's not him, it's somebody with something big to hide, and I don't want Marti going anywhere near him. There's no telling what he'd do to her. I mean, after what he did to me...well, it doesn't bear thinking about."

"Yeah, I agree. Did you get his address? I'll see if I can match it to a name."

"Yeah, I got it," Harry said as he reached into his inside jacket pocket for his spiral book. He flipped through the pages, stopping at the correct one. "It's 11643 Strongs road and the town is also named Strongs. I spotted the local power company as I was driving down M-28. It's Cloverland Power Cooperative. But I didn't get a phone number for them."

"That's okay," Mitch said as he copied down the information. "I'll get their number. How about his license plate?"

"No. That's what I was after when he attacked me out in his yard. But it's a Jeep, Grand Cherokee. How many of them could there be in Strongs, Michigan?"

"Well, if it's like most of the little towns in the U.P., probably not many. I'll see what I can dig up on it." He closed his notebook and tossed it onto his desk. "Well, if you're ready, let's go see Darlene. Hopefully she can get something good enough to put into AFIS. If he's as nasty as he seems, it would surprise me if we don't get a hit."

Darlene Warner was glad to see Harry and greeted him with a strong hug, the emotion of which nearly brought him to tears. She eagerly took the glass, agreeing to test it for fingerprints and enter any results into AFIS on her own time, then send the results to Mitch. However, she wouldn't allow Harry to pay for anything; such were her feelings of kinship with him.

When they left the lab, Mitch offered to take him for an early lunch, but Harry declined, citing a late breakfast. In truth, he hadn't had that much for breakfast, but as far as he was concerned, it was time to get out of there. Mitch was his one enduring friend, and there was a sense in which he loved him, but visits to the department since he'd been forced to retire were always difficult; leaving him in a state he couldn't quite describe. On the one hand, he was more than glad to see his old friends and associates. On the other, it was an all too poignant reminder that there would never be a place there for him again. And it provoked in him a semi-elated, semi-depressed mood that always seemed to morph into no elation, all depression by the time he got back to his lonely apartment.

When Harry got to his car he set out for home. There wasn't much more he could do on the case until Mitch got back to him with the address and car information and Darlene got the glass processed and the fingerprints made their way through AFIS. That, of course, assumed there would be usable prints on the glass.

When he'd first become a detective, all detectives needed to know how to lift a set of prints. That was in the days before the so-called CSI divisions. Still, he had to admit, things had changed for the better. And there was no one better than Darlene. If there were usable prints on that glass, she could get them off.

Before he had lunch, Harry spent half an hour at the gym, most of it on the treadmill. It would be a while before his shoulder was up to any kind of significant work again. The workout made him feel good and, after he arrived at home, he cleaned his apartment and did his laundry. Then he took a shower and afterward put on sweat pants and a T-shirt before taking a short nap on the sofa. He had just finished eating his supper when the phone rang.

"Harry? Hi, it's Marti. I, uh...wondered how you made out today. Or is it too soon to ask?"

"Well, it is a little soon. Mitch is checking out the guy's address with the local power company and I have a fingerprint specialist checking the glass. I may hear from Mitch as early as tomorrow, but I doubt there'll be any news on the glass for a few days. She's doing it as a favor to me on her own time."

"Oh." He heard what sounded like dejection in her voice.

"You're hot to get this guy aren't you?"

She took a shuddering breath. "I hardly slept all night last night, thinking about this. And the more I think about that picture, the more sure I am that it's Greg. And the more I think about it, the more I think it's just like something he'd do! I'm just livid about it and I want to go up there and throttle him—if it's him. And...I think it is, but...I want to be sure."

"Listen Marti, I want you to stay away from that guy. Just let me handle—"

"*No!*" she interrupted indignantly. "I want to go up there and face him! I want *him* to know that *I* know he's alive and that he didn't get away with it! I want to see the look on his face! I want him to pay for what he did!"

"Just simmer down a minute. Okay?" he said gently in an attempt to assuage her anger. "Let's just suppose for a minute that it is Greg up there. You know he left for a reason. Now I'm not saying that you're the reason, but he's been perfectly content not to have had any contact with you for over five years now. Apparently he's established a new identity for himself and he has a vested interest in not being found out. I mean, look at what he did to me. What do you think he'd do to you if you suddenly appear on his doorstep? Let me handle this. After all, that's what you're paying me for. If I can prove it's him I'll get the police involved and he'll get his comeuppance. But you need to stay away from him until he's in custody."

"Look, Harry, I think I know him a *little bit* better than you do!" she retorted, her voice trembling with her growing indignation. "I was married to him for *five years* you know! Humph, if it's him, I'm *still* married to him! And I am *not* some little girl who needs somebody to tell her what's in her own best interest. I'm a grown woman, thoroughly capable of thinking for myself!"

He heard her sniff and could tell she had begun to cry. "You okay?" he said softly.

"Noooooo. My best friend is...dead because of him."

"Have you been thinking about her all day?"

"Yyyess."

"Then I can see why you're upset," he said with compassion in his voice. "Listen Marti, I know that you're a grown woman and I know that you can think for yourself. I'm sorry if I conveyed the impression that you weren't or that I didn't know that—I certainly didn't mean to. I'm just concerned for your safety, that's all."

She sniffed. "And I'm sorry I flew off the handle at you. You didn't do anything wrong. I'm just...just...overwrought, I guess. Thank you for c-caring about me."

She began to weep in earnest and he heard her put the phone down and then blow her nose several times. It was well over a minute before she came back on the line.

"I'm sorry I got after you, Harry. Please forgive me."

"Hey," he said gently. "There's nothing to forgive. Listen, why don't I come over and sit with you for a little while? Or, if you don't want me, I'd be happy to call Liz or Jo for you. I'm sure they know how hard it is for you to go through all this again."

She made a small, involuntary sound in her throat as she exhaled. "You're a nice guy Harry, but I'll be all right...really. I'm already starting to feel better. I guess I just needed somebody to vent on and you were handy. I'm sorry."

"I'm not. I'm glad I could be there for you. You sure you're going to be all right?"

"Yeah," she said quietly.

"Listen, I'll call you the minute I know anything. Okay?"

"Okay."

"Then we'll make a plan about what our next steps should be. Okay?"

"Okay."

"Maybe you..." He hesitated for several seconds.

"What?"

"I was going to suggest that maybe you should think about calling it a day and get some sleep, but I don't want you to think I'm telling you what to do."

She chuckled. "No, you're right. I was thinking the same thing myself. It's not been a very good day for me."

"Good. Get some sleep. And I hope tomorrow is a better day for you."

"I will. Goodnight, Harry."
"Goodnight, Marti."

Chapter 13

"I HOPE YOU DON'T MIND, but I'm not going to church this morning," Marti said, walking into the kitchen in her robe and slippers. "I just don't think I can f-face anybody right now. It's, it's too soon, I...I didn't get any s-sleep last night, and—"

Jenny set her coffee mug on the counter and drew her friend into an embrace, gently laying her hand on the side of her head as it rested on her shoulder. "Of course I don't mind," she tenderly interrupted. "Nobody's expecting you to do anything right now and God certainly understands how—"

"Oh, Jen. What am I...going to do?" she wept out.

"Shhh, Shhh, It's all right, It's all right, I'm here for you," she said softly as she stroked her hair. "You don't have to do anything right now except let us take care of you. We'll get through this...together. That's what sisters are for. Now, let me pour you a cup of coffee. It'll make you feel a little better to get something warm into you."

Jenny walked Marti over to a chair in the dinette and gently sat her down before going back into the kitchen, retrieving a mug from the cupboard and filling it. She brought the mug to the table, set it in front of her friend and then hugged her with one arm, the sides of their faces touching, before she stood again. "Let me wake up Liz and call Clay to tell him he's on his own today. Then I'll make us some breakfast..."

THE RAUCOUS NOISE BROUGHT Marti out of her bedroom into the hallway where Liz stood holding the telephone handset at her side—oblivious to the screeching off-hook alert that said the person on the other end had hung up long ago.

"Liz?"

She didn't answer, but continued to stand there transfixed, a vacant look on her face.

"Liz?" Marti spoke again, a little louder, her voice tinged with alarm. "Liz, what is it?"

It wasn't until she actually touched Liz's wrist while reaching for the handset to hang it up that she came out of her apparent trance. "Oh!" she said vacantly, her preoccupation giving way to awareness as she quickly hung up the phone.

"Liz, what is it? What's wrong? Who was it on the phone?"

Liz didn't respond, but stood there, her distress apparent on her face, her eyes searching, as if trying to find the answer somewhere in the distance.

Marti's hand went to her mouth as she gasped. "Oh!' she said, inhaling. They found him, didn't they? They found Greg."

"No."

Her friend's obvious distress was causing Marti's anxiety to build. "Who was it on the phone, Liz?"

Again, Liz was silent and seemed to be searching for a response.

"Liz, *please?*"

"It was Mitch," she said gently, coming to Marti with her arms open. There's been an accident. It's Jen—Jenny. She's dead."

SUDDENLY MARTI WAS WIDE awake and short of breath, her heart beating so hard that it hurt as it bounded in her chest. Then the tears came and she moved back the covers, sitting on the edge of the bed to once again weep out her agony over her dear friend.

She switched on the bedside lamp before pulling two tissues out of the box. After not having had this dream since...she couldn't remember when, this was the second night in a row it had awakened her with an anguish unabated by the passage of time.

Missing and Presumed Dead

She could still feel the dreamed touch of Jenny's cheek against hers and it seemed so unfair to be having these vivid dreams again after so long. The two things they accomplished were to bring back painful memories of a husband who had used her, and to enlarge the already giant void in her heart; intensifying her feeling of loss for the one who had sought her out to be her friend and sister.

She blew her nose again and collected her spent tissues, throwing them in the wastebasket as she made her way to the bathroom to splash some cool water on her face and get a drink. Then she returned to her bed, questioning whether it had indeed been a wise idea to enlist Harry's services to find the man Gary had seen up north.

Not that Harry was the problem. Harry was a nice man—at least to her. It was the not knowing, the never having truly known, about Greg, and the fresh opening of wounds that had never really healed. This was turning out to be much harder than she had foreseen. Still, maybe this painful exercise would finally bring her the closure she continued to seek after so many years. She hoped so.

Harry. There was a man who was carrying some baggage. He tried hard not to show it, to hide behind his tough cop persona, but inside he hurt. She could sense it—feel it in her heart. If he'd just confide in her, maybe she could help him find the closure he needed. But who was she trying to kid? She was depending on him to help her find her own closure.

It was 11:05 p.m. when she shut off the light and laid back down, pulling the covers over her. She'd been awake for just over an hour, just longer than she'd been asleep. And it didn't look like sleep would come again anytime soon.

Greg. That rotter. Harry was right about one thing: he would get his comeuppance; she'd see to that—assuming it was him, hiding up there in the U.P.

It was well past three a.m. before she finally drifted back to sleep.

Chapter 14

TUESDAY CAME AND WENT with no word from either Mitch or Darlene. Having spent his entire working life as a cop, Harry knew the story: it's nice to be able to help a friend, but the official work comes first. His request would be relegated to lunch hours or other periods when they weren't on the county's time. And that's the way it should be.

Actually, he considered himself fortunate to be getting any help at all. If it weren't for his relationship with Mitch and Darlene, he doubted he'd even be granted access to their offices—much less get any help. PIs are not generally held in fond affection by cops.

Still, memories die hard. And in his mind's eye, he could see himself behind his desk, phoning the power company to run down the address information or walking into Darlene's lab to see how things were going. It made him itch to be 'back in the saddle,' but that, he knew, was not going to happen. A door had closed and there was no way he could get it open again. At some level he had come to accept that. At another, it was the source of unrelenting frustration. He was made to be a cop and he was good at it. His mind still knew how to investigate, but his body could no longer pass the physical.

If he were a PI he could pick his cases, avoiding the ones he was physically incapable of doing. But he couldn't use Mitch as a resource all the time. Couldn't and wouldn't. Mitch was in this, probably at Liz's urging, because of his friendship both with him and with Marti. After all, he and Clay Ramsey had virtually rebuilt that little house where she lives and done it largely at their own expense.

Mitch was a good guy—the only guy who showed up every single day that he lay in that hospital bed, the only guy who stood by his bedside and prayed right out loud for him, the guy who had his whole church praying for his recovery. He couldn't use Mitch. Couldn't and wouldn't.

He wondered, though, how good of an investigator he could really be without all of the official resources he'd once had at his disposal. The door, after all, was closed. Maybe he needed to quit hanging around by the door and move on to something else. But what—stocking nuts and bolts at some home improvement superstore? The prospect was anything but enticing.

BY 9:30 ON WEDNESDAY morning, Harry was back in his apartment with the information Mitch had obtained for him, including driver's license photos. Darlene, according to Mitch, had managed to extract three sets of usable prints from the glass, but had not had the time to process them through AFIS yet. Those results would be a day or two away.

Rather than call Marti immediately as he said he would do, he decided to scan the photos into his computer and experiment with an idea that had occurred to him the night before. If he could obtain the results he was looking for, she would be glad he waited.

When he finished, he called her at work and they agreed to meet for lunch at Torrey's English Grille. She hesitated because the place was expensive, but he prevailed with her. He didn't tell her, but he'd decided to just pay for their lunches and not bill her.

He was already seated in a booth when she arrived at 11:35 a.m. and he waved to catch her attention as she scanned the dining room from near the hostess station.

She threw her coat on the seat and then slid in across from him. "Nice place. You eat here a lot?"

"No, not really; too rich for my blood. I suggested it because there tends to be less chaos here than in your average lunch venue; more conducive to a quiet meeting. How about you?"

"No, first time for me," she said, opening a menu.

She looked good, very good, in a navy blue pantsuit and pink top, under the one-button jacket that she wore open.

"The grilled chicken Caesar salad is good, if you like that kind of thing."

"Yes, I do. Sounds good."

She closed the menu and set it near the edge of the table just as the waiter arrived to take their orders. She waited until he was out of earshot before speaking again.

"So, what did you find out?" She gave her head a shake and used both hands to flip her hair away from her eyes.

"Well, we got a name to go with that address up in Strongs: Wayne McCarthy."

Her countenance fell. "So it's not him, then—Greg...Wait a minute!" she said, her expression brightening. "Maybe it *is* him and he just *rents the place* from this Wayne guy...McCarthy!"

Harry smiled briefly at the way her face animated when she got excited, but then produced the blow-up he'd made of McCarthy's driver's license photo and slid it in front of her. "No, he's the guy I saw up there, the guy that...uh, the same guy Gary Hammond saw."

"Oh," she said, her countenance falling again.

She sat there, with her elbows on the table, her forehead resting on her fingertips. And Harry couldn't tell if she was looking at the picture or had taken up a silent lament. He was about to produce the next blow-up from his portfolio when she spoke again.

"You know, it sure looks like him. I mean, take away the beard and lighten his hair a little bit..."

Harry produced the next picture and slid it in front of her, beside the first one. "That's his driver's license photo. Here's Greg's last driver's license photo taken the year he went missing."

She studied the two photos side-by-side, touching first one and then the other with a fingertip, tracing the bone structure in the faces.

He produced a third picture from his portfolio. She looked up as he held the picture in front of him with his left hand. "Now, come here," he said, gesturing to her with his right hand.

She got out of her seat and slid in next to him. Her hip bumped his and his heart jumped so hard he thought it would leave his chest. He could smell her perfume and feel the heat radiating from her and suddenly he found it difficult to breathe.

He was surprised, and he knew he had to say something—soon, but he wasn't sure if he had enough breath to be able to form words.

She turned her head and looked at him. "You okay?"

Whew! He thought. *Gotta talk now.* He cleared his throat and took a deep breath, exhaling as he moved a little to his left. "Yeah," he breathed, putting his right arm on the back of the seat behind her, being careful not to touch her. *I can pull this off if I don't touch her.*

He laid the picture before them. "I got to thinking about driver's license photos, how they always make you stand on the line to shoot your picture. That means that all driver's license photos are pretty much the same, in terms of perspective, distance from the camera, that kind of thing. And I thought, why couldn't I superimpose one photo over another? So that's what I did. I loaded Wayne and Greg's pictures into my computer and kind of merged them into one. What you're looking at is Greg overlaid on Wayne. I'm no expert at this, so it's pretty crude, but I think we've got a fairly good match." He ran his index finger quickly over the eyes, cheekbones, and mouth of the image, making an imaginary 'Z,' then swiped it down the nose before removing his hand.

Marti studied the photo carefully, also running her finger over the ghostly looking, merged features. Then she shook her head and smiled. "You're good. Do you know that? You are *really* good!"

Harry laughed. "Well, driver's license photos being what they are, it's by no means conclusive, but—"

"No, I agree," she interrupted. "It's not conclusive, but it's close—very close. Close enough to go up there and confront him."

The waiter arrived with their lunches and gave the two of them a knowing look, smiling as he set the plates before them. Marti blushed, and when he was out of earshot whispered, "I should get back on my own side."

Harry wanted to object and say that she didn't have to, but he kept his mouth shut as he cleared the photos off the table and placed them back into his portfolio. When she resumed her seat, he picked up her plate in both hands and gave it to her. She sat it down and bowed her head, extending her hand to him. He reached out and picked it up as he too bowed his head and they prayed silently for their food.

"I'm thinking I can take Friday off," she said after swallowing a bite of her salad.

Harry raised his eyebrows. "What for?"

"For going up there to confront him. I've got plenty of vacation time—seeing as I hardly ever use it—so I know it won't be a problem. We could come back on Saturday."

"Whoa, wait a minute. I'd like to get the results of the fingerprints back first, just to be sure what we're up against. Now, it's possible they could be in by tomorrow or Friday, but—"

"So where's the problem, then?" she interrupted.

"Well, as I was starting to say, I have to be in court on Friday morning. I've got to testify in a case from when I was still on the job. Plus, I think our plans should be contingent upon what the prints reveal. I mean, what if it turns out the guy is some dangerous criminal?"

"Oh." Her countenance visibly fell again.

"Look, I know you're disappointed, but you've already waited this long, what difference will an extra few days make?"

She didn't reply, but continued eating.

"Please don't be angry with...me." He was surprised as he heard the words coming out of his mouth.

"I'm not angry," she replied tersely.

"Why do I get the impression that you are?"

"I don't know, Harry."

He took a deep breath and exhaled it. "Look, Marti, I need you to trust me on this, okay? I thought we were friends."

She continued eating in silence until she finished her lunch. Then she wiped her mouth with her napkin, placed it on her plate and pushed the plate aside. "I've got to be getting back," she said, picking up her purse.

She opened her purse, removed her wallet from it and snapped it open.

"I'll get it," Harry said.

"That's all right," she replied, laying a $10 bill on the table.

She put her wallet back into her purse and set the purse on the corner of the table as she slipped out of her seat and then into her coat.

"Uh...I'll, uh...call you as soon as I get the, uh...fingerprint results."

"Yeah," she said flatly, picking up her purse. "You do that."

She turned and left the restaurant.

Harry took another deep breath and slowly blew it out through pursed lips; hanging his head as he traced absent mindedly on the tabletop with his index finger.

That went well, he thought. *What's the big deal about waiting a few days to be sure? Can't she see I'm just trying to protect her? I probably should have told her about him trying to kill me. That's what I get for trying to spare her feelings, I guess.*

Mitch's words suddenly played back in his mind: *"I think she likes you."* *Yeah, right, Mitch; she likes me just fine. She wouldn't even acknowledge that we are friends. That's how much she likes me.*

He blew out another breath as the waiter stopped at the table with the check.

"I can take that up for you whenever you're ready, sir."

"I'm ready now," Harry replied, taking out his wallet. He removed enough money that, when combined with what Marti had left, would pay for their meals and provide a generous tip, and slipped it inside the small folder containing the check.

"Will you be wanting change, sir?"

"No, keep it," he replied sadly.

"Thank you, sir. Have a nice day."

"Yeah," he replied flatly as the man turned and left.

Harry slid out of the booth and stood.

Somehow, in spite of his defenses, he knew she had gotten into his heart. He could tell by how much it hurt as he, too, left the restaurant.

Chapter 15

HAVING LOST SLEEP TO the same dream for the third night in a row and after her falling out with Harry, Marti was not at all sure she was up to going to church on Wednesday evening. But she went. And, after choir practice, stayed behind and spent some time talking with Liz and Jo.

"How are things going with your investigation?" Liz inquired.

"Oh...I don't know," she lamented.

"Harry not working out for you?"

"No, it's not that. He's done a great job of finding him; got pictures and everything. I'm all but certain that it's Greg."

"So what's the problem, then?"

"Well, I can't get him to go back up there with me to confront him. He got Greg's...well, *the guy's,* fingerprints on a glass and turned them in to somebody he knows at the sheriff's department to be processed. He *says* he wants to wait for the results to come back, but I don't think that's it. He got into a scuffle with him when he was up there last week and I'm pretty sure he's afraid to go back up there again."

"Oh, Marti," Liz responded with gentle incredulity. "I really doubt that. He might be afraid, but that wouldn't keep him from going back up there. Take it from a cop's wife: all cops have times when they're afraid, but you can't be a cop for as long as Harry has without learning to conquer it. He's no coward, Marti. If there's one man Mitch respects, it's Harry. And that just wouldn't be the case if he were a coward. My guess is it's exactly what he says it is. He's waiting for the fingerprint results; being thorough—cautious. That's what Mitch would do. If you're a cop, and you want to go on living, it doesn't pay to be unnecessarily bold."

"That's kind of what Clay says about flying," Jo added. "'There are bold pilots and old pilots; but no old, bold pilots.'"

"Yeah," Liz laughed. "Mitch says the same thing about cops. One of the first things you learn as a cop is to be sure of what you're doing before you do it. Make sure you know everything you can know about a situation before you go in. It's how you stay alive."

Jo spoke again. "You know, Marti, Harry never knew Greg. I mean, all he's got to go on is the evidence he's been able to dig up. He's not going to be near as sure as you are, just by looking at pictures." Liz was nodding in agreement.

Marti's face took on a pained expression as she squeezed her eyes shut and shook her head in small side to side movements.

"What's the matter?"

"Oh...you're right, Jo," she moaned. "You're both right. And I was so mean to him today: I gave him the silent treatment and wouldn't let him pay for my lunch. I insulted him and I know I hurt his feelings. Ohhh," she moaned again, putting her face in her hands.

"You *care* about him, don't you," Jo observed, exchanging a look with Liz.

The pained expression was still on Marti's face when she raised it. "I guess I do," she said, nodding, tears beginning to form in her eyes.

"Oh, honey," Jo said, capturing her in an embrace. "You'd better call him and tell him you're sorry."

"First chance you get," Liz added, exchanging another look with Jo as she continued to hold Marti.

"I guess I'd better."

THURSDAY TURNED OUT TO be a busy day for Harry. He spent the early part of it at the sheriff's department going over his old case file in preparation for his court appearance, and much of the remainder of it at the county prosecutor's office being drilled over and over again on his testimony. It was late afternoon when he finally left there and he was tired, but he decided to do his weekly grocery shopping on the way home, not knowing what his schedule would look like the next day.

On the way home from the market he went through the drive-thru of a fast food place and got a big hamburger and an order of French fries, knowing that they weren't good for him and not caring. He ended up having to reheat them in the microwave because, not having full use of his right arm, it took him so long to carry in his groceries and put them away.

It was fully dark when he finished eating, and he closed the drapes before checking his answering machine. No messages. However, cycling back through his Caller ID he saw that he'd received seven calls from Choice Care HMO, beginning early in the morning and going through late afternoon. He recognized it as the place where Marti worked.

He shook his head. *That woman just does not give up. Well, I don't have the results on the prints yet and I don't know when I'm going to have them. So, sorry, Marti, I don't have any news for you today.*

He thought about calling her anyway. *No. If she wanted me to call her back, she would have left me a message. And she didn't. Clearly, she doesn't want to have anything to do with me if I can't tell her what she wants to hear. And I can't. So there's no sense in calling her. Besides, I don't think I can bear to hear her voice right now.*

NONE OF THE DEFENSE'S NINE objections during Harry's testimony on Friday were sustained. Finally, after being strongly cautioned by the judge, they requested and were granted a half hour recess.

When court reconvened, the defense, with the concurrence of the prosecution, outlined the plea deal they'd made during the recess. Harry was dismissed.

When he got home he checked his answering machine and found a message from Mitch stating that the fingerprint results were in. He erased the message and returned the call, agreeing to meet Mitch for lunch, and immediately set out in his car.

He arrived at about 12:20 p.m. and found Mitch already seated.

"We got a hit, but only on one set of prints," Mitch said after they'd ordered their meals. "But I'm sure it's our guy."

"Must be a pretty good hit if you're sure."

"It is," Mitch replied, producing a booking photo of a young man. "The prints go back to one, Gregor Alansky of Rockford, Illinois. He was arrested when he was eighteen for possession of greater than one ounce of marijuana and intent to deliver. He pled down to possession and got ninety days in the Winnebago County Jail." He slid the picture in front of Harry. "Recognize him?"

"Oh yeah. That's him all right. A young him."

Harry continued to study the image for a moment, paying particular attention to the name on the booking plate the young man was holding. "Gregor Alansky. What is that, Russian or something?"

"I don't know, could be. Sounds like maybe it's Slavic, but I don't know." Mitch flipped a page in his spiral book. "He legally changed his name to Greg Forrester, but he's also been known as, Gregory Allen and Alan Gregory."

"You mean he's got more than just the possession beef."

"Yeah. Seems he got married when he was in his early twenties to a 52-year-old widow who used her inheritance to put him through Northwestern's Real Estate Management program and supposedly set him up in business. Nothing came of it though, and when the money ran out so did he. She filed a complaint with the local authorities, but he'd done nothing illegal, so nothing could be done. She divorced him, but by then it was too late.

"As Greg Allen, he swindled a 64-year-old widow in Iowa out of her savings. And as Alan Gregory, he married a 50-year-old widow in Rochester, Minnesota. It took him two years to clean her out and she committed suicide after he took off. Her kids—"

"Tried to have him prosecuted," Harry interrupted. "But there was nothing the police could do because he hadn't obviously broken any laws and was no longer in the jurisdiction anyway."

"Right. Larceny by false pretense, but try to prove it."

"Yeah, the old sweetheart scam. And, as Greg Forrester, it looks like Marti was his unsuspecting victim number four. Did he ever really work for her uncle?"

"Good question. My guess is, probably yes. He had to have found out about her somehow and that makes sense. Do you know the name of the company? I'll see if I can find out."

"No, I don't know it. I'll have to ask her and get back to you."

They both worked on eating their lunches, and it wasn't until Harry finished that he spoke again. "You know, something about this just doesn't seem right. It's got a weird feel to it."

"What do you mean?"

"Well, the name for one thing. He always used some derivation of his right name in the past: Greg or Alan. He told Gary Hammond his name was Alan Coombs. He told me his name was Alan Chambers. And he was always Greg or Alan something with the women he bilked. Why is he deviating from that pattern now and calling himself, Wayne McCarthy?"

Mitch wiped his mouth with his napkin and then pushed his plate aside. "Good point. Once these guys find a formula that works they usually stick with it."

"And another thing: with the other women, he just took off. Why, all of a sudden with Marti, does he go to all the trouble to fake his own death?"

"I don't know. You think maybe he might have cared about her and wanted to be sure she got the insurance?"

"I doubt it. Apparently they weren't, uh...consummating their marriage on anything like a regular basis. And she had to deal with a couple of floozies who wanted to profit from his insurance after hearing the news about the explosion. I don't think he loved her at all."

Mitch made a wry face and shook his head.

"What?"

"Oh, I was just remembering how heartbroken she was. That dirty..." He shook his head again as he strongly exhaled. "She's a good woman. She deserves better than that."

Harry nodded. "Well, she's angry now. I mean, *really* angry—hot to go after him."

"Can you blame her?"

"No. I just wish she'd cool down a little bit, you know. I'm afraid, if I take her up there, she'll go after him. I tell you, Mitch," he said, shaking his head. "He is a violent guy. I don't want to see her get hurt."

"Well, that's why she's got you."

"Yeah," he said flatly. "Listen, uh...I wonder if that woman in Iowa is still alive."

"Bigamy?"

"Yeah. If she's still alive and never divorced him or if we can prove she was alive and had not divorced him when he married Marti, there's no contract, no marriage as far as Marti is concerned. That would give us grounds to go after him and her grounds for a civil suit. Maybe she can get back some of her inheritance."

"Yeah, it's worth a look. I'll see what I can find out."

When Harry got home he tried to call Marti at work, but discovered she had taken the day off. He began to get an uneasy feeling in the pit of his stomach when repeated calls to her home throughout the afternoon also went unanswered.

Chapter 16

MARTI GOT UP AT EIGHT A.M. on Friday morning. Having the day off, she had not bothered to set her alarm and was glad for the two hour's extra sleep. It had been a difficult week—mostly due to the emotional strain of the dreams. But her sleep last night had been dream free and she felt better for it and, she knew, for her decision to confront Greg.

After breakfast, she did her dishes and packed an overnight bag. Then she scrounged around for a map and for the slip of paper upon which she'd written Greg's address, before leaving for the U.P. at about 9:30.

By three p.m. she was driving west on M-28. It was a cold day, 24 degrees according to the thermometer in her car. And although the roads were clear, there was about two inches of snow on the grassy areas. She'd never been in the U.P. before and somehow had expected there would be more. But two inches was two inches more than they had in Grand Rapids and winter had not yet really begun.

She saw the sign indicating she had entered Strongs Corners and slowed, but still managed to drive past Strongs road before seeing it. Continuing on a short distance, she turned around in a motel parking lot and drove back the way she had come, turning south when she reached the corner.

Strongs Road was level for a little way and there was a cluster of houses right near the intersection. However, after about a quarter mile, the road declined in a fairly steep hill and the houses gave way to moderately dense woods.

She drove on slowly, looking back and forth out the side windows for mailboxes or any thing else that would indicate she'd found Greg's house. There was nothing but dense woods on the west side. With the exception of a few places where a car could pull off, the trees came almost to the edge of the pavement.

The road leveled out, and after going for about a mile and a half, she encountered a drive on the east side and slowed even more until she spotted a sign indicating that it led to some kind of camp that was closed for the season.

Finally, after going more than half a mile further down the road, she spotted a mailbox on her left. She slowed, looking for the house number, but was unable to make it out because it was on the opposite side of the box from the way in which she had come.

She continued on, and after about another half mile she was out of the woods and into an open area that, at least on the left, appeared to be marshy. There was no good place to turn around so she followed the road in a right-hand curve and drove on until it ended a couple of miles later at M-123.

She turned around in the intersection and drove back, stopping when she reached the mailbox. The address read, 11643. She had been nervous since turning onto this street, but now she could feel her heart beating in her chest and her resolve waning as she sat there trying to decide what her next steps should be. She closed her eyes and took several deep breaths, trying to bolster her courage, and was startled when a large SUV sped by her, going in the opposite direction. It shocked her, jarring her out of her reverie and she quickly put the car in gear, drove north to M-28 and turned left.

Klein's Motel was about a half mile west of Strongs Road, on the right. It was a classic 50s-60s vintage roadside motel with ten drive-up units contained in a single long structure. The office, which was a separate building to the left of the units and perpendicular to them, appeared to also be the home of the owners. A large sign welcoming snowmobilers was bolted underneath the name sign which stood near the entrance to the gravel parking lot where she'd turned around only several moments before.

Marti parked in front of the office and got out of her car. She moved her shoulders around to stretch them as she scanned the lot. There was a pickup truck parked in front of the next to the last unit and one other car, next to hers, which turned out to belong to the owner.

She went in and prepaid for one night's stay in unit four. Then she parked her car in front of the door and, using her key, let herself in.

The place was clean but Spartan. The knotty pine paneled room contained a double bed, a small writing desk, a Kennedy style rocking chair and a television. There was no phone. A gas space-heater was built in to the right-hand wall, which was a 'bump-out' to accommodate a small bathroom with a shower stall. There was no restaurant in the place, but there was a diner across the street, which the motel owner highly recommended.

She threw her overnight bag on the bed and turned up the heat a little before freshening up the bathroom. Then, her courage returning, she put her coat back on and left, checking the door on her way out to be sure it was locked.

As she neared the driveway she once again felt her resolve giving way, but she pressed on, short of breath, her heart beating hard and fast again as she pulled in. She realized then that his sensors had probably detected her arrival and that he would be prepared for it. So, making no pretense, she exited her car and slammed the door before walking to the house.

The garage door was down and the place was quiet as she went up onto the stoop. The screens were still in the storm door and the inside door was standing about a quarter of the way open. *That's just like him,* she thought. *Door standing open, doesn't have his storm windows in yet. He probably still leaves his socks and underwear lying on the floor, too. If anything ever got done around our house it was because I did it.*

A noise came from within and she turned her ear to the screen to listen. She heard the footfalls of someone running. Then she heard a door slam and almost simultaneously smelled the acrid odor of fireworks on the puff of air created by the other door slamming.

"Hello?" she called.

No one answered.

"Helloo!" she called again, louder and then knocked on the storm door.

Again, no one answered.

She turned her ear to the screen again and listened. It was hard to tell, but she thought she heard a sound. She held her breath and listened carefully. She heard it again—faint and raspy.

She pulled open the storm door and gingerly stepped in, pushing open the inside door as she entered. The acrid smell was more intense now. "Hello?" she called again to no response as she let go of the door knob.

The room was large, extending the entire width of the house. On the right, it was a living room with a leather sofa, several leather easy chairs, and a large flat-screen TV. To the left of the door was a dining room. No one was in sight, but she could hear the raspy noise a little better now. It seemed to be coming from her left.

She could see that the dining room morphed into a kitchen on the other side of a counter with stools around it, so she walked that way, trepidation building within her as she followed the sound.

She saw the blood first, lots of it on the kitchen floor. Again, she could feel her heart beating hard in her chest and she wanted to turn and run, but the knowledge that someone needed her help compelled to continue on.

Then she saw him—Greg—laying on the floor, gasping for breath, a fearful gray-yellow pallor to his face. His eyes darted to and fro, like a frightened animal backed into a corner, until she came into his view. Then they locked on her, the pupils large, dark pools. His mouth moved as he tried to speak, but he couldn't get enough breath to make himself heard.

Her fear gave way to her natural compassion as she rushed to his side and knelt down. His mouth was moving, but no sound was coming out as she cradled him in her arms, lifting him slightly.

"Marti," he rasped out in a soft whisper.

"I'm here, Greg. Don't try to talk now. I'll call 9-1-1."

He opened his mouth, she thought to speak, but it had fallen open when his spirit left him. Greg was dead.

She laid him back down and ran to the phone, lifting the handset and dialing 9-1-1. But nothing happened. She waited several seconds and hung up. *Maybe they don't have 9-1-1 service up here.*

She looked down and caught a view of her clothing. When she saw that she was covered with blood, panic took over and she fled the house.

Chapter 17

"CHIPPEWA COUNTY SHERIFF'S Department."

"Uh...yes...I'd like to report a crime. I think somebody was murdered."

"Okay. And what is—"

"I was calling on homes in the area along M-28 today and I pulled into this driveway, but there was already a car there. Anyway, I parked behind it and walked up to the door and I could hear this woman in there screaming and a man was yelling back. Then I heard three shots, and the man screamed, so I got out of there."

"Where was this?"

"11643 Strongs Road, near the junction of M-28 and M-123."

"Give that to me again."

"1-1-6-4-3 Strongs Road. Take 28 west, almost to the junction of 123 and turn left. It's about a mile and a half, two miles down, on the left."

"Okay. And who—"

"Anyway, I was heading back north on Strongs, and I wasn't wasting any time, when she went roaring by me. I don't think she knew I'd been there because she didn't even look in my direction, but flew on up to 28 and then turned left.

"And who are—"

"So I followed her at a distance and saw her pull into Kline's Motel, just a little west of Strongs Road, and rush into one of the rooms."

"Did you get the room number?"

"Yes. It's room four. And I also got her license plate number. It's an older green Camry, I don't know what year, with a Michigan plate, and the number is 2-2-3-K-R-D."

"Are you there now?"

"No. I thought I should get out of there before she came out again."

"And what is your name?"

"I'd rather not get involved, if you don't mind. I don't want to be her next victim."

"We really need to get your name," the dispatcher replied to a dead line.

Chapter 18

MARTI WAS SHAKING SO BAD that she could barely get the key into the lock in the door of her motel room. And once she got the door open, the key wouldn't come out. She forced herself to slow down and turn the key until it was straight up and down in the lock before removing it. Then she rushed in and slammed the door, relocking it from the inside and standing with her back against it, her hands still on the knob as she tilted her head up, breathing through her mouth, so she could get enough air into her lungs.

She wasn't sure how long she had been standing there when she finally let go of the knob and stepped into the room. She took off her coat and threw it over the rocking chair. Her breathing was a little better now, but she was still badly shaken as she closed the drapes over the picture window and then went back and pulled the curtains together over the window in the door.

Now what do I do? It seemed like she'd asked herself that question a hundred times just since she'd arrived back at her room. And the only answer that came was to get out of there, as fast as she could and as far away as she could.

She hurried in to use the bathroom and immediately glimpsed herself in the mirror. The front of her cream-colored turtleneck sweater was covered with Greg's blood. She looked down and shuddered as she again saw that her jeans and shoes were also covered with it.

Panic surged through her. She wrenched off her clothing, dropping them on the bathroom floor. His blood had even soaked through to her skin.

Quickly, she picked up her sweater from the floor and turned on the cold water. Then she started scrubbing as she held the garment in the flow, but the blood had begun to dry and the stain was set.

She couldn't do this any more. Her hands were shaking so bad that even her forearms were shaking. She had to get that blood off her skin. Right now!

Dropping the sweater, she reached in and turned on the shower. Then she let the sink fill with cold water while she waited for the shower to get warm. She pressed the sweater down into the water, but it kept floating back up. She turned it so that the blood stained front of it was facing down before she plunged it in one last time.

The water from the shower poured down on her and she adjusted it as hot as she could stand as she moved to let it hit directly on the area where the blood had been. Then she washed her hair and scrubbed herself mercilessly with a soapy washcloth to be sure she'd removed every vestige of Greg's blood. Still, she felt sick at her stomach as she trembled inside. She could feel the trembling all the way from her breast bone to her spine and down through her legs, which felt like they wouldn't go on supporting her. *I've got to sit down. No! There's no time! I've got to get out of here! I've got to get clean and I've got to get out of here!*

Marti had bent over to wash her feet when she felt it coming. *"Ohhh!"* she screamed as she burst out of the shower to throw-up in the toilet. She stood there for a moment, trying to catch her breath; the spasms in her esophagus making her retch several more times even though there was nothing left to come out. When she returned to the shower she let the water run into her mouth and rinsed it several times before she continued to bathe.

I never should have come up here. I should have waited for Harry. I wish he were here, he'd know what to do now. Oh, Greg! Greg, what happed to you? What happened to us? I never wanted this to happen. Never, never, never. What's wrong with me? I drive my husband away and now I've hurt Harry and he won't even take my calls. Oh Lord, what's wrong with me? Is my whole life going to be this way? Please Lord, I'm 46-years-old. My life is more than half over. Is it going to be like this forever?

The water had gone from hot to warm to cool before she finally shut it off and opened the curtain. She looked out as she picked the nearest towel off the rack and dried herself. The bathroom was a mess. Her bloody jeans and shoes, and her underwear were lying on the floor; which was wet from when she'd fled the shower to throw-up. Her good sweater was soaking in the sink, the water pink with Greg's blood. She realized then that trying to clean her clothing was a lost cause. She'd have to do what she could to get her shoes clean because they were the only pair she'd brought with her, but the rest of it was beyond help.

She wrapped the towel around herself and double folded the edge of it in front of her so it would stay put. Then she went into the room and retrieved the plastic bag she'd brought for her dirty clothes. Returning to the bathroom, she reached into the sink and pulled the plug to let the water drain.

She shuddered again as she wrung out her sweater as best she could and put it in the bag. Then she sponged off her shoes under running water and dried them with tissues, which she threw into the toilet before flushing it. After that, she checked the pockets of her jeans and removed her car keys before putting them in the bag with her sweater. Finally, she picked up her panties and bra and examined them. They were stained with blood, so she put them into the bag.

After tying the bag shut, Marti set it by the front door and then went back into the bathroom to thoroughly wash her hands and forearms and blow-dry her hair. While she was in there she also brushed her teeth and rinsed well before going back out into the room.

As she was getting dressed she saw the outside lights come on and realized it was starting to get dark. She looked at the clock. It was 5:45 p.m. Greg had been dead for more than an hour and a half. She put her shoes on and wanted to get down on her knees and pray for him as she'd done so many times while they were married, but it was too late. All the opportunities were gone. His fate, whatever it was, was beyond being able to change now. She was sad, but felt guilty that she was unable to cry for him.

She switched on the light by the TV, picked up her keys from off the bed and put them in her pocket as she reached for her coat with her other hand and put it on.

Marti checked herself in the bathroom mirror before she turned for the door, shutting off the light on her way out. She picked up her purse and overnight bag and shut off the light by the TV. Then, picking up the bag of clothing, she left her room.

As she closed the door, she spotted a dumpster near a small copse of evergreens close to the front corner of the parking lot and decided to drive over to it to throw away the bag containing her ruined clothing. She unlocked the car doors with her remote and put her overnight bag in the back seat. Then she got in, placing the clothing bag on the floor in front of the passenger seat. That's when she saw it: the steering wheel also had blood on it from where her hands had touched it when she drove there from Greg's house.

She almost lost it again as her mind replayed the scene. Was there no end to it? She'd never seen so much blood before. And all of it from the man she had once loved and committed herself to for life.

This time her tears did come. *Oh, Greg...why?*

When she regained her composure, she reached between the seats and pulled several tissues from the box she kept on the back floor behind the passenger seat. She dried her eyes before wetting the tissues with some of her drinking water and cleaning off the steering wheel. She drove to the dumpster, got out of her car and lifted the plastic lid, cringing at the smell and holding it up with only her thumb as she threw away the bag and tissues.

A Chippewa County Sheriff's patrol car pulled into the lot, swung wide to drive in front of the units and then parked in front of the office as she was returning to her car. The deputy got out and walked into the office as she was fastening her seat belt. A part of her wanted to drive over there, follow him in and tell him everything that had happened. But another part of her, the part that had been urging her to get out of there, was screaming loudly. Greg was dead. And nothing she could do or say would change that. If she hadn't gotten his blood on her, she would already have been more than an hour gone. So she put the car in drive and left the parking lot, turning on her lights as she turned left to go east on M-28. She would call them. But not until after she was well south of the Mackinaw Bridge.

Marti took a deep breath and gave a sigh of relief to finally be on her way. It had been a mistake to come up here, she knew that now. Five years ago, her emotions had run the gamut through the stages of grief: shock, denial, anger; and a deep depression, that only her faith and the love of her friends had been able to see her through. Clay had been so kind—not holding her responsible for Jenny's death—that even now when she thought about it, it brought tears to her eyes. But she had never been able to get to the stage of full acceptance because she'd never had a sense of closure about Greg. She realized that that had been the driving force behind the impetuosity that had brought her up here, but it had been a mistake. There was no closure, only a deep sense of sadness for Greg, and guilt that her love for him had so long ago gone cold.

Then there was Harry. Her impetuosity had created within her an attitude that somehow made it okay for her to go against her new nature and hurt him. She determined that she would go to him in person—stand outside his door until he let her in if necessary—tell him she was sorry and ask for his forgiveness. *And, while I'm at it, I need to get down on my face and ask God to forgive me too.*

As she approached Strongs Road she saw the flashing red and blue lights of a sheriff's patrol car, which was parked kitty-corner in the middle of the road. A pickup truck and a car were stopped in her lane and the deputy was talking to the driver of the truck. Another deputy was standing near the rear of the patrol car with a flashlight, presumably to talk to drivers going the other way, but there were no cars in the westbound lane.

She slowed as the deputy stepped back from the truck and the driver steered around the patrol car in order to be on his way. He was talking to the driver of the car as she pulled up behind it and stopped.

Soon, that car also moved on and she idled up to where the deputy stood, stopped and put down her window.

"Evenin' ma'am. May I see your driver's license and registration please?"

Marti picked up her purse from off of the passenger seat and removed her wallet from it. She opened it to expose her license and held it up where the deputy could see it.

"Please take it out of the wallet, ma'am."

She removed her license and gave it to him. "What's going on, officer?"

"And your registration, Ma'am," he went on, ignoring her question.

Marti reached over, opened the glove box and dug around until she retrieved her registration. When she sat up again the deputy had moved back and was standing with his legs spread and his knees slightly bent, holding his gun in both hands and pointing it at her.

"I need you to step out of the car, ma'am."

"What is this? Please, you're frightening me."

His eyes were wide and his rate of breathing had significantly increased as he spoke again, more firmly. "Keep both your hands where I can see them and reach out and open the door from the outside!"

Marti's hands were shaking as she complied with his order.

"Now, step out of the car!"

She stepped out. *"Please,* you're frightening me." Tears were forming in her eyes.

"Turn around and face the car!"

"Please," she said as she turned around."

"Now, take one step back, spread your legs, and put your hands on the roof!"

As she complied with his order the other deputy, who turned out to be a tall woman of slight build, stepped behind her and somehow interlocked her left leg around Marti's left leg. She grasped first Marti's left and then her right wrist, and with fluid motion, handcuffed them both behind her back. Then she searched her, patting her down and paying particular attention to her pockets, waistband, and around her ankles. When she turned Marti back around the other deputy had holstered his pistol and was snapping the thong that held it in place.

Marti was crying now; shaking badly and trying to catch her breath. "P-please...what are you...d-doing?" she wept out.

"You are Martha Forrester. Is that Correct?"

"Yes."

"And this is your car. Is that correct?"

"Y-yes."

"Martha Forrester, I am placing you under arrest on suspicion of the murder of Wayne McCarthy."

"*What?*" she took a shuddering breath.

He reached inside of his jacket and produced a card from which he read: "'You have the right to remain silent. If you give up that right, anything you say can and will be used against you in a court of law. You have the right to an attorney and to have an attorney present during questioning. If you cannot afford an attorney, one will be provided to you at no cost. During any questioning, you may decide at any time to exercise these rights, not answer any questions or make any statements. Do you understand these rights I have just read to you?'"

"Yes. P-please, I...I d-didn't kill anybody." She sniffed hard and shook her head while blinking rapidly to clear the tears from her eyes.

"That's for the detectives, and I suspect, the courts to determine. Our job is to detain you and bring you in," he replied as the woman deputy led her to the patrol car.

She opened the back door and held Marti's head as she struggled to sit down without the use of her hands. The door closed and Marti could hear them on the police radio, canceling roadblocks that had been setup in other places. Then she saw another patrol car approach from the west and turn on its light bar as it slowed to a stop. A male officer exited and strode over to where the two deputies who had arrested her were standing. They spoke together for a few moments before the female deputy came back and joined her in the back seat.

"Do you have a tissue?" Marti asked, blinking her eyes and sniffing.

"No, I'm sorry, I don't."

Marti sniffed again. "What's going to happen to my car and my purse?"

"Your car and everything in it will be impounded. Deputy Riley, the man who just arrived, is going to wait for the tow truck."

"I didn't kill anybody."

"Look, what I think doesn't matter. I don't have the authority to let you go. So you might as well save your breath and tell it to the detectives."

Marti hung her head and concentrated on breathing deeply, in the hope of being able to keep from crying. *Oh, Lord. Father, I'm in trouble, big trouble and I need your help. Please help me. In Jesus' name, amen.*

The deputy who had pulled the gun on her got in the driver's seat and shut the door. "You ready to go?" he said to the female deputy as he put the car in drive.

"Ready."

He turned around in the intersection and headed the car east on M-28 before picking up the microphone clipped near the front of the radio. "Dispatch, car twelve."

"Go ahead, twelve."

"We have a female suspect in custody and are leaving the corner of Strongs Road and M-28, en route to the station. Our mileage is 4-1-9-4-7 point 6. Can you give us a time check?"

"10-4, twelve," the disembodied female voice came back. "Your time is 6:19 p.m."

Chapter 19

"HELLO?"

"Harry? It's Mitch. I just heard from Marti and—"

"Oh," he interrupted. "I've been trying to reach her all day."

"Yeah, well, she's up in Sault Sainte Marie. In jail."

"In jail?"

"Yeah. They arrested her for killing Greg—Wayne McCarthy."

"Oh, *good night!* I *told* her to stay away from him and let me handle it."

"Well, apparently she wasn't listening."

"I *know* she wasn't listening! She was angry with me about it. The last time I saw her she refused to even discuss the matter; she just got up and walked out on me."

Harry took a deep breath and sighed. "Well, she's gone and done it now. Maybe next time she'll listen."

Mitch didn't reply and the silence began to grow uncomfortable between them before Harry broke it. *"What?"*

"She needs you, Harry. Certainly you don't think she did it."

"Of course not, but the real question is, 'does she *want* me?' Why are you defending her, anyway? I thought you agreed with me on this."

"I do agree with you. It would have been far better for her to have let you handle it. But just because you and I agree about something doesn't change the facts about what actually happened. And I'm not going to abandon her just because she made a mistake!"

"Look Harry, you've known her for, what, two, three weeks? I've know her for the better part of ten years. She and Liz are close, like sisters, and I *know* what kind of woman she really is. And what you've seen in the short time you've known her is not it.

"This whole business has seriously affected her. Ever since that...Hammond guy saw Greg up in the U.P. she has not been herself. Worse than that, she confided in Liz that she's been having nightmares almost every night and not sleeping. Now surely you, of *all* people, can understand the kind of effect that can have on a person. And, just in case it's escaped your notice, *you* have not been the most pleasant person to be around for at least a couple of years now!

"Look, Harry, you're a friend, a darn good friend, and the best cop I've ever known. And I have no intention of abandoning you just because you got a raw deal and are having a hard time coming to terms with it. I know the man you really are still lives inside of you someplace and that someday he'll be back—at least I hope so. And he would no more abandon her than I would. So the *real* question is, are *you* going to stop feeling sorry for yourself and step up the plate and help her? She needs you, Harry!"

Once again silence ensued, growing so palpable between them that if Mitch hadn't heard Harry breathing, he would have guessed that he'd hung-up. His mind was in turmoil. He'd just chewed-out his mentor and, in spite of the fact that it was something he felt Harry needed to hear, he felt bad for having done it.

Finally his guilt got the better of him and he broke the silence. "Look, uh...I'm sorry. I was out of—"

"No!" Harry quickly interrupted. "Don't apologize." He took another deep breath and sighed. "I had that coming, and uh...faithful are the wounds of a friend, I guess. I'm the one who owes you an apology: I'm sorry, Mitch. Of course I don't believe she did it and yes, of course I'll help her. What did you tell her?"

"Thanks, Harry. It's good to have you back. As I'm sure you know, there wasn't much time to talk. So I basically just told her not to say anything to me over the phone or to anybody else until she got a lawyer. Sounds strange, I know, coming from a cop and all, but that's pretty much all I said, except that I would contact you and you'd get up there as soon as you could."

"And she was good with that?"

"Yeah. She's expecting you. Really Harry, she's not the way you think."

"Oh, I know that. I knew she was okay the minute I met her. I just didn't want to admit it to myself, lest it challenge my sorry notion that all women are basically evil. You told her the right thing; at least it's the thing I would have told her. I guess I'd better get my act together and get up there."

"Thanks, Harry."

"Hey. I'm the one who should be thanking you. Thanks, pal. It's good to be back. I'll stay in touch, but now I'd better get going."

IT WAS JUST PAST TWO a.m. on Saturday morning when Harry pulled into the nearly full parking lot of the Essex Hotel in Sault Sainte Marie. In his haste to be underway he had not bothered to call for a reservation and was glad to be able to get a single on the third floor.

He hung his clothing in the closet and stowed his socks and underwear in a dresser drawer before falling into bed. He was tired, and under ordinary circumstances he'd already have been asleep for four hours or so, but his mind was still hyped from having to be alert for the drive, and in spite of the hour, sleep did not come easily to him.

Turning half onto his side, he scrunched the pillow under his head in an attempt to get comfortable as his thoughts turned to Marti: *She's probably never even seen the inside of a jail before, much less been incarcerated in one. She must be scared to death.*

What happened, anyway? Obviously she found him (I never should have given her the address), but what happened? Did he attack her, like he did me? He's a powerful guy and she's not very big. She never could have fended him off...unless she had a gun. No, she's not the type. She's probably never even touched a gun; much less know how to use one. A knife? No, something like that would never enter her mind. But what happened? They certainly wouldn't have arrested her without some kind of probable cause.

I wonder if she's seen a lawyer yet. Probably not. They probably won't arraign her until Monday. She must be so scared. How am I going to get her out of this?

He realized then that he was engaging in useless speculation and forced his mind off the subject. Still, it was well after three a.m. before he finally dropped off to sleep.

SHE HAD LAIN IN HER bunk since lights-out—at least that's what they called it—the place never went completely dark, but had not slept a wink. The bed was uncomfortable and the place, beyond having a strong and unpleasant odor of pine cleaner, had a hollowness about it that was positively spooky. Every time a door closed, which was frequently, or someone walked down the polished concrete floor, the sound of it echoed throughout the cellblock.

She desperately wanted to know what time it was, but they'd taken away her watch and, as far as she could see, there were no clocks in the place.

Actually they'd taken away everything she owned, including her clothing, leaving her with only an oft-washed orange jumpsuit that had obviously been sartorially conceived for a much larger woman—or even a man. And seeing herself in it only added to her sense of humiliation and isolation.

The minutes had crept by like hours and the hours like days as she waited out the night while alternating between praying and crying. But it must be morning now. She'd heard the noise of what must have been the shift change, maybe an hour ago. Surely now someone would discover that it had all been a horrible mistake and it wouldn't be long before they'd be coming to let her out of this cell, give her back her belongings and let her go home.

The door banged shut again and the echo of footsteps harbingered someone's approach. The severely overweight twenty-something woman stopped outside her cell as a loud buzz and click indicated that the door had electrically unlocked.

"On your feet, Forrester; detectives want to talk to you."

Marti stood as the uniformed woman entered holding a pair of handcuffs. *So much for the thought of them letting me go.*

"Hold out your hands."

Marti held her hands out in front of her as the woman, Hanson, according to her name tag, bent slightly to apply the shackles. Her scraggly, copper-colored hair had an acrid odor, in spite of it being mostly tucked up inside of her brown baseball cap and Marti tilted her head back and to the side to escape the smell.

"Let's go," she said, stepping behind her and giving her a light push on her back.

Marti instinctively turned in the direction from which the woman had come and walked to the cellblock door, waiting as it was buzzed unlocked. Then she allowed herself to be directed to a small room with a table and two chairs. Hanson turned on the light and pulled out a chair, guiding Marti onto it before leaving without further comment. She heard the door latch and then lock as she laid her forearms on the table.

The place seemed permeated with the pungent odor of cigarette smoke and Marti made a face, scrunching her nose as she looked around. There was a camera mounted about midway along the left-hand wall and just below the ceiling tiles; it seemed to be pointed right at her. A half-full ashtray was sitting in the middle of the table.

She stood and picked up the ash tray using both hands to carry it to the corner of the room and sit it on the floor. Then she went back and sat at the other side of the table; not so much to avoid the camera, but because it made her uncomfortable to have her back toward the door. Besides, it looked like the camera could move to pick her up no matter where she sat.

She waited, and waited, for what seemed like a long time. She had purposely looked for a clock on the way to the room, but had not seen one. It was somewhat disorienting and she wondered if they did that intentionally to keep people off balance.

At last the door opened and a dark-haired, thirtyish man in plain clothes walked in, followed by a blonde, uniformed woman who appeared to be a slightly younger.

"Good morning, Ms. Forrester. I'm Sergeant Jason Stark and this is Deputy Erin Tierney. You can call me Jason. Is it all right if I call you Martha?"

"I usually go by, Marti." These were the first words she'd spoken since the night before and she was surprised at how shaky her voice was.

"Erin, can you remove her handcuffs?"

The woman complied and then returned to the place where she had been standing near the door.

Marti had been fighting against terror since she had been arrested the night before, and having to wear handcuffs had given her an overwhelming sense of dread that she could only describe as claustrophobic. The kindness she was now being shown and the act of removing the handcuffs greatly ameliorated her; even to the point of allowing her to breathe easier, and the emotional release brought tears to her eyes.

"Okay, Marti," Jason said while sitting down in the other chair. "Before we begin, I want to be certain that you have been made aware of your rights. Were your rights read to you yesterday?"

She blinked several times and wiped her eyes with the backs of her hands. "Yes."

"Did you understand your rights as they were read to you?"

She sniffed. "Yes."

"Is it your desire to exercise any of those rights at this time?"

She took a deep breath to muster her courage. "What is this all about? I haven't done anything to anyone."

"Well, Marti, the evidence says otherwise," he said gently. "We have your bloody fingerprints on the telephone and on the door jamb, among other places in Wayne McCarthy's house at..." he consulted the papers he had brought in with him. "11643 Strongs Road, out in Strongs; the house where Mr. McCarthy was found shot to death. Are you denying that you were there?"

Marti could feel her fear beginning to build again and didn't answer.

"We also found traces of Mr. McCarthy's blood on your shoes, in your car, in the motel room you were staying in and on your blood-soaked clothes that you threw in the dumpster there. That's what the evidence says. Now, you've got some serious trouble here, Marti, and we want to help you, but you've got to help us do that. You've gotta be straight with us about this or there's absolutely nothing we can do for you."

Marti took a deep breath through her mouth and shuddered as she let it out; her mind racing as she contemplated her predicament. She had been so frightened when she fled Greg's house that it had never occurred to her she was leaving bloody fingerprints everywhere. In the end, she had tried to help Greg not hurt him. But even she could see how damning the evidence against her was.

Her elbows on the table, she rested her forehead on her fingertips as she sat there fighting her tears and trying to get control of her breathing. What could she say? How could she convince them that she had had nothing to do with this? *Oh Lord, please help me know what to...*

"What did you do with the gun, Marti?"

"*Gun?* What gun?" She put her arms back down.

"The gun you shot Wayne McCarthy with."

"*Please,* I didn't do this. I don't know *anything* about a gun. In my whole life, I've never even *touched* a gun. *Please* you've *got* to believe me." She put her left hand over her mouth as she began to cry softly.

"Marti, the evidence says otherwise. Now, maybe it was an accident, or maybe he attacked you and you were only defending yourself; I don't know. But if you didn't do this, how do explain away the evidence? Come on, Marti, you've gotta help me here."

Marti took another deep breath and shuddered as she blew it out through pursed lips. *Mitch is right, I shouldn't say anything to them.*

"I think I need that lawyer now."

"You think? Are you sure? We could clear this up very easily if you'd just answer a few questions for us.

Confession is good for the soul, Marti. You're going to feel a whole lot better when you get this out."

"No, I want a lawyer. Please get me a lawyer."

"All right," Jason snapped, sliding out the chair with his legs as he stood.

He turned to Erin. "Cuff her and take her back to her cell," he said tersely, and stormed out of the room.

HARRY TURNED OUT OF THE hotel parking lot onto the I-75 Business Spur and drove the short distance to a McDonald's. It was almost 9:30 a.m. and he'd slept longer than he's intended, but he took the time to quickly eat two breakfast burritos and drink half of a large coffee. He took the other half with him as he set out again; driving east on the Spur and then turning left to go north on Ashmun Street.

He remembered seeing a book store on Ashmun, and he stopped there, picking up three magazines and two books he guessed Marti would like. Returning to his car, he continued north on Ashmun, turning right onto Maple and right again to go south on Court Street to the sheriff's department and jail.

He walked to the desk and stood there for a few seconds before the young deputy looked up from her paperwork. "Yes?" she said brusquely.

"I'd like to see Martha Forrester. I understand she's an inmate here."

Her look bespoke her annoyance that he would make such a stupid request. "Visiting hours are Tuesdays and Fridays, one to three and seven to nine," she said flatly as she returned to her paperwork, dismissing him.

He produced his identification and held it out so that it was in front of her face. "I'd like to see the shift supervisor, please."

She looked up at him again, took his ID card, examined it and gave it back. "Look, uh...I'm sorry to be short with you, Lieutenant Brannan. I worked last night and I'm supposed to be off today, but I had to come in to cover for someone who called in sick. How 'bout I do you one better? I brought her in last night and I happen to know that Sergeant Jason Stark is assigned to her case. I saw him come in this morning and I think he's still here. How 'bout I see if I can locate him for you?"

Harry smiled. "Sure."

She picked up the phone and placed a call, talked for a few seconds and then hung up. "He'll be out right away."

"Thanks."

"I'm really sorry about being short with you."

"That's okay. Low seniority?"

She nodded. "I started in March."

"What's your name?"

"Pat. Pat Kavanaugh."

"Things will get better, Pat."

"I know," she said, nodding, a sad expression on her face. "It's just hard to make my kids understand—and my husband."

Suddenly she looked like she might cry and Harry laid his hand on top of hers and gave it a gentle squeeze.

"My girls were looking forward to us going Christmas shopping with Grandma today and they're disappointed. And my husband's mad at me..."

Harry gave her hand another gentle squeeze and let it go as he saw a man walking toward them.

"Lieutenant Brannan?" the man said as he approached.

"Retired," Harry said, extending his right hand.

"Sergeant, Jason Stark. What can I do for you?"

The men shook hands. "I'd like to see Martha Forrester. I understand you're the detective assigned to her case."

"That's right. What's your interest in this, anyway? She your girlfriend or something?"

"Well, she's my friend...and she happens to be a woman, if that answers your question. I drove up here from Grand Rapids early this morning and I was hoping you would extend me a professional courtesy and let me see her."

"Well now, you still haven't told me what your interest is in this. So why would I want to do that?"

"Okay," Harry said softly, refusing to take the bait. "I'm here to find out what happened and to do whatever I can to help her. I also bought these books and magazines," he held up the bag. "And I planned to give them to her so she'll have something to do to occupy her time. That's about it."

"Visiting hours are Tuesdays and Fridays, one to three and seven to nine. My suggestion is you come back then," he said as he turned to leave.

"That's it?"

"That's it," he said, turning back. "Look, I'm under no obligation to let you in there and I'm certainly under no obligation to help you work against me. So, like I said, 'visiting hours are Tuesdays and Fridays.' Come back then."

"I think we're both interested in the same..."

Jason held up his hand. "Look, do yourself a favor and go home," he said, turning.

"Yeah, thanks for your help!" Harry said to his back. "Better chance of a conviction when you don't let a little thing like the truth get in the way, right?"

Jason stopped and turned, his red face evincing his anger. "Look, I'm going to cut you a break, old man, because you used to be a cop. Get outta here...now...before I find a reason to throw you in there with her."

Jason stormed out of the room as Harry turned to leave.

Chapter 20

"LIEUTENANT!"

Harry stopped and turned as Pat Kavanaugh stepped out from behind her desk. He started in her direction and stopped as they met half way between the desk and the door.

She handed him one of her business cards and pointed to a phone number she had written on it. "Call me in about an hour. He should be gone by then and I'll see if I can get you in to see her."

"Thanks. Thank you very much! You sure you're not going—"

"I can't talk now," she interrupted as she turned to hurry back to her desk.

HARRY WAS STANDING BEFORE her desk again at 11:50 a.m. "You're not going to get in trouble for this, are you?"

"I don't think so. Our beloved Sergeant Stark is gone now and Sergeant Drake, the shift supervisor, is a nice guy. I think he'll let you in to see her. We just won't mention that you were here earlier. He'll be out in a few minutes."

"Why are you doing this, anyway?"

"Good question: I don't know. I guess partly because Stark is a jerk. But it's more than that. I don't know how to describe it, but something about this just doesn't seem right to me. Call it woman's intuition if you want, but I don't think she did it. I mean, she was just too surprised, too taken aback, too...I don't know—innocent I guess. In any case, I think she deserves to have somebody in her corner. But it's also something you said to Stark. We *are* after the same thing here, and that's truth. Sometimes that makes our job as cops harder, but it makes it a whole lot easier to sleep at night."

Harry smiled as he nodded. "I like you. What you call intuition, I call a cop's gut. You, Deputy Kavanaugh, have got the makings of a good detective. You should pursue it."

She gave a small, self-effacing smile and blushed slightly. "Thanks."

HARRY HAD BEEN WAITING for about ten minutes in the small conference room when Marti was ushered through the door at not quite 12:30 p.m. Her countenance was severely fallen and she looked beleaguered in her oversized, orange jumpsuit.

He stood as she entered the room, suddenly realizing that something had changed inside of him since he'd spoken with Mitch on the phone. His heart lunged in pain at the sight of her.

He took a deep breath. "Oh, Marti—"

"I'm sorry, Harry," she interrupted, not looking at him and holding her head slightly down. "I wanted to tell you that, and I tried to call you six or seven times on Thursday, but you weren't home—"

"Marti—"

"It was *shameful* the way I treated you, and I could tell I hurt your feelings."

She wiped away tears with the backs of her hands. "I'm sorry, Harry. I am so, so sorry," she struggled to say as she began to cry in earnest.

"Oh, Marti," Harry said, stepping forward and gathering her in his arms.

He held her while she wept. "Shh. It's all right. Don't worry about it. It's all forgotten. We've got to concentrate on getting you out of here, now," he said softly as he stroked her hair.

At length she began to regain her composure and Harry cupped her face in his hands, stepping back from her slightly. "You okay?"

She nodded in small movements. "I got your shirt all wet."

"Don't worry about it," he said gently, pulling her face toward him and kissing her forehead before letting her go.

He could tell she was startled, but she didn't say anything. He was startled too. He hadn't planned to do that. Even so it made his heart beat so hard it felt like it might leave his chest.

There was a box of tissues on the table, and he pulled a couple of them out and gave them to her, hoping she didn't detect the slight tremor in his hand from what had just taken place.

"Thank you," she said before drying her eyes and blowing her nose. She looked around for a wastebasket and then stuffed the spent tissues in her pocket.

Harry pulled out a chair for her and held it as she sat down. Then he sat in the chair next to her, turning it so that he was facing her.

"What happened, Marti?"

She slid around on the seat. "I don't know," she said shaking her head. "I was sure from your description that it was Greg. And I came up here on Friday to confront him."

She was becoming agitated and was lightly hitting the tops of her legs with her palms. "But, but...he was already dead—or almost. And I, I—"

Harry scootched his chair forward until their knees were almost touching and picked up both of her hands in his. "Take it easy, now," he said compassionately. "It's going to be all right. So, you went to his house. Did you knock on the door?"

"No. It took me a little bit to find the place. And when I finally did I was scared to drive up his driveway. So I went and got a room at a motel. Sometimes, if I'm scared, I do something else until my courage comes back." She was fidgeting in the chair.

Harry gently squeezed her hands. "So you went back."

"Yes," she nodded. Then, with his gentle encouragement, she went on to tell him the whole story."

"I feel so guilty. He was my *husband* and he died in my arms and I couldn't feel anything more for him than if it had been some stranger. What's *wrong* with me?" she squeaked out, pulling her hands free and using them to cover her face as she cried.

Harry gave her a couple of more tissues and waited until she dried her eyes and blew her nose. Then he took her hands again.

"Listen to me, Marti," he said with gentle firmness, squeezing her hands. "There is *nothing* wrong with you. You are good. You're a fine and beautiful woman with a good heart and he was not worthy of you. Your love and your marriage meant nothing to him. He used you, just like he used at least three other women before you. And the fact that you couldn't bring yourself to feel anything for him is a testimony to you. You have every right to hate him, but hate is not in your dictionary."

She gave a wan smile. Harry laid the palm of his left hand gently against her right cheek.

She looked up again and covered his hand with hers; caressing it and giving it a gentle squeeze before letting it go.

"He had three other women before me?"

"I'm afraid so, Marti. It's called, the sweetheart scam, and he was apparently a master at it," Harry said gently. He went on to tell her all that he and Mitch had found out.

"I feel like such a fool," she said when he finished.

He squeezed her hands again. "You're no fool, Marti."

"I'm glad you're here, Harry."

"Me too. And I'm going to do everything in my power to get you out of here. Now, tell me what they've done with you so far."

"Well, the first thing after I got here a man sprayed something out of an aerosol can on my hands. Then he shined a light on them. It was kind of purple."

"Mmm, a trace-metal test. It's a test they run to see if you've held a gun recently."

"But I didn't!"

"I know. But the fact that they ran the test is evidence in your favor."

She nodded. "Then they swabbed the backs of both my hands, and along the top of my index fingers and thumbs and the web area in between with some stuff that didn't smell very good."

"It's a weak nitric acid solution that they use to test for gun shot residue. When you fire a gun, unless it's a really well-made gun, a fair amount of the combustion residue can blow back onto your hand. This test detects that residue. If they find any, it's evidence that you've fired a gun recently."

"So that works in my favor too, right?"

"Probably. The test is not as well-regarded as it once was because too many things can interfere with it: for example, the fact that you took a shower. Did you tell them that?"

"Uh-uh," she shook her head."

"Good. They'll most likely test your clothing too...and find nothing. This is all good for you, and we'll definitely want to let your lawyer know it. And the fact that Stark asked you what you did with the gun almost certainly means they don't have it—"

"Even if they did have it, my fingerprints wouldn't be on it," Marti interrupted.

Harry smiled. "True, but often the shooter wears gloves or wipes the gun clean; that is if you can find the gun at all. That they most likely don't have it, and that the only evidence surrounding it is that you've neither shot nor held a gun argues powerfully in your favor."

"So they'll let me go?" she said, her face brightening some.

Harry picked up her hands again. "Well, we're not out of the woods yet. The fact that your clothing has blood on it that will turn out to be his—"

"It is his blood, and they already know that," she interrupted.

"You and I know it was his, but there is no way *they* could know it conclusively yet. They were lying to you this morning when they led you to believe they knew it was his."

"They can do that?"

"It's not illegal, and some cops regularly do exaggerate to strengthen their position in the mind of a suspect."

"Humph," she uttered, shaking her head. "You ever do that?"

"Well, I'd be lying if I told you I never did it. On the other hand, it never was my practice. I've done it a few times, but only when I felt I had enough other evidence to make me believe the suspect was truly guilty. If you don't have a good body of evidence and you keep hammering away on a suspect, you run the risk of coercing them into admitting to something they didn't really do. And that does not serve the interest of justice. But it's a moot point anyway because the blood will turn out to be his. And that, when added to the presence of your bloody fingerprints, means—"

"They won't be letting me go any time soon," she said, the sad look returning to her face. "What's going to happen to me?"

"Well, you'll be arraigned, most likely on Monday, to—"

"What does that mean?"

"It means that you'll have to appear in district court. You'll be informed of the charge against you, and the judge will determine if there's enough evidence to hold you in jail or let you out on bail. The prosecuting attorney will argue against that and your attorney will argue for it."

"Kind of like on TV."

"Kind of. But you won't be asked to plead guilty or not guilty unless you end up in circuit court. Instead, you'll be advised of your right to a preliminary hearing. That's where they'll determine if the evidence against you constitutes enough probable cause to bind you over for trial in circuit court. If there is, you'll be arraigned again, a trial date will be set and—"

"And I go to prison for the rest of my life."

"Not if *I* can help it, you won't! Look, Marti, I'm going to eat, sleep and breathe this thing until I can prove to them that you're innocent!

"Thanks, Harry," she said in a small voice. "I know you didn't sign up for this."

"I'm not going to abandon you, Marti. I'd like to think that we—"

There was a knock on the door and a man stuck his head in. "Mrs. Forrester?"

"Yes," Marti answered.

He stepped into the room, closed the door behind him, and spoke as he walked toward her. "I've been appointed to be your attorney. Donald Ripley," he said extending his right hand. "Please call me Don."

Don Ripley was in his mid-sixties. He was a robust man, just under six feet and maybe two-hundred pounds, with thinning gray hair. His baritone voice had the strength and resonance of an old-fashioned orator, giving him a certain "presence" in the room.

She shook his hand. "Don, this is Harry Brannan. He's a detective."

"Mr. Brannan, you certainly know better than to question her after—"

"No no no," Marti interrupted, picking up Harry's hand. "He's my friend."

Harry stood and extended his hand. "I'm retired. I came up here from Grand Rapids to help Marti. They let me in as a professional courtesy."

"Ah, well, good to meet you," Don said, shaking his hand. "I'm kind of retired myself. Semi-retired, I guess you could say. The county occasionally throws a case my way."

"I see. What's your background?"

"Criminal. Criminal and civil. Could have made more money in corporate, but I'd have been dead forty years ago from the boredom."

Harry laughed as he turned his chair back toward the table and sat down. Don walked around to the other side and sat across from Marti.

"So do you know anything about where we stand?" Harry asked.

Don cleared his throat. "Well, the judge and the A.P.," he looked at Marti, "the associate prosecutor, were not too happy about being bothered on a Saturday, but that's their problem.

"The A.P. is a man named, David Bostwick. He's young, but he's good. He's going to charge open murder; mostly because he doesn't have the gun—at least not yet. If he did, it would be murder-two, but as it is, he's going to let the jury decide."

Marti didn't gasp, but as Don spoke, she inhaled audibly and held her breath while biting her lower lip and grabbing hard onto to Harry's hand.

"Heyyy," Harry said gently. "Easy now, it's all right. It's the best we could have hoped for under the circumstances." She let go of Harry's hand and exhaled, her chest heaving as she caught her breath. Harry got up and stood behind her, placing his hands on her shoulders. He bent his head down and spoke very softly near her ear. "It's going to all right; it's going to be all right."

She worked at getting her breathing under control before she was able to speak again. "What does this mean?"

Don spoke up. "Well, In Michigan there is really only first or second degree murder. But in order to prove first degree, he has to prove premeditation; which at least right now, he can't do. In order to prove second degree, he has to prove intent. If he had the gun and could prove it was yours or found your fingerprints on it or could prove you fired it, he could do that, but he doesn't have the gun. Michigan law does not require him to choose between first or second degree. He can just charge, open murder and let the jury decide based on whatever proofs he can provide."

"And if they find me guilty?"

"Are you?"

Marti shook her head. "No," she said forlornly. "I didn't do it. I did *not* do this."

"That's good to know. I'd defend you anyway, but it's good to know. But to answer your question, first degree is mandatory life without parole. Second degree is up to the discretion of the judge, but it would probably be at least fifteen years."

Marti shook her head.

"I could probably get him to agree to a plea deal. I'm guessing he'd go manslaughter. Man-one is fifteen years, max."

This time Harry spoke up. "No! She didn't do it! And it's a travesty that she's had to spend even this long in jail! I don't want her to spend one second longer than absolutely—"

Harry took a breath and then looked from Don to Marti. "I'm sorry. I have no right to speak for you."

"No. Go on. I don't want to spend any longer in here than I have to either."

"Well," Don said. "We don't have to decide now. I'm just guessing, but I don't think his case is all that strong. His so-called witness called from a pay phone and didn't give a name, so I think all he's got is the physical evidence. We'll find out whatever else on discovery."

Harry cleared his throat. "Listen, uh, could I work for you—as your investigator? I mean, I'll do it for free. I just don't think the judge will sit still for the county paying for it because I'm not licensed as a PI."

"You any good?"

"He was a lieutenant," Marti proffered.

Harry smiled. "Well, I was a detective for 27 years and I closed most of my cases."

Don nodded. "Good enough for me. Consider yourself employed."

The men shook hands on it as Harry spoke again. "First thing, I'd like to hear the voice of that anonymous witness. Do you think you could subpoena a copy of the tape?"

"Mmm, I like the way you think. Yeah, I'm sure I can. But it won't be until after the arraignment."

"Why is that important?" Marti asked.

"Because there has to be a reason why the call was anonymous," Harry said. "Maybe the caller was just afraid, but maybe it was the real killer using your presence there as an opportunity to confuse the matter by shifting the attention of the police on to you. Maybe it's nothing, but it's a place to start. At this point we don't even know if it was a man or a woman."

"I see."

"When is the arraignment?"

"Nine o'clock Monday morning," Don replied.

Harry could feel the muscles in Marti's shoulders tense and he massaged them lightly as he continued speaking. "They've done trace-metal and GSR tests on her, and probably on the clothes she was wearing by now, too. Those will come back negative and that will give you some ammo for Monday."

Don nodded. "Yeah. Yeah, we can use it."

Harry sat back down. "Listen, Marti. Is there a way I can get into your house? I'm going to head back to Grand Rapids and I want to bring back your most conservative dress for the arraignment. I'll come back in time for Don to get it to you on Monday morning."

Marti nodded. "I keep a spare key under a big rock to the right of the little door that goes into the garage. Call Jo Ramsey when you get there. She knows where it is and our taste in clothes is pretty much the same. She'll know what to pick out."

"Okay," he said, standing up. "You want me to call your daughter?"

She shook her head. "No. Not just yet. Let's see how things go on Monday," she said, also standing up.

"Okay, I'm away, then. Take care of her, Don. I'll call you on Monday morning. Can I get one of your cards?"

Don gave him a card and Harry slid it into his shirt pocket. Then he picked up Marti's hand and gave it a gentle squeeze. "Goodbye, Marti."

She pulled him into an embrace, tears forming in her eyes as she snuggled her head next to his. "Don't be long," she whispered.

"I won't," he whispered as he pulled her close. "I'll be here for you. I will not abandon you, Marti."

Chapter 21

THIS IS A FINE MESS! And it's my own stupid fault. I should have known she'd come back. For crying out loud, she drove all the way up here; it's not like she'd just turn around and go back home. I should have waited. I should have guessed she would come back and waited for her to finish her business with him before going anywhere near the place. After all, he lived alone; and the place is so remote it may have been months before somebody found him.

Maybe it works in my favor. No matter what the cops find, I've already planted the seed that she did it. And when they find out she was his wife that will just cement it in their pointy little heads. After all, they always suspect the spouse first, right? So this may just work in my favor after all.

Of course it may not, too. It just depends on what he might have left lying around and whether they find it—and if they do, if they can tie it to me. But then I didn't see anything—at least nothing lying around in plain sight. Of course I didn't have that long to look before she showed up again.

Another stupid move! I should have just waited upstairs—hid in a closet or something until she left. Of course, she may have come upstairs...

Then I could have grabbed her. Oh man! That's what I should have done! I should have grabbed her! I could've easily made it look like murder-suicide. Then I would have had as long as I wanted to search the place. Duhhh!

Too bad I couldn't get the gun into her car. That would have really done it. No. She probably locks her doors. I should have looked. No, too risky. I might have been seen. And what if I set off her car alarm? Maybe I should toss it into the ditch along the side of his road. No. If they've already searched there and the gun turns up after she's already in custody, they'll know she didn't do it. I should have thought of that yesterday, before I called them.

Now what do I do? I'm sure not going to get in there any time soon with the cops crawling all over the place. And I'm sure as heck not going to spend another night sleeping in the back seat. Man, I like to froze to death. Small price to pay for not leaving a paper trail, I guess. But who knew it would be so darn cold?

I might as well go home. I can try again next week. Things should have cooled down a little by then. Maybe I can get into the house and spend as long as I need to search it out. No maybe about it! I will get in there! And if it's there, I'll find it!

And no more freezing my butt off in the car! I'm staying in a hotel. Now that he's dead it won't matter if I leave a paper trail.

Wow, I've got to get some gas. I should have enough to make it to Saint Ignace. At least I hope so. I'll look for a busy place where they're not likely to remember me. And I'll pay cash.

Chapter 22

ORDINARILY, ON A LONG DRIVE, Harry might have played the radio or CD player, but this time he drove the near five-hour trip to Grand Rapids in silence. He needed time to think.

Greg's death had significantly changed the complexion of things. First of all, Marti was in jail for murdering him. That was just plain wrong.

After having been a cop for thirty years, "good" was not an appellative he was inclined to bandy about indiscriminately when it came to people. Yet when he'd described her earlier in the day as being good, he knew he believed it with all his heart. She might be headstrong, but she didn't have it in her to do something like this—or to lie. And that was part of the problem: he knew it in his heart—not in his head. It didn't make it any the less true, but it made humbug of the notion of her being a mere unit, a factor in a problem. He knew he was less than objective where she was concerned.

She was very much more attractive than she knew, and he had been naturally drawn to her from the moment he'd met her. At first, though, professional detachment and the defenses he had built around his heart had made it fairly easy to disregard that attraction. But getting to know her through their subsequent meetings and phone conversations had produced in him something very difficult to ignore. He realized that as he recalled the tinge of jealousy he'd felt upon seeing the pickup truck parked in her driveway and the concomitant feeling of elation when it turned out to be Jo Ramsey. Then much more so with the episode in the restaurant, when she slid in next to him and accidentally bumped him with her hip. That had sent his heart rate through the roof. But the thing that took the ramparts down was his conversation with Mitch and the ensuing realization that he couldn't see who she really was because he wouldn't let himself see it.

She was very much more attractive than she knew, not because she had a poor self-image, but because she wasn't fixated on herself. In fact, it wasn't in her nature to think much about herself at all. And the reason why she was so intent on bringing an end to this business about Greg was because it was forcing her, contrary to her nature, to focus on herself.

He realized, then, that she was a woman without guile; that she was good and decent and true. And in the resultant crashing down of his man-made walls, the attraction he felt toward her turned into something very much deeper.

He remembered her embrace, the feel of her in his arms, her breath against his ear as she whispered to him. This was a woman worth knowing, a woman worth having.

He wondered if she felt the same, if she could feel the same. Right now she was afraid and vulnerable; perhaps her embrace was a reaction bespeaking only that. Perhaps she thought of him as only a friend. After all, she and Liz were cronies from way back, and Liz hugs all her friends. And didn't Marti say she was 'pulling a Liz' on him when she hugged him last Sunday night? He grimaced.

"Don't be long."

Suddenly he was in her arms again; feeling her pressed up against him, hearing her words whisper again in his mind. And he knew he'd move heaven and earth, if that's what it took to free her from that cell. But where to begin?

He knew from long experience that there is always some kind of connection between a murderer and his or her victim. It may be an indirect connection, as in the case where a jealous husband kills his wife's lover, or even more indirect as in the case of murder for hire. But the connection is always there. The trick is finding the one right connection among all the many connections in a person's life. And that is the stock and trade of detective work.

Murder is almost always the result of some kind of offence committed by the victim. The offence may be real or it may be imagined, but in the mind of the murderer or the one who instigates the murder, an offence has been committed.

Statistically, in the case of married couples, the remaining spouse virtually always starts out high on the list of suspects. The list of possibilities for the victim having committed some kind of 'offence' is almost limitless.

The same thing applied even more so to couples who had divorced; the offence in these cases being the divorce and the 'victim' having taken up with another. This put the lie to the concept of no-fault divorce.

He knew Marti was innocent. But he also knew that once Stark discovered that Wayne McCarthy was really Greg Forrester, and the facts surrounding his disappearance, five years ago, he would grab onto it like a pit bull and not let go.

The problem was Greg and finding out what he had done that, in the mind of his murderer, was an offence that made him worthy of death.

That the man was a philanderer didn't help matters. On the other hand, the prevailing attitudes about extramarital sex, at least among those who engage in it, have put it on a more or less recreational level. No promise, real or implied, need be made; it is what it is, and the participants go about their business afterward with no expectation of commitment. As attitudes go, this one tends to lessen the possibility for an offence to occur. After all, a woman who allows herself to be picked up in a casino isn't looking for commitment. How did those ads for Las Vegas go—what happens there, stays there? In other words, do whatever you want; nobody's going to find out. Interesting, if disgusting, ad copy, but not always true—all it takes is one offended husband. What is it the Scripture says, "...be sure your sin will find you out."?

Still, while he couldn't dismiss the idea entirely, his gut was telling him that it wasn't likely to be the aftermath of a one-night stand or an irate husband.

That left other causes. Might he have done something to one of his neighbors? Not likely; his nearest neighbor was two miles away. Did he cheat someone? Did he run somebody off the road? What did he do for a living? Who might he have offended there? And why now, just at the time when Marti happened to show up? He'd never been one to put much stock in coincidence, but you never know. All he had was questions.

What he needed was answers. If he could find out Greg's offence—*why* he had died, he would almost certainly find out simultaneously who had killed him. That's what it was going to take to get the charges against Marti dropped. And the place to start was Greg's house. He had to get in there. He'd have to break in. And crossing a police line to do it would be risky. But it was a risk he'd have to take if Marti was to be freed.

Chapter 23

IT WAS ALMOST 6:30 P.M. when Harry got to his apartment. He hadn't eaten yet, but not wanting to waste any time, he immediately looked up the Ramsey's phone number and placed the call. By seven o'clock they were entering Marti's house.

"How is she doing?" Jo asked.

Harry shrugged. "About as good as could be expected, I guess. She's trying to put a good face on it, but I know she's afraid. I wish, for her sake, she'd never gone up there."

"Yeah, but that's Marti. She never was one to let grass grow under her feet."

"Humph." He made a wry face. "I'm finding that out."

"Hey, don't give up on her!"

"I'm not going to abandon her, Jo. I'll be there for her. And I *will* get her out of this if it is at all within my power to do so."

Jo tilted her head to the side as she looked at him. "You care about her, don't you?"

He exhaled through his nose and gave her a wan smile before looking away.

"It's okay, you know."

He gave her another half-smile. "What, is it written on my forehead or something?"

"No. It's what you said. Or more the *way* you said it."

"Ah. Well, you're very perceptive. I do care about her— very much, if you want the truth. But I, uh...don't know if she feels the same. Is that dumb, or what?"

"I don't think it's dumb. I think it's just fine. You're not one of those strong, silent types are you?"

"What do you mean?"

"I mean, don't hide your light under a bushel. If you have feelings for her, you should let her know. You might just be pleasantly surprised."

"Yeah, well, we'll see."

"So, what did you want me to pack for her?"

"Mmm. Good question. I don't want her to appear at her arraignment in jailhouse orange. I want to convey her innocence. Having said that, I don't mean something Victorian because that would be a caricature. And if she has some kind of a power suit she wears for work I don't want that either. Neither do I want something that would make her look sexy. Something conservative will do nicely; something like she might wear to church."

Jo nodded her head. "Well, as far as I know, she doesn't have a power suit. She does have a black dress which I'm sure you'd admire, but I, uh, won't pack that. Let me go up to her room and see what I can find."

"Thanks. If she has a garment bag, you might want to put it in that. They won't let her have regular clothes in the jail so her lawyer will have to bring it to the courthouse for her. You might want to throw a few other things and some underwear in an overnight bag. I can just hang on to that in case they let her out on bail."

"Okay. I'll be back down in a few minutes," she said as she started up the stairs.

Harry wandered into the kitchen and noticed that the light was flashing on Marti's answering machine. The display indicated there were four messages; the first one having come in at 8:05 p.m. the previous evening. He pressed the play button.

"Mom, it's Cam. You there...Call me when you get in— unless it's too late."

The second came at 9:55 a.m. that morning. "Mom, it's Cam. If you're there, pick up...Mom?"

When she called the fourth time, at 4:15 p.m. her voice had taken on a more frantic tone. "Mom! Mom, are you there? Mom, it's Cam! Please pick up! Mom? Are you okay? *Please* pick up if you can! .....Mom?"

He looked at his watch. 7:19 p.m. Her last call had been just three hours ago. What to do? Marti had not wanted him to call her. But he could tell from Cam's tone that she was ready to send out the militia. He pulled his spiral book from his inside jacket pocket and had started to look for her number on the caller ID when the phone rang.

"Hello, Forrester residence."

"Who is this?" the female voice came back.

"My name is Harry Brannan, and you must be Cam, Camille."

"Who are you and what are doing in my mother's house?"

"I'm your mother's friend and I—"

"What? She's not in a relationship. She would have told me!"

"Well, we're not in a relationship—exactly—"

He told her the whole story, in brief.

"I'm coming up there! I should be able to get there tomorrow some time."

"Cam, there's no sense in doing that. She appears in court on Monday morning, and I'm hoping they'll let her out on bail. If that happens, I'll have her call you. If not, I'll call you myself. But for you to come up here now wouldn't accomplish anything and would be a waste of your time and money."

There was a long silence on the other end.

"Cam, are you there?"

"I want a call on Monday morning—the very instant you know something!"

"I'll call you. I promise."

"Let me give you my numbers."

Harry wrote her work and home numbers in his spiral book."

"Give..." Her voice broke. "Give her a h-hug for me and please tell her that I love her and that I'm p-praying for her."

"I will," Harry said gently. "And you try not to worry, okay?

He hung up the phone and put his head down, resting his forehead in his left hand as he exhaled through pursed lips.

"You handled that well," Jo said, startling him.

He turned toward her and leaned back against the counter top as he gave another large sigh. "I hope so. This is hard, you know? When you're a cop, you just go after the bad guys and you usually don't worry too much about people's feelings. But I know there's no way Marti could have ever done anything like this, and it hurts me to see her in jail." He sighed again. "And it hurts to hear her daughter crying on the other end of the phone." He hung his head.

Jo laid the garment bag over the back of a dining room chair.

"Is it okay if I give you a hug?" she said as she approached him.

Harry allowed her to hug him.

"I think you're just the right man for this job," she said as she released him.

"I hope you're right, Jo."

"Have you eaten yet?"

Harry shook his head.

"We haven't either. So, why don't you follow me home and let us feed you?"

"You sure?"

"Yep. Of course, Clay has decided to cook tonight. But he's not too bad. Really. And he always makes enough for a crowd."

IT WAS PAST 9:30 P.M. when Harry arrived back at his apartment. His visit with Clay and Jo had provided a good ending to an otherwise no-so-good day. Clay's chicken and barley chili had filled his stomach. And their prayers for him and the time they all spent in prayer for Marti had filled his heart. He'd even agreed to go to church with them the next day.

But now, as he prepared for bed, the encouragement he'd felt earlier in the evening began to give way to an awareness of the daunting task that lay ahead of him. Never before had he felt like he had so much personally at stake on the outcome of an investigation.

IT WAS LIGHTS OUT and Marti used a folded-up tissue for a bookmark as she closed the book Harry had gotten for her. What a day it had been. Don Ripley had seemed like a nice man. He had lots of experience and he seemed to genuinely believe in her. That made her feel good.

And what had happened to Harry? She had expected him to be angry with her for coming up here against his advice. But the way his voice sounded when he became indignant about her having to spend time in jail, the tender way in which he'd held her, the heart bouncing kiss on her forehead, bespoke the depth of his concern for her. This, too, made her feel good. But she knew that if she were to be set free, it would be because God had delivered her. And it was to that end she prayed.

Chapter 24

"ALL RISE!...THE 91ST District Court of Chippewa County, Michigan is now in session; the honorable Jefferson Rhodes presiding."

He doesn't look like a Jefferson, Marti thought. *A Jefferson would be tall and austere; slender with lots of white hair and tortoise shell glasses. This man should be a Max or something, with his round face and halo of gray hair.*

She took another slow, deep breath through her nose; watching the fabric of the navy print dress Jo had picked out for her rise as her lungs filled with air. *Calm down. Just breathe slowly and deeply through your nose. This is no time to hyperventilate. Who cares what he looks like?*

"Be seated," the judge said as he stepped onto the dais and took his seat at the bench.

She stole a look behind her as she sat and saw that Harry had slipped into the front row, just barely to her right. He was almost, but not quite within her reach. Her mind traveled back down the already well-worn path to Saturday and she longed to feel his hands on her; gently massaging her shoulders as he'd done then, or holding her in his tender embrace. Now that her day in court had come, she wondered if she would ever feel those things again.

The clerk stood and handed a file folder over the front of the bench to the judge. He opened and quickly perused it. "Martha Forrester, please stand."

Marti and Don Ripley both stood and faced the bench as the judge read.

"File number, R-0-9-5-6-2-8-F-Y, the people of the state of Michigan versus Martha Celeste Forrester. Ma'am, are you that person?"

"Yes sir."

"Ma'am, it is claimed that on or about November eleventh, this year, in the village of Strongs, Chippewa County, Michigan, you did murder Wayne McCarthy. That is a felony offence that carries a maximum possible penalty of life in prison without parole. Do you understand?"

"Yes sir."

He thumbed through the pages in the file, stopping at the one he wanted and briefly perusing it. "Ma'am, you signed a rights form setting out your legal rights. Is that correct?"

Marti gave Don a brief quizzical look and he nodded. "Yes sir," she said.

"Did you read the rights form, discuss your rights with your attorney, and do you understand it?"

"Yes sir."

"Do you wish to have me read any or all of those rights to you now?"

Marti shook her head.

"You have to answer verbally, Ms. Forrester."

"No sir, I don't need to have you read any of my rights to me."

"Let the record show that council is present in the courtroom: David Bostwick for the prosecution and Donald Ripley for the defense. Gentlemen, are you ready to proceed?"

Both attorneys signified that they were.

"All right," Judge Rhodes continued. "I'm going to defer the matter of a plea until the preliminary examination. I assume, Mr. Ripley, that Ms. Forrester is not waiving her right to a prelim."

"That's correct, your honor."

"Good. Now," he spent several seconds looking at his calendar. "Given that the Thanksgiving holiday falls at the end of next week, we'll schedule the preliminary hearing for two weeks from today: Monday, November 28th, at one o'clock p.m. Is that agreeable?"

Both attorneys signified that it was.

Now, let's discuss the matter of bail: Mr. Bostwick.

"Judge," David Bostwick said as he stood. "Sheriff's deputies, acting on an anonymous tip, found Wayne McCarthy, of Strongs, shot to death in his home this past

Friday, November eleventh, at 5:37 p.m. Subsequent findings by the medical examiner place the time of his death at approximately 3:30 p.m. that same day. The anonymous caller, while unable to identify the defendant by name—"

"Objection!" Ripley stood as he spoke. "Your honor, if the caller was anonymous, as Mr. Bostwick has stated, then the prosecution has no knowledge as to his or her ability to identify my client by name."

"Sustained."

"I'll rephrase, your honor...the anonymous caller identified the make, color, and license plate number of the defendant's automobile. In addition, the place she was staying, Klein's Motel, unit four, was also identified.

"Once the police confirmed that Mr. McCarthy had indeed been shot to death in his home, they immediately began to setup road blocks east and west of the motel on M-28 as well as north and south of the motel on M-123. A sheriff's patrol car also went to the motel, but found unit four unoccupied. The deputy obtained Ms. Forrester's name from the motel's registration card, and immediately radioed it to the roadblocks. Ms. Forrester was subsequently apprehended in her car, eastbound on M-28 at approximately 6:10 p.m.

"Further investigation by the police revealed the defendant's bloody fingerprints on a kitchen countertop, a telephone, the front door jamb, and door knob of Mr. McCarthy's house. At this point, based on protein and enzyme variants, we can say that there is a greater than 90% probability that the blood was that of Wayne McCarthy.

"This same blood was found on the driver's side floor mat of the defendant's car, on the soles of her shoes, and on several items of clothing that had been disposed of in a dumpster at Klein's Motel—"

Don stood. "Your honor, the defense stipulates that Ms. Forrester was at Wayne McCarthy's house on the day in question."

"Mr. Bostwick?"

"Given the seriousness of the crime, judge, the evidence, and the fact that the defendant has no apparent ties to the community, the people are requesting that she be remanded to the county jail, without bond.

Marti took another deep breath through her nose and concentrated on keeping her head up and not 'looking guilty,' as she had been coached by Don. But it was difficult. David Bostwick had done her much harm. If she were the judge, she would be giving strong consideration to his request right about now. She wanted to cry, but fought her tears as she concentrated on her breathing. She needed to pray and compromised by keeping her head up while she closed her eyes.

Father, you know that I didn't do this. I pray, Lord, that you will empower Don by your Spirit to speak convincingly on my behalf so that the judge will let me out on bail and ultimately that these charges against me will be found to be false. In Jesus' name, amen. She looked back toward the bench.

"Your turn, Mr. Ripley," Judge Rhodes declared, turning his head in Don's direction.

Ripley stood. "Your honor, there is no question about whether Ms. Forrester was at the decedent's house on the day he died. She was—she freely admits it. She knew the man and she went there to visit him.

"There is no question about whether her bloody fingerprints on the counter top, or door, or telephone are in his blood. They are—she freely admits it.

"In fact it was she who discovered him dying on his kitchen floor.

"In fact is was she who cradled him in her arms as he lay dying, and did everything in her power to help him.

"In fact, it was she who tried to call 9-1-1, but was unable to get through. And it is our contention that when the facts come out, the fingerprint evidence will reveal this."

He stepped out from behind the defense table. "Is it the act of a guilty person to kill someone, and then go to a motel room, and spend at least an hour there before deciding to leave? No. A guilty person would put as much distance as he could between himself and his offense; and in the shortest amount of time that he reasonably could.

"And what about the means of death? A gun is a weapon that kills from a distance. If Ms. Forrester had shot Mr. McCarthy, there would be no need for her to get even so much as a drop of his blood on her person or on her clothing. The fact that she did is evidence, your honor—evidence that she happened into a crime scene after the fact, evidence that she came to the victim's aid, that she did everything in her power to—"

"Judge," David Bostwick said as he stood. "It is always very interesting to hear Mr. Ripley orate, but does he have a point here?"

"Donald?"

"I do, your honor. The point is that Mr. Bostwick does not have the gun that killed Wayne McCarthy. The point is that the police ran trace-metal and gunshot residue tests on Ms. Forrester and they all came back negative! And Mister Bostwick knows that—"

"Your honor," Bostwick stood again. "We all know that the reliability of gunshot residue testing has been questioned in recent—"

"Nevertheless, David, the tests were run. Is Mr. Ripley correct in his assertion that the results were negative?"

"Yes, but she may have worn gloves or—"

"Your honor," Don interrupted. "Would the assistant prosecutor have us believe that my client wore gloves to shoot Mister McCarthy, and than took them off so she could get his blood on her hands and leave bloody fingerprints all over the place?"

The few people in the gallery snickered as Don turned his head, giving Bostwick an inquiring look, and Marti took her first really unconstricted breath of the day.

David Bostwick's face was red as his eyes locked with Don's. "Ripley, you're playing this for all your—"

"Mr. Bostwick," the judge interrupted. "Please address your remarks to the court."

"Yes, your honor," Bostwick said while sitting down.

Don turned back toward the judge. "Your honor, the defense requests—"

"Save it, Donald. I'm not going to dismiss the charges."

"Your honor, I was going to ask that a reasonable bond be set. The only thing the prosecution has shown is that Ms. Forrester was at Wayne McCarthy's house on the day in question; something she freely admits."

"That may be, Mr. Ripley. But bond is set at one million dollars."

"Your honor," Don said gently while tilting his head slightly to the side. "Ms. Forrester works as a secretary. For her, a million dollars is equivalent to a remand."

The judge looked at David Bostwick, took a deep breath and blew it out slowly through pursed lips before looking back at Don. "Don't make me regret this, Donald. Bond is set at 500 thousand dollars on the proviso that you, Ms. Forrester, assuming you are able to pay it, do not leave the jurisdiction, and that you present yourself at the Sheriff's Department each and every day by nine a.m."

"Your *honor,*" David Bostwick protested.

"Next case," Judge Rhodes said as he banged his gavel.

Chapter 25

THE REPORT OF THE GAVEL was still echoing in the courtroom as Harry stood. A female deputy strode the three steps from her place near the jury box to the table where Don and Marti sat. Marti had seemed to deflate as the amount of the bond was announced and Harry wanted to get to her, wanted to hold her and tell her that everything would be all right, before they took her back to her cell.

"It might as well be a million," she agonized to Don as they, too, stood. "I don't have that kind of money and I don't have any way to get it."

The deputy had her hand around Marti's arm before Harry could get around the half-wall to where she stood, and Marti resisted slightly, turning toward him. "Come on, Forrester," The deputy intoned, tugging on her arm. "Let's not make this any harder than it needs to be."

Marti's look became even more forlorn as the deputy led her away. She turned her head toward Harry as the deputy paused to open the door at the front of the courtroom.

In that instant, Harry's eyes locked with hers. "I'll find a way," he said loud enough for her to hear.

"Order," Judge Rhodes said loudly as he once again banged his gavel.

Don came around the half wall and Harry fell in step with him. "I suppose they won't let me go back to the cells to speak with her."

"No, sorry, attorneys only, but I can give her a message."

"Tell her that I'm heading back to Grand Rapids and I'll be back just as soon as I can raise the money...and, uh...tell her I...tell her to keep her chin up, I guess. I'll wait out here for the garment bag."

Harry stowed the garment bag in his trunk and drove back to the hotel to check out. He hadn't bothered to unpack his bag the night before, figuring he probably wouldn't be staying for more than one night, and time was of the essence. It was already past ten a.m. and he wanted to be home before the bank closed. Once he was under way, he used his cell phone to call Cam, finally reaching her at her work number:

"Cam? Harry Brannan."

"Oh, Harry, I'm so glad to hear from you. How's my mom?"

"About as good as could be expected, I guess. They wouldn't let me go back to see her. However, they did set bail for her."

"How much is it?"

"Half a million dollars."

The line went silent, and with the road noise Harry wasn't sure if the connection had dropped. "Cam, are you there?"

"Yeah, I'm here. Sorry, I just was taken aback at the amount. I don't know how I can raise that much. I mean, even our house isn't—"

"We don't have to raise the whole amount. Fifty thousand, plus collateral will satisfy the bond."

"If Roger and I cash in our retirements, we might be able to raise about half of that. And I...I just..." She sighed, "I don't know."

"Just let me worry about it, okay? I'm on my way back to Grand Rapids now, and I'm pretty sure I can raise the money."

"Are you sure about this?"

"I'm pretty sure, as sure as I can be."

"No. I mean, why are *you* doing this?"

"Because she's frightened. Because she needs help and I promised her I would do everything in my power to help her. Because she didn't do anything wrong—she doesn't belong in that awful place. I'm doing this for the same reason you would do it, if you could. Look, Cam, I'm coming up on the bridge and I have to get my toll ready. I'll have her call you just as soon as I can get her out of there."

Harry rang off, dropped the phone in his jacket pocket, and dug out four dollars for the toll to cross the Mackinaw Bridge.

By three p.m. he was back in his apartment. Without bothering to take off his coat, he booted his computer and checked his bank accounts, writing down the numbers of the CDs he would cash-out to supply the needed monies. From there he went to the bank.

Upon leaving the bank, Harry drove to Choice Care HMO and was able to meet with Marti's department manager before she went home for the day. He didn't tell her Marti was in jail, but explained that her former husband had died unexpectedly, that many arrangements needed to be made and there was no one else to make them. It was a lie and Harry felt bad about it, but the woman approved vacation days, with a request that Marti call in as soon as she was able.

It was dark when Harry got back to his apartment. Having gone the whole day on coffee alone, he was hungry, but there was still much to do before he could allow any time for himself.

He searched through his records and found the deed to the apartment building, along with its most recent property tax valuation to prove the value of it. He locked these items, along with the cashier's check for the bond in his brief case. Another call to Jo Ramsey and he was on his way to Marti's house to pick up additional clothing, which he packed in one of his own suit cases and stowed in trunk of his car.

It was near nine p.m. when he arrived back at home and Harry decided he was too tired to eat a meal. He settled on four soda cracker squares and a dose of pain killers to quell the ache in his shoulder and knee, and went to bed.

Chapter 26

HARRY WAS BACK IN Sault Sainte Marie by 2:30 on Tuesday afternoon. The Essex was busy, but he managed to get a single on the third floor. He stowed his luggage there before heading over to post the bond for Marti's release.

It was nearing four o'clock when she entered the lobby where Harry was waiting. She was wearing blue jeans and the same dusty pink top she'd had on the first night he'd been to her house—the clothes she must have been wearing when she was arrested. When she spotted Harry her face lit up and she ran to him, dropping her overnight bag and coat as she flew into his arms. "I missed yooou," she said, holding him tightly in her embrace.

Harry held her tight, lifting her feet from the floor. "I missed you, too," he said, setting her down. "Let's get you out of this place."

"You don't have to ask me twice," she said as Harry helped her into her coat.

He picked up her bag and led her out to his car, holding the passenger door open so she could enter, and then stowed her bag in the trunk with the rest of her luggage before getting in and starting the car. "You hungry, or do you feel like doing a little work?"

"Well, I am hungry, but what do you have in mind?"

"I'd like to touch base with Don to see if he's been able to get a copy of that 'anonymous' call, reporting the crime. I'd like to listen to it and have you listen to it to see if it can provide us with any clues. After that we can get something to eat. Of course, if you're starving—"

"No, no, that's a great idea. Let's give him a call. We can always eat later," she said as Harry pulled into a space in the hotel parking lot and shut off the engine.

"I've got some extra clothing for you in the trunk. Given that the judge said you can't leave the jurisdiction, I thought you could use some extra things to wear. However, I want to put your mind at ease that I was not pawing around in your dresser or closet or whatever. I called Jo and got her to pick things out for you."

"Oh, thank you," she laughed. "I appreciate that. I was wondering what I was going to do."

"If you're ready, why don't we go inside? I'll stop at the desk and see if we can line you up with a room. Then I'll come out and bring in your luggage."

"Uh...do you think maybe I could stay with...you? Look, uh...please believe me; I'm not suggesting anything untoward—"

"I know that."

"It's just that...being in jail...you have no idea what that's like. Nobody up here knows us, and I...just don't want to be alone."

Harry exhaled audibly. "I can understand that. All right, then...I promise you that you'll have absolutely nothing to fear from me. That I'll respect your dignity and protect your good name."

"Thanks, Harry. And thank you for saying that. I know you would have done it anyway, but I appreciate that you said it and that you care about my reputation."

"Well, to be fair with the hotel, I am going to have to add you onto the room. I guess I can tell them you're my wife and take your luggage with me to make it believable."

Harry took Marti up to his room before bringing in her luggage and getting her registered. When he returned to the room she was talking on the phone. "Thanks, Sweetie. I'll talk to you soon. Okay, bye."

She hung up and turned toward Harry. "I hope you don't mind, but I called Cam."

"Oh, no. I'm glad you did. I spoke with her yesterday and told her I'd have you call as soon I got you out."

"Yeah, so she said. She also said she spoke to you on Saturday night when she called the house. Thanks for calming her fears—although she views you as this big mystery man. Believe me; you've got her interest *really* piqued."

Harry laughed. "Well, good. I've never been a mystery man before and I kind of like it."

"About the bond money—"

"We can talk about that later," Harry said, pulling a business card from his pocket. "Right now we should call Don and check on that tape."

Harry called Don, verified that he had the tape copy and got directions to his house. Twenty minutes later, he and Marti were sitting across from Don in his home office.

Don removed a cassette player from his desk drawer and loaded the tape. "I hope you don't mind, but I asked them to put this on a cassette. I know the technology is a little out of date, but I'm too old to figure out all that new-fangled computer sound-file stuff." He pressed the proper button on the machine and the tape began to play.

When it was finished, he pressed the stop button and then hit rewind. "What do you think?"

"Well," Harry said. "It's definitely a man's voice. But it sounds muffled, like he has something over the handset."

"Yeah, that's what I thought, too."

"What do you think, Marti?" Harry asked. Does the voice ring any bells with you?"

Marti shook her head. "No. Could we listen to it again?"

"Sure," Don replied.

"Listen carefully to his voice," Harry said. If you can't identify the voice itself, listen to his inflections and the way he puts his sentences together."

Don pressed the play button and they all listened again.

"Anything?" Don asked as the tape came to an end.

Marti shook her head again. "No. Sorry. But I can tell you that nothing he said was true."

Harry picked up her hand. "That's okay. It was a long-shot anyway. At least we know the killer was a man."

"You think he was the one who did it?"

"Absolutely," Harry said as Don nodded. "The whole thing is a fabrication with the sole object of getting the police to focus on you. I think it scared him when you showed up. He panicked and ran and thought he should call the police before you had a chance to report the crime."

"I tried to call 9-1-1, but the phone didn't work. Maybe I did something wrong. I was pretty panicked myself...I've never...seen so much blood." Tears began to run from her eyes and she removed her hand from Harry's to open her purse.

Don held a box of tissues over his desk and Harry pulled a couple of them out and gave them to Marti.

"Thanks."

She put the used tissues in her jeans pocket and snapped her purse closed as Harry turned to Don. "Do we know, officially, whether the phone was working? I didn't think of this before, but there has to be a reason why the phone didn't work when she tried to call 9-1-1."

"I don't know, but I can certainly find out. Bostwick made a point about her bloody fingerprints being on the phone—"

"Exactly. But if the line had been cut—"

"What does that mean?" Marti asked.

Harry picked up her hand again. "It means that if the line was cut and you knew it—meaning that you had cut the line—there would be no reason for you to try to call 9-1-1."

"Ergo, no reason for your fingerprints to be on the phone," Don said. "The fact that they were on the handset and on the 9 and 1 buttons argues in favor of your innocence—assuming the line was cut. It's not conclusive, but it's one more thing in your favor."

Marti smiled. "I wouldn't know a phone line from a chorus line, but I'm glad you two are on my side."

Chapter 27

"WHERE WOULD YOU LIKE to eat?" Harry asked, as they left Don's house. "I still have your dress in the trunk if you want to go someplace fancy."

"I thought you said you were 'a meatloaf kind of guy.'"

"I am a meatloaf kind of guy, but I can also do fancy. I just thought that...what with you having to suffer the indignity of being in jail, I'd try to do something really nice for you."

She turned her head and looked at him, tears forming in her eyes. "Thank you," she squeaked out, putting her hands over her face as she put her head down and began to cry.

Harry pulled off the road into a parking lot and stopped the car. He removed a couple of tissues from the console and slipped them into her hand as he put his right arm around her shoulders. "Hey," He said softly. "What's the matter?"

After a few minutes, she stopped crying, dried her eyes and blew her nose. "Sorry," she said, blowing out a breath through pursed lips. "I'm just a little emotional, tonight, I guess. I'm not used to being treated this way—not that people treat me badly." She blew out another breath. "It's just the contrast, I guess. That jail is such a horrible place—hard and lonely—then you treat me like...I don't know, like I'm royalty or something."

Harry pulled her toward him and spoke softly near her ear. "You deserve to be treated well—all the time...at least, I think so."

"Thank you," she said, sitting up straight as he took his arm from around her. "Now, I have something to tell you, Harry: I'm just a simple woman. And being out of that jail is really nice. That you care about my dignity and reputation is really nice. Being listened to and not talked down to is really nice. That you treat me like a lady is really nice. So I can do fancy—if I have to. But the truth is I'm a meatloaf kind of girl, and I've learned how to be content that way. Honestly, I've never acquired a taste for fancy."

Harry smiled. "Okay. How about we find a comfortable looking place and see what the food is like?"

"Sounds good to me."

"WHAT DO YOU THINK my chances are," Marti asked as they ate their meals.

"I'd say about forty-sixty, right now. Bostwick has evidence, but it's circumstantial. We can offer rebuttal evidence, but that's also circumstantial. If Stark is any kind of cop at all, he's working hard trying to establish what your relationship to Wayne/Greg was. If he finds out you two were married—"

"Then I'm sunk. Even I know that."

"Not necessarily. But I would feel a whole lot better about this if I could find out *why* Greg was killed. It would almost certainly lead us to who did it. Is there anything you can think of, anything at all, that might that might shed some light on this?"

Marti shook her head as the waitress dropped off the check. They both got out of the booth and Harry helped Marti with her jacket before picking up the check and leading the way to the cashier's station.

When they were underway Marti said, "You don't suppose it could be something as simple as robbery, do you?"

"I doubt it," Harry replied. "Why choose that particular house? Why cut the phone line, assuming it was cut? Why call the police instead of just getting out of there as fast as he could? Of course, you could ask *that* question for any of those circumstances."

Harry pulled into the hotel parking lot and stopped under the canopy. "Do you have your door-card with you?"

"Yess," she said tentatively. "Why would I need it?"

"To let yourself in the room. I'm going over to the house to see if I can dig up some evidence."

"Well...I'm coming *with* you."

"No you're not. For one thing, it might be dangerous. For another, I'm going to have to break-in, which is against the law. If we should get caught over there, do you realize—"

"I don't care! I'm coming with you, and that's that!"

"Oh Marti," Harry agonized. "Don't you ever do what you're told?"

"Not since I turned sixteen."

Harry laughed. "I believe that."

"Look, Harry, I appreciate that you want to protect me, but I'm probably better equipped to recognize what might be evidence than you are. And besides, two of us can get more done in less time."

"I'm not going to win this argument, am I?"

"Nope," she said, facing the front and folding her hands in her lap.

"All right," he said, putting the car in gear and driving away.

"You're not angry with me, are you?" Marti said, some moments later, as they turned to go westbound on M-28.

"No. I just wish I had some idea of what we might be looking for. It would make this a whole lot easier."

"Harry?"

"Hmm?"

"We're pretty close friends, aren't we? I mean, since we've known each other, we've become pretty close, haven't we?"

"I'd like to think so."

"I want to tell you something, but it's hard for me to say."

"A friend should be able to tell a friend anything, right?"

"Right. Umm," she took a breath. "Greg was into sex, I mean really into it. And I know from the women who showed up after he went missing that he'd had at least two affairs while we were married. But I also know there were more than just the two. I mean, I don't know who they were, but a woman...just knows. So if he didn't care that *he* was married, I'm pretty sure he wouldn't care if the woman was married. But what if her husband found out?"

"Well, it's certainly possible, but the timing seems like it would be too much of a coincidence."

"What do you mean?"

"Think about it. Why now? Why not six months ago—or next week? Why does it happen on the exact same day you come up here to confront him? It just doesn't seem like a coincidence to me. It seems to point the idea that whoever it was knew Greg, but thought, like everybody else, that he was dead—until Gary Hammond saw him in that casino."

"Oh, I see where you're going with this."

"That may also answer the question about why he called the police. If there is something in the house that could be tied to him, he would benefit by shifting their attention onto you. I wonder who, besides you, Hammond told about seeing him. Another question is why did Greg fake his death in the first place?"

"I just assumed that he wanted to be rid of me."

"I think most guys would consider themselves lucky to have you. Of course, we know now that Greg wasn't most guys. But, still, it doesn't make sense to me. I mean, why go at all? He had a nice home, a beautiful wife, a good job, a certain amount of respect in the community; by any meaningful standard of measure, it doesn't make sense. There has to be another reason—some kind of inciting incident that made it either advantageous or necessary for him to leave and to leave when he did."

Harry turned left onto Strongs Road and slowed as they reached the house, continuing on until they came to an opening in the woods about two hundred feet south of the mailbox. He turned off the lights and got out, proceeding on foot into the opening. Returning, he backed the car in among the trees and shut off the engine.

Chapter 28

HARRY OPENED THE CONSOLE and removed his holstered pistol.

Marti's face registered her shock. "Is that a gun?"

"Yes. It's okay, I'm licensed to carry it and I know how to use it."

"Harry, I'm frightened."

"Well, there's nothing to be—"

"Please, Harry...put it away."

Harry put the gun back into the console and closed the lid.

"Thank you."

"What is it?"

"I'm...just frightened, that's all."

"You want to talk about it?"

"No...no, no, no," she said, visibly shaking.

Harry gently held her left forearm. "It's all right. We'll just leave it locked up, okay?"

"Thank you, Harry."

They exited the car and Harry led Marti by the hand as they walked carefully through the woods toward the house. The south end of the place came into view and they stopped before entering the clearing. Harry whispered to her, "You wait here while I make sure nobody's around. I'll be back as soon as I can."

She nodded her head as he set out toward the front of the house.

Harry walked slowly, staying under cover of the trees, while spying out the house. The place was dark, and he could see the crime-scene tape stretched across the front door as well as the door to a breezeway connecting the garage to the house.

He came to the driveway and, bending low, scooted quickly across it into the cover of the trees on the other side, continuing on slowly around the garage and to the backside of the structure. The back entrance to the breezeway also had yellow tape stretched across it.

To the left of the breezeway and centered on the house was a concrete patio with a second floor deck above it. French doors, leading into the house, were centered on the deck. The lower patio had no such doors and was apparently accessible only from the breezeway.

The place was completely dark and Harry walked quickly back to where Marti was waiting. "Everything looks good." He whispered, holding out his hand. "Come on."

Marti put her hand in his and he led her through the woods until they were across from the back entrance to the breezeway.

"Now what?" Marti whispered.

"You wait here while I get the doors open. If everything's okay I'll come out and get you. If alarms start going off, make a bee-line for the car. I'll catch up with you as quickly as I can." He took his keys out of his pocket and handed them to her. "Wait a few minutes. If, for some reason, I can't get to you, take off."

"I'm not going to take off and *leave* you here."

"Well, you probably won't have to. The place looks unoccupied. But just in case they've got a deputy in there or something, you do not, under any circumstances, want to be caught here."

"Harrrry!"

"Shh," he whispered. "I'll be back for you in a few minutes."

Harry bent low and hurried across the clearing to the breezeway entrance. A storm door was the only door, and from the hinges he could tell that it opened out. He pulled on a pair of latex gloves, tried the latch and found it unlocked. So he pulled the door open until it hit the crime-scene tape. The opening was maybe a little more than a foot. He carefully, but firmly pulled the door against the tape, stretching the tape until the door was open far enough for him to enter.

He walked across the breezeway to the side door of the house. It was too dark to see any details of the lockset so he removed his flashlight from his jacket and trained the beam on the door. There was no deadbolt and the entrance set appeared to be of the standard variety with a key slot centered in the knob.

Harry tried the knob; the door was locked. He reached into his back pocket, removing his wallet, and from it removing a dollar-bill-sized piece of cardstock, laminated in plastic. He lined the end of it up with the center of the knob and pushed it into space between the door and the door jam. It met a little resistance when it hit the latch so he pushed a little harder until the latch receded into the door. He gave the door a push with his foot and it swung open. He replaced the cardstock in his wallet and returned it to his back pocket before stepping into the house.

From the light of his flashlight, he could see that he was in the kitchen. The outline of Greg's body was still on the floor. He skirted around it and mostly covered the beam of the flashlight with his hand while he checked out the house. When he was satisfied it was safe he went back out to the breezeway and found Marti waiting by the door.

He pushed open the storm door. "What are you doing here?"

"I didn't hear any alarms or anything so—"

"Well come on in," he said pushing the door open as far as he dared.

Once they were in the kitchen, Harry closed the door. When Marti saw the outline on the floor she froze. Harry put his hands on her shoulders and turned her until she was facing the dining room, then sidestepped with her until the kitchen was out of her view.

"Here are your keys." She said holding them out.

He took the keys and put them in his pocket before taking another pair of latex gloves out of his jacket pocket. "Thanks. Here. Put these on."

Marti pulled the gloves on. "Where do we start?"

"Why don't we start upstairs and work our way down?"

Marti nodded as he took her hand and led her to the stairs.

The second floor was a loft, covering slightly more than the back half of the house and making for a very tall ceiling in the living and dining rooms. A wrought-iron railing spanned almost the entire width of the edge, except for an area above the kitchen. Once they were in the loft, Harry trained the beam of his flashlight up and down the hallway. There were three doors that appeared to enter rooms and a bi-fold door in the end of the wall over the kitchen. They walked to the bi-fold door and Harry opened it: A linen closet.

The next door revealed a bathroom with a separate bath and large glassed-in shower. The middle door led to a large, plush bedroom with French doors leading to the deck, a California king-sized bed on the right-hand wall and a large flat-screen TV mounted on the wall shared with the bathroom.

The final door led to an office, into which they walked. Harry closed the door and walked over to the window, looking out before closing the blinds. He trained his beam near the door. "How about switching on the light."

Marti turned on the switch and they both stood there for a moment while their eyes became accustomed to the brightness.

The place looked like an executive office. A large cherry-wood lateral file cabinet sat under the window and held an expensive-looking stereo on its top. About three feet in front of the file cabinet was a matching cherry-wood desk, facing the door. In front of the desk was a leather sofa with its back against the door wall.

"Where do we start?" Marti asked.

"Why don't you take the filing cabinet and I'll take the desk."

"What are we looking for?"

"I don't know. Papers—anything out of the ordinary or anything that catches your attention, I guess. Something Greg shouldn't have."

Marti began to search through the files and Harry started on the desk, pulling out drawers and checking their contents, checking underneath the drawers and behind them and in the drawer cavities for something that may be taped there. He found nothing incriminating.

"How are you doing?" He asked Marti.

"Not much, I'm afraid. I've gone through the whole top drawer and it's just bills and receipts, stuff like that. The bottom drawer doesn't have anything in it at all."

Harry checked underneath and behind both file drawers and in the drawer cavities, but found nothing. "Let's look in the cushions of the sofa," he said, closing the top drawer.

Marti went for the sofa as Harry checked the backside of a picture hanging on the wall. Again, they found nothing. He gave Marti his flashlight. "I'm going to pick up the end of the sofa. Why don't you see if anything is underneath it."

She got down on the floor as Harry lifted the sofa end. "I don't see anything," she said.

"Can you see up into the sofa?"

"No. There's some kind of fabric stapled on the bottom."

Harry set the end of the sofa down. "I'll get my jackknife out and—"

"Shh," Marti whispered. "I think I hear something."

Harry reached out and hauled Marti to her feet as he hit the light switch, plunging the room into darkness.

She pressed the flashlight into his hand. "Do you hear it?" she whispered.

"Yeah. It sounds like somebody's trying to get into the house."

"What do we do?"

Harry took her by the hand and led her out of the room. The noise was louder in the hallway and sounded like it was coming from the kitchen door.

A flashlight beam blazed into the dining room and Marti gasped loudly. "Come on," Harry whispered pulling her down the hallway to the bedroom.

Chapter 29

HARRY DRAGGED MARTI INTO the bedroom, closing them in and pulling her to the French doors, where he fumbled with the latch, trying to get it open in the dark. Suddenly it released and he yanked her out onto the deck. She stood there, transfixed. "Get over the railing," he whispered loudly.

Marti stepped over the railing and stood on the edge of the deck, her heels hanging in midair as she clung to the railing. Harry put her hands on two of the wooden balusters. "Let yourself down, hang on to the bottom rail, then drop off and run like hell."

He bent over the railing, holding her wrists as she let herself down, and then went over himself after she'd dropped off. He could hear her running as he, too, dropped to the ground, sending a searing pain into the bone above his artificial knee. He staggered, almost losing his balance as he heard the French doors burst open.

Harry took off at a limping run after Marti. He was mostly across the clearing when a shot rang out. He kept running. A second shot. The bullet stung his side. He stumbled, but recovered and dashed into the woods.

Marti had run the opposite way from where the car was parked. He knew he was running in the same general direction, but he'd not actually seen where she went. He stopped behind a tree, leaning on it as he gasped, his breath making large plumes of vapor in cold night air. If the guy was coming, it would be a dead giveaway. He unzipped his jacket part way and pulled it up so it was covering his mouth and nose, trying to get his breathing under control while he listened. Nothing. He listened for several minutes more. Still nothing. His side burned where the bullet had hit him, but it didn't have that awful feeling of a deep wound like his shoulder had had a couple of years ago. It didn't seem to be bleeding too badly, either; at least he wasn't drenched in blood. That was good because there was no time to waste worrying about it.

Harry started off again in the same direction, removing his flashlight from his jacket pocket and switching it on. He played it back and forth it in a wide arc in front of him as he pressed slowly on; looking for Marti or any sign she may have passed by.

This isn't getting me anywhere, he thought after going about a hundred yards. There'd been no sign of Marti and he didn't know if he was even on the right track. The uneasiness in the pit of his stomach was beginning to crescendo. Was he too far east, too far west; was she behind him somewhere, laying injured? It was cold—seventeen degrees, according to the thermometer in the car. How long could she last out here in that leather car coat she was wearing?

He switched off his light and bowed his head: *Lord God, I'm sure you don't want to hear from me, but I'm not praying for myself. Marti is out here someplace and I don't know where she is. I don't know if she's lost or if she's injured...all I know it that it's cold—very cold, and I'm...so afraid for her. Lord, please help me find her, or help her find me. And help me get her someplace where it's safe and warm. I'm not asking you to do this for me, but for her, and for her daughter and her grandchildren.*

Harry switched on his light again and continued limping in the same direction he'd been going. Up until now he'd not wanted to call out for fear of alerting the shooter, but there'd been no sign of the guy. Worse, there'd been no sign of Marti either. He called her name.

Was that a noise? He stopped, listening. The same sound again. It was somewhere ahead of him. He hurried on, almost falling as the ground declined sharply. Harry caught hold of a tree, hanging on with one hand as he shined his light down, scanning it to and fro. He was on the rim of a hill. The sound came again—Marti's voice—somewhere to his right. He limped as fast as he could, going from tree to tree, training the beam of his light downward, until at last he spotted her, sitting against a tree near the bottom of the hill.

Harry hurried toward her. "Thank God you're safe!" he said as her reached her.

"I th-think m-m-my ankle's b-broken. I-I'm s-s, so c-c-c-cold."

Harry knelt beside her. "You're soaking wet."

"There's w-w-water d-down—"

"Shh, don't try to talk." He took off his jacket.

He unbuttoned her coat, got hold of the collar and wrenched it off of her, pulling first on one sleeve and then the other until it came away. Her whole body was shaking.

He unbuttoned her top.

"W-what are...d-doing?"

I'm sorry, Marti, but you're soaked through to the skin. We've got to get this stuff off from you before you freeze to death.

He removed her top, then pulled off his own shirt and put it on her, followed by his jacket. He zipped it up part way and reached inside, removing his gloves from their pocket and putting them on her hands before zipping the jacket fully closed.

He moved toward her feet. "Which ankle is it?"

"T-this one," she said, moving her right leg.

He gently grasped her trembling ankle between his thumb and forefingers. "Try to move it from side-to-side."

She tried and it moved.

"I think it's only sprained," he said. "Let's see if we can get you on your feet."

Harry walked around behind her, put his hands under her arms and helped her up. "See if it will bear your weight."

She put some pressure on it. "H-hurts," she said, nodding her head,

"It's going to hurt. Can you walk on it?"

"D-don't th-th-think so."

Harry leaned her against the tree and picked up her wet clothing, stuffing her top into a sleeve of her coat and putting his flashlight in his back pocket. He held her coat in his left hand, putting that arm around her waist as he ducked under her right arm, holding her right wrist with his right hand, and together they set out for the car.

It was slow-going up the hill and they had to stop several times to rest. But when they reached level ground he picked up the pace, moving as fast as he could with her through the woods. He stopped, out of breath, when they reached the clearing where the house stood.

Harry spied out the house from the cover of the trees. The place was completely dark and seemed to have been abandoned.

"How are you doing?" he breathed.

"Still f-freezing, b-but not as b-bad. You m-must be ice c-cube now."

"Not too bad—must be all the hard work."

"Looks like th-they're g-gone."

"Yeah."

Harry moved out into the clearing with her as they continued on. When they reached the car, he walked her directly to the passenger side door and unlocked it with the remote. He pulled the door open and sat her inside, putting his hand on her head so it wouldn't bump on the door frame, then lifted her legs and helped her get situated in the seat before pulling out the seatbelt and buckling her in. He hurried around to the other side, pulled open the back door, threw in her coat and pulled a fleece blanket off the floor behind the driver's seat. Slamming the back door, he got in on the driver's side and started the engine, almost simultaneously reaching over and turning the heater up to full blast.

"B-blanket?"

"Hey, this is Michigan. I always have a blanket in the car," he said as he wrapped it around her legs.

Harry put the car in gear and pulled out from among the trees, turning left onto Strongs Road and driving out to M-123 before turning on the lights.

By the time they turned onto the I-75 ramp Harry was warm, even in his T-shirt. Marti was sitting with her head down and hadn't spoken since they'd gotten underway. He reached over and touched her arm. "How are you doing?"

She kept her head down. "I'm still cold, but at least I'm not s-shivering so much."

He gently squeezed her arm. "Marti, are you okay?"

She looked at him with sad eyes. "I did the best I could. P-please don't be angry with me."

"Oh, Marti, don't think that. I could never be angry with you. I'm sorry for barking orders at you, but I could see you were frightened and didn't know what to do, so I just...took over, I guess. Please believe me; my only thought was for you and for your safety."

Tears were streaming from her eyes and he reached over and grasped her hand. "Ohhh, don't cry...or you'll have me doing it—and I have to drive."

She smiled, sort of, but the tears kept coming. Harry dug in the console for a packet of tissues and gave them to her.

"Thanks," she said, taking off his gloves and pulling out a couple of tissues.

"What happened to you, anyway? I heard you running, but I was too busy trying to get off that deck to see you."

She dried her eyes and blew her nose. "You told me to run so I ran. Then I heard shots, and I was *so* scared. So I just k-kept running...until the ground disappeared from under my feet. I came down on my right foot and it twisted off to one side. After that, I went t-tumbling down the hill. There's a marsh or a swamp or something down at the bottom. I hit it pretty hard and went through the ice. It took me a while, but I m-managed to crawl up to where you found me.

"I didn't know where I was and I was s-so cold. I prayed and prayed that you'd find me."

"Yeah, I prayed that I'd find you, too."

"God answered our prayers."

"Well, more likely, He answered your prayers. Hey, we're here," Harry said as he turned into the hotel parking lot. "I'm going to pull around to the side so we can get you right into the elevator without having to go past the desk."

Chapter 30

HARRY HELPED MARTI INTO the room and sat her on the bed before going into the bathroom and turning on the water in the tub. When he returned, he switched on all the lights. "Let's get your shoes off."

She laid back, propping herself up on her elbows, as he removed her shoes and peeled off her wet socks. "You've got a bruise starting on the outside of that ankle."

"What does that mean?"

"It means you've torn some muscle fibers...and that it's going to hurt for a while."

"Lucky me," she said flatly.

Harry helped her up to her feet and got his jacket off her. "Come on. Let's get you into the bathroom."

Marti put her right arm around his neck and they made their way into the bathroom. He sat her down on the edge of the tub. "Do you need any help?"

"I think I can get undressed by my—you have blood on your shirt—lot's of blood."

"Yeah, I know. One of the bullets nicked me. It's just a scratch. It's already stopped bleeding."

"*Ohhh*...let me look at it."

"Not now. You need to get in that tub and get warm," he said, leaving the room and pulling the door mostly shut behind him. "Holler if you need anything."

He picked up her overnight bag and opened it on the bed, finding her pajamas and blow dryer. The only socks she had were anklets so he got a pair of socks from his own bag and stacked them with her items.

He took them to the bathroom door. "I'm going to put your PJs on the counter. I'll keep my eyes closed, okay?"

"Okay."

He placed the items on the counter and pulled the door back mostly closed. "I'm heading out to find an elastic bandage for your ankle. "I'll make sure the door's locked."

"Get something for your side while you're at it."

"Good idea," he said, pulling up his shirt and checking his side for the first time. It was more than a scratch, but not much more. He let his shirt down, put his slightly damp jacket on and left the room.

When he later let himself back in he could hear her humming from the open door of the bathroom. Her hair was dry and she was dressed in her pajamas, hanging her used towel over the shower rod. "You sound better," he said, dropping his bag on the bed and taking off his jacket.

She hobbled over to him. "I feel better—a hundred percent better. Thanks for the socks."

"You're welcome." he said. "Let's get a look at that ankle."

She sat on the foot of the bed and scooted herself back so that just her lower legs were hanging off the end. Harry removed his sock from her foot and wrapped the elastic bandage around her ankle. "Sorry to be gone so long, but it took me a while to find a place that was open."

"That's okay. I needed a good soak and, no offence, but I was more comfortable knowing you weren't here."

"I promised you that I wouldn't violate your trust," he said, clipping the bandage in place and pulling the sock up over it.

"It really wasn't about you...but let's just leave it at that. Okay?"

"Whatever you say."

Harry gathered his night clothes and went into the bathroom to shower and change. When he returned she was still sitting on the end of the bed. He looked at her. "You okay?"

She nodded. "Let me look at your side."

"Oh, it's just a—"

"Harry, please let me help you."

"All right," he said, standing with his side to her and lifting his shirt. "I got some alcohol wipes. They're in the bag."

She removed a foil packet from the box, tore it open and dabbed the wipe over the scratch.

"*Whoa,* that stings."

"Sorry, but the last thing you need is an infection."

"I know. Thank you," he said, taking the used wipe and throwing it in the waste basket.

"Thank you."

"What for?"

"For letting me help you."

"I didn't know it was that important to you."

"Well, it is. This whole thing is my fault. I came up here against your advice and got myself in a jam, and I wouldn't have blamed you if you just let me fend for myself, but you come up here and pay...my..." She began to cry.

Harry gathered her in his arms. "Shh," he whispered. "None of that matters now. The important thing is that you're safe. Listen, this is *our* problem, together, not your problem alone. You don't need to worry about the money. You don't need to worry about a thing, right now. We'll find a way out of this. By God's grace, we'll find a way."

He continued to hold her, rocking from side to side, comforting her until she regained her composure.

"I got your shirt all wet," she said, stepping back from him.

"I'll never wash it again."

She smiled and chuckled as Harry pulled a couple of tissues from the box on the night stand and gave them to her.

She sat back down on the foot of the bed and blew her nose as he folded open the covers. "Come on," he said, helping her to her feet. "Let's get you tucked in."

"*Nooo,*" she protested, as he sat her down on the sheet. "This is your room. You take the bed. I'll take the chair."

"I can't do it, Marti. There's just something in me that won't let me do it. Look, I'm an expert at chair sleeping. I spent over a year sleeping in a chair after my shoulder surgery. Besides, I took a hydrocodone so I'm not going to be doing a lot of sleeping tonight anyway."

She looked up at him. "What's that?"

"It's a pain pill—Vicodin. I hurt my knee dropping off that deck."

"Ohh, Harryy."

"It'll be all right," he said, pulling the covers up over her. "I just need to get off from it for a while."

He turned on the light in the bathroom and pulled the door mostly closed, then got a blanket from the dresser before turning off the room lights and sitting in the chair.

Chapter 31

"HARRY, ARE YOU SLEEPING?"

He pressed the backlight button on his watch: 12:10 a.m. "No."

"I can't get to sleep either. Will you sit with me for a little while?"

"Sure," he said, pulling the chair over until it was touching the bed. He sat down. "Is this too close for comfort?"

"No, it's fine. I'm not frightened of you, Harry," she said, inching herself closer to the chair.

"That's good, because earlier, when you said you felt that we'd become close, I felt that, too, and I wouldn't want you to be afraid of me."

She smiled. "I want to know about you, Harry. I mean, I've told you practically my whole life story, but all I know about you—"

"Marti, there are things in my life that are not very pretty, and you...and your friendship are important to me. I don't want to do anything that will—"

"It's important to me, too," she said, reaching out and taking his hand. "And that's why you can't keep these things to yourself anymore, Harry."

He put his head down and sighed, exhaling through his nose.

"I know about Lisa and about how you were in ICU for three days, in a coma, while she was off with another man. I know about the divorce—"

Harry looked at her with sad eyes.

Marti returned his gaze, saying nothing.

"She was, uh...thirty-one and I was forty-five. So we really didn't have anything in common, except she had a little boy." He smiled. "He was nine, and name was Curt. I got to know him through Kids of the Future, a mentoring program sponsored by the department." He put his head down, sighing again. "I don't know if you can understand this, but I loved that little guy."

"Oh, Harry, of course I understand," she said, squeezing his hand.

He sniffed. "I took him to a baseball game one night and he fell asleep in the car on the way home so I carried him in the house and helped Lisa get him into bed. The next morning I woke up in her bed. It wasn't something I planned or that was even in my mind, but it happened."

"She seduced you?"

He gave a mirthless chuckle. "It takes two, Marti. I knew what I was doing and I knew it was wrong. But I also knew, at some level, that my future relationship with Curt was in play, too. So it was...I don't know, complicated, I guess, at least for me. She was okay with it, but I'm just old fashioned enough to feel guilty about sleeping with a woman and not being married to her."

"So you got married."

"Yeah. Now, aren't you glad you asked?"

"When I had Cam I wasn't married."

"I suspected as much...but that's not who you are now, Marti."

"No, but I wanted you to know that you're not the only one capable of making a mistake—even a big mistake. But God is rich in mercy, Harry."

He put his head down, resting the bridge of his nose on his index fingers. "I know you want to believe that, Marti—"

"I do believe that. I believe it with all my heart. God has not ceased to pour out his grace on me—even up here, in all this mess I got myself into. And you're part it, Harry. He sent you to me. I want you to believe that."

Harry sniffed, loudly. "He took my wife—twenty seven-years-old. Ohhh..." He turned his head.

"Harry!" she said, reaching for him as he stood and then rushed into the bathroom.

He pulled two tissues from the box and leaned against the counter, drying his eyes and then blowing his nose—for all the good it did.

Marti pushed the door open and stepped into the room.

He dropped his expended tissues into the wastebasket. "Sorry," he said, breathing through his mouth. "It was a long time ago. I didn't know I had any tears left."

"I'm the one who's sorry, Harry. I didn't know. I should have known, I guess, knowing the kind of man you are—"

He sniffed again. "Just what kind of man is that?"

"A man with a tender heart," she said, boosting herself up with her arms to sit on the countertop. "A man who can love a child, not his own. Maybe I sensed that in you and that's why I feel close to you, I don't know, but I felt so close to you that night at church, when we were singing together. And your heart was breaking and...I could feel it...breaking my heart." A tear ran down her cheek.

He pulled a tissue from the box and gave it to her. She lifted it to her eyes as he bumped his forehead against hers. "We're a fine pair, aren't we?" he said softly.

She put her arms around him. "I don't want to have secrets. I want to be there for you. But maybe I'm wrong to pry."

He stepped back. "No. You know what? It's all right; although there really isn't much to tell: Linda and I grew up together, and somehow we just knew we belonged to each other. I mean, neither one of us ever dated anyone else—we really didn't even date each other, at least not in the conventional sense, we were just...together, if that makes any sense to you."

She nodded.

"We lived in Farmington Hills (suburban Detroit) and I had just gotten my first big assignment as detective. I was part of an organized crime task force, and I was pushing pretty hard trying to prove myself, I guess. Anyway, one day my car blew up—a bomb...someone put a bomb in the car and hooked it to the ignition."

"But you weren't in it."

He shook his head. "No. We only had the one car, and Linda had a doctor's appointment—her first prenatal appointment."

"Ohhh," Marti groaned, turning her head.

"Yeah. The question I keep asking is, 'why?' Why her? I mean, she loved the Lord with all her heart. Why not me? I was the one who was supposed to be in the car. Why not a day sooner, or a day later? I've been a believer since I was sixteen and I know I've committed sins, but I cannot recall where I have deliberately set out to sin. I have racked, my, brain, trying to figure out what I did to offend God, and I don't know what it is, unless I was...arrogant, or something."

Marti took a breath and blew it out. "I don't know what to say, Harry, except some questions don't have answers—at least not answers we're privy to down here. I do know, though, that God did not take her to punish you—or her. That's just not who he is."

"I would love to believe that, Marti."

"Why did my dad have to die in Viet Nam? Why did my mom take off the day after I graduated from high school, leaving me with two months rent and a baby on the way? Why did Greg pull his shenanigans and end up getting himself killed and I get blamed for it? Why did Jenny have to die?

"I wish I knew the answer."

She took hold of his hand and spoke softly. "I think you do know the answer, Harry: Bad things happen because there's evil in the world. I mean, you've spent your whole career dealing with the consequences of sin."

"Yeah, well, no doubt about that."

"But understand, that's not the way God created things; evil came in as a result of sin. When God made man, he gave him rule over the earth. But something happened when man obeyed Satan in the garden that legally transferred that rule to Satan. That's why Jesus said of him that he's the ruler of this world."

"So you're saying God didn't take her."

"No. He took her. With open arms he lovingly received her. You know, when you sign up with Jesus, you're not signing up for an earthly kingdom. Remember he said that his kingdom is not of this world. That's why we lay up treasure in heaven, that's why our reward is in heaven—that's where our citizenship is. So I know, because she believed, Linda is with Jesus, and I know she's experiencing a kind of joy that we will never know until we get there, too. But I think her joy would be made full if you could understand and be happy."

Harry took a breath and, putting his head down, blew it out, a silence ensuing between them.

Marti sat there, tears welling in her eyes and finally running down her cheeks as she reached out her hand, touching him. "Please say something, Harry. Please don't break my heart."

He grasped her hand and gently held it. "I think you're a very wise woman."

She laughed through her tears. "Well," she blew out a breath, "it's nice that you think so."

"I do think so. May I hug you?"

"Oh, I wish you would."

He turned, facing her, and pulled her close, sliding her forward on the counter as her arms came around his back. "I want you to know something," he spoke softly near her ear.

"What?"

"I love you."

"I know," she said, pulling him closer. "And I love you."

Harry pulled his head back so he could see her face.

She gave a wan smile. "Don't you think it's time you kissed me?"

"It's way past time," he said, pressing his lips onto hers, holding her tightly against himself as she responded, feeling the love radiate from her and the beauty of her spirit as he relished in the softness of her lips, sensing this as a sacred moment.

When at last their kiss broke they were both breathless and Harry felt weak at the knees as they continued to hold each other. He nuzzled his head against hers and whispered. "So you *knew* I was in love with you?"

"Well, I hoped," she said softly. "You've been carrying my heart around with you since that day at the restaurant."

"Ohhhhh," he breathed, pressing his lips onto hers again.

He continued to hold her close when their lips parted. "And you've been carrying mine around since that night at your church."

"Ummm," she said, pulling him into another long and passionate kiss.

"You know, we should stop this and get some sleep," she said, softly, when they parted. "It must be one o'clock."

Harry looked at his watch. "Almost," he said, scooping her up in his arms. He turned sideways with her as he carried her out of the door into the main room, her arms coming around his neck as their lips met in another long and passionate kiss.

"We've *got* to stop this," she whispered in a shaky voice as he laid her in bed. Her arms clung to his neck as he tried to stand, and he cupped her face in his hands as he gave her another brief, soft kiss.

When their kiss broke, he pulled the bed covers up over her. "You're right; we've got to stop this...for righteousness sake. But, if you don't mind, I'm going to keep that chair as close to you as I can get it."

Harry pulled the bathroom door mostly closed, once again casting the main room into semi-darkness. He returned to the chair, pulling the blanket over him as Marti moved closer to the edge of the bed, her face just inches from his. She smiled and closed her eyes and his heart melted within him.

Chapter 32

HARRY CHECKED HIMSELF in the mirror one last time before walking into the main room. He smiled to see that Marti was awake. "Good morning," he said softly. "Did I wake you?"

"Morning," she said sleepily. "No, I always get up around six."

He bent down and kissed her lips. "Here's a proper good morning."

"Ummm, you shaved," she said, rubbing her hands over his face. "I'll take another one of those."

Harry sat on the edge of the bed and bent down to kiss her, wrapping his arms around her and pulling her up to hold her as her arms went around him. "I love you," he whispered near her ear when their kiss broke.

"Ummm, I love you," she said softly.

He held her hand as she swung her legs over the edge of the bed. "How do you feel about breakfast?"

"Hungry," she said, stretching. She stood. "Oooo, I forgot about my ankle."

He picked up the bag Jo had packed and placed it on the foot of the bed. Marti removed the items she needed and hobbled into the bathroom.

When she came out, she was dressed in black jeans and an emerald-green chenille sweater. "Does this look okay?"

Harry whistled. "You look absolutely stunning."

Her eyes brightened. "Thank you, sir." She smiled as she sat on the foot of the bed and scooted back until just her lower legs were hanging off the end.

He removed his socks from her feet and then unwrapped the elastic bandage from her ankle. "The bruise is a little darker, but the swelling isn't too bad. I think we'd better keep it wrapped, though," he said as he rewrapped the bandage around her ankle. "I'll help you with your socks and shoes."

MARTI TOOK A SIP of her coffee. "You don't suppose it was the police who came to the house last night."

"No. A policeman would never discharge his weapon unless it was to protect his life or someone else's. Even then he'd give a warning, if at all possible." He reached into his jacket pocket, produced a small object and handed it to her.

"What is this?" she said, examining the object.

"It's a bullet, a slug without the casing. It's the bullet that hit me last night. I found it in the lining of my jacket this morning while you were getting dressed. It looks like a .32 caliber to me—not something any police agency would use."

"So..."

"So I'd bet money it's from the same gun that killed Greg."

"So the person who killed him came back? Let's take this to the police. Then they'd know I didn't do it."

"It proves nothing by itself."

"You could show them your side."

"It still proves nothing. I'd let you shoot me if I thought it would get you out of this."

"Oh, Harry, don't even think such a thing."

"I know *you* would never do anything like that, but it's not an uncommon thing. I'll give the bullet to Don and maybe it will be useful as he builds your case—especially if they find the guy and he still has the gun."

"So, was it just a case of the killer returning to the scene of the crime?"

"No." Harry smiled. "That pretty much just happens in the movies. He wouldn't risk coming back and being found out unless there's something in that house he doesn't want to fall into the hands of the police. He's after something, and that's a clue for us because now we know what's going on."

"We do?"

"Yeah, unless I miss my guess it was blackmail. Greg had something on somebody and he'd been making him pay. That would also explain why he had no apparent means of supporting himself. I didn't think of this before, but I'm going to see if Don can get a court order to let me go in the house legally. Now that I have an idea what's going on, I may be able to find evidence of the mail-drops he would have had to use to hide his current name and location from the person he was blackmailing. That way I could prove what really happened. Maybe I'll even be able to find the blackmail evidence."

"You're *not* going back there," she said, shaking her head. It was a statement, not a question.

"I *have* to, Marti. If I'm going to get you out of this, I have to find out who really did it, or I have to find enough exculpatory evidence to provide reasonable doubt so you won't be convicted. I'll take my gun, but I have to go back."

"If you'd had your gun last night, you might have already caught him. I know you left it in the car just to please me."

Harry reached over the table, picked up her hand and smiled. "You're here with me and you're safe. That's the only thing that's important to me."

"I love you," she mouthed.

Still holding her hand, he half stood and, bending over the table, kissed her forehead. "Come on," he said, getting out of the booth, "we'd better get over to the sheriff's department so we can let them know you haven't flown the coop."

Harry started the car and put it in gear. "When we get back, I'm going to give Gary Hammond a call to find out who else he might have told about seeing Greg."

"Oh, that's a great idea."

"How about you? Do you recall if you told anyone about this?"

"Not that I can think of, except for Liz and Mitch, Jo and Clay, of course. But I can't think that they would have told anyone else."

"Yeah, I doubt that, too. We'll just have to see what Gary has to say."

When they reached the sheriff's department, Harry opened the car door so Marti could get out. He helped her as she hobbled into the building, and he recognized Pat Kavanaugh as they came up to the desk. "Hi, Pat. On desk duty again, huh?"

She looked up. "Oh, hi, Harry. Yeah, just for today, though. I'm off tomorrow, then on night patrol the rest of the week What can I do for you?"

"Pat, you remember Ms. Forrester. She's out on bond and the court has set a requirement that she present herself here every day before nine a.m."

"Yes, I'm aware of that," she said, fingering through a small stack of papers on her desk and pulling out the one she wanted. She looked up at Marti. "I'm sorry to have to tell you this, Ms. Forrester, but your bond has been revoked. My instructions are to take you into custody."

The color drained out of Marti's face as she turned toward Harry. Her eyes rolled back in her head and she tried to catch herself on the shelf over the desk as she fainted.

Harry caught her in his arms. "Whoa," he said, picking her up and carrying her to a chair, the deputy following close behind him. "Pat, can you get her a glass of water."

Pat scurried off as Harry gently sat Marti in the chair. He opened her coat and unbuttoned the top button of her sweater before gently lowering her torso so her head was between her knees.

She was coming around as Pat returned, and Harry took the glass and held it to her lips as she took a couple of sips. Tears were streaming down her face as he handed the glass back to Pat.

"I'm sorry, Ms. Forrester, but I need you to come with me. I don't have a choice in this," Pat said.

"Do you know why her bail was revoked?" Harry said.

Pat shook her head. "It doesn't say."

"Can you give us just a few minutes?"

Pat nodded and stepped back a couple of steps as Harry hunkered down before Marti, taking both of her hands in his."

"I can't go back into that horrible place," Marti wept out.

Harry fought against his own tears. "Oh, sweetheart, I would go in there for you if I could."

"No, no, you're my only hope, now."

"No, keep your hope in the Lord and pray for me."

Marti nodded her head, unable to speak for crying as Harry lifted her to her feet and held her. "Shh, shh, listen to me," he said, stroking her hair as Pat turned her face away. "Come Christmas time, I'm going to take you to Colorado so that you can have the joy of being with your family again and holding Callie and Ben on your lap." He took a couple of shaky breaths. "And I'll get to meet Cam and tell her what a wonderful mother she has. And, and you'll have the...best Christmas ever. And it will be my gift to you...my gift of love."

He removed his handkerchief from his pocket and gave it to Marti. She wiped her eyes and blew her nose and flung herself back into Harry's arms, clutching the handkerchief in her hand. "I'm going to hold you to that."

He continued to hold her until she recovered herself. "Are you okay?" he said at last, letting her go.

Marti nodded.

"All right, Pat. Thank you for waiting."

Pat sniffed. "I'm sorry," she said, walking toward Marti.

Marti looked directly at Harry. "I love you," she squeaked out.

"I love you," he replied. "Pray for me."

"I will," she said, nodding her head. "Please pray for me."

"You know I will, sweetheart," he said as Pat took her arm and led her away.

Chapter 33

IF I KEEP THE TOP of my head about even with the top of the steering wheel, I can stay out of sight and just nicely see over the dashboard. I wish he'd step on it, though. It's darned uncomfortable sitting this way.

Ahhh, there he is, and......hold it......hold it......*yes*, he's alone. Great! That takes care of her; one down and one to go.

That was a stroke of genius—letting the cops know she was his wife. Of course, I wouldn't have had to do it at all if they weren't such hicks. How many times am I going to have to call them?

I could have sworn I hit that guy, last night. The way he stumbled, the way he limped. But there he goes, driving out of the parking lot. Of course, it's better not to hit him at all if I didn't kill him. The last thing I need is for him to end up in the hospital and have them dig a bullet out of him and match it to the ones from Forrester.

Man, I never thought about that. I probably shouldn't have shot at all. I shouldn't have panicked. But hell, I wasn't expecting anybody to be there.

Why were they there, anyway? I can't believe she knows anything about this. She's so darn straight-laced she'd stumble all over herself going to the cops with it.

So if she doesn't know anything, then he most likely doesn't know anything either. They were probably just on a fishing expedition. And they couldn't have been in there legally or I'd have seen their car in the driveway— which means they're not going to tell anybody about what happened. Good.

I have got to find those pictures. Hopefully, I've got him tied up for a few days, trying to get her back out of jail. If not, I'll just have to deal with it. I've already wasted one night and I, sure as hell, can't stay up here forever. It's find them, or fix it so nobody can find them. If he comes back...well, that's his problem. Nobody will ever find his body in those woods.

Chapter 34

HARRY DROVE DIRECTLY FROM the sheriff's department to Don's house, not bothering to call in advance. Don's wife led him to the dining room where the attorney was drinking a cup of coffee. "No, I haven't heard a word from anyone," he replied to Harry's question. "Hold on, I'll give them a call."

Don's wife poured Harry a cup of coffee. He sipped at it while he waited.

"They got an anonymous tip on Monday," Don said, resuming his seat. "They know McCarthy's real identity and that Marti was his wife."

"Oh, great," Harry said, rubbing his forehead. "Is that enough for them to revoke her bond?"

"It's debatable. They didn't ask and we're under no obligation to tell, but armed with that information, they did some additional digging. They know about the boat explosion and they've tied the purchase of," he looked at the paper in his hand, "a one-pound container of Pyrodex (whatever that is), four five-gallon gas cans, and a twelve-volt light bulb for a car tail light to a credit card belonging to Marti. They're saying that a bomb could be made from those materials."

Harry shook his head and slowly blew out a breath. "Pyrodex is an accelerant, a smokeless black powder substitute used by guys that shoot muzzle loader rifles. I guess you could make a bomb out of it."

"Their theory is that she tried to kill him five years ago and, realizing she missed, came up here and finished the job."

"Don, you know she didn't do either of those things."

"Well, I doubt that a woman, a secretary, would have the requisite knowledge. But she may have had a boyfriend..."

Harry shook his head. "No. No. Her heart is pure gold. She would not cheat on her husband, no matter how bad he was. She doesn't have an untrue or unkind bone in her body. It's just not in her DNA. I'd literally stake my life on it so don't give up on her."

"Obviously, you're in love with her."

"Yes. But that doesn't make it any the less true."

"Oh, I believe you," he said. "She's an innocent. On balance, she's just not the type."

"Thanks, Don. Listen, can you get me permission to go into that house to look for evidence?"

"Yeah, the defense should be allowed to go in there. I'll work on that."

"Good. I've got to head back to Grand Rapids. I have an idea that might put an end to their bomb theory. I'll try to be back tomorrow."

"Sounds good. I should have your clearance by then."

Harry drove back to the hotel to collect his belongings and check out. But when he got to his room, he decided to take only his razor and personal items so he could avoid the check-in hassle if he got back in the middle of the night. Besides, Marti had been there: her luggage was there, her blue jeans, now dry, were hanging on the drapery rod over the heating blower, her toothbrush and blow dryer were on the bathroom counter. He couldn't pack them up. He plopped onto the unmade bed and half lay down, placing his head on her pillow. The smell of her shampoo filled his nostrils and once again she was in his arms...

The phone rang. He picked it up on the second ring. "Hello."

"Harry? It's Cam. Can you put my mother on?"

"I'm sorry, Cam, I can't." He went on to explain what had happened.

She exhaled loudly. "As if things weren't *bad* enough. I can hardly *believe* this! What are you *doing* about it?"

"Calm down. You think I like this any better than you do?"

"She's my *mother*. She gave up *everything* for me. She's my...mother," her voice trailed off.

He heard her sniffle. "I'm sorry, Cam—"

"No, I'm sorry. I just feel so...powerless—stuck here, twelve hundred miles away—"

"Cam, I've got to get out of here. I've got to get back to Grand Rapids to try to derail this bomb theory thing. Then I've got to get back here and get into that house to see if I can find something to clear her. And I've been up most of the night already, and at some point I've *got* to get some sleep. But there just aren't enough hours, and I can't leave her in there—"

"Whoa, Harry, slow down. You're not going to help her at all if you have a stroke."

He blew out a breath. "Yeah, okay. But I do have to get going. I should be back tomorrow, I'll call you then."

Chapter 35

HARRY FILLED HIS GAS TANK in St. Ignace and pretty much ignored the speed limit once he was south of Mackinaw City. He transitioned to southbound US-131 at Reed City and placed a call to Mitch.

"Hey, Harry. How are things going? You sound like you're in your car."

"Yeah, I'm on my way back. Things have really hit the fan." He went on to explain the situation.

"Oh, brother," Mitch said. "The good-for-nothing not only blows up her boat, but uses her credit card to buy the explosives so if there's any question it will look like she did it."

"That's about it. Look, I want to talk to Vicki Thomas, tonight. I'm just about to Big Rapids now and I'm flying low so, if the troopers don't catch me, I'll be there in less than an hour."

"Do you want me to set it up with her?"

"No. I want to surprise her. But I'd like you to come along and bring your badge. Think about it, though, because this is anything but official."

"I don't have to think about it, Harry. I'll do it. Just don't kill yourself getting here."

"Thanks, but I feel like the Dutch boy, trying to plug up holes in the dike. She's alone and frightened and I feel like I need to be up there, doing everything I can. But I don't even know what I'm looking for. Now this business pops up and it seems like there just aren't enough hours in the day."

"You think you can make it to my house by 5:30?"

"Yeah."

"Okay, I'll be waiting for you."

Harry recognized Vicki Thomas' red Miata in the carport as they pulled into a spot in front of her building.

They walked to her door and Mitch rang the bell, holding his badge so she could see it from the peep-sight.

She opened the door. "Yes?"

"Ms. Thomas, I'm Lieutenant Ferguson from the sheriff's department and this is Harry Brannan. We'd like to speak with you for a few minutes, if we may."

"What's this about? I haven't done anything wrong, have I?"

"We don't think so," Harry said. "But we'd like to ask you some questions about your previous employer."

"Scott Jacoby?"

"No, ma'am. Greg Forrester."

"Ohhh. You know he's dead, don't you?"

"Yes, ma'am. May we come in and sit down?"

"Oh, sure, I guess so," she said, leading the way."

Her face took on a strange look as she sat in a chair and laid her hands in her lap. "You don't think I had anything to do with Greg's death, do you?"

"No ma'am," Harry said, sitting on the sofa next to Mitch. "But we do know that you were romantically involved with him."

"Is there some law against that? I mean, he said he was going to divorce his wife—said she'd gone all religious on him. The liar. I mean, you tell me, how long is a girl supposed to wait. I'm sorry he's dead, but I was getting ready to dump him anyway. I found a new job and everything."

"Yes ma'am. We're not concerned about that, and we know that you had nothing to do with his death. But we also know that you purchased a list of items for him: gas cans, a light bulb for a car tail light, and Pyrodex."

Her rate of breathing picked up and she swallowed, visibly.

"Ma'am we know that you used his wife's credit card and that you forged her name."

Her breathing became shaky and more rapid.

"Ma'am?"

"Look...he told me it was okay...that he needed the stuff...and, and...I don't even know what that pyro-stuff was—I had to get somebody to help me find it—"

"Ma'am—"

"Look, I'll pay for it...with interest."

"Ma'am, we're not interested in that and we're not interested in having you prosecuted, but we could use your help."

She sighed, the relief showing on her face. "Sure."

"Would you be willing to swear a deposition to the effect of what you did for a guarantee of not being prosecuted?"

"I guess so, as long as I'd be protected. Why is this so important after all this time?"

"Because Greg was not killed in that boat explosion. He blew the boat up himself and went into hiding. However, he recently was killed and his wife is being held for it. We know she didn't do it and your sworn testimony can help her."

"That's just like him. That son of a..." She grimaced, "Yeah, I'll do it—gladly."

"Thank you, Ms. Thomas..." Harry closed his eyes and sighed.

"I'll be in touch with you about that deposition," Mitch said. "Thank you so much, Ms. Thomas."

"You okay?" Mitch said when they were back in the car.

"Yeah," Harry said. "Just, uh...I was thanking God...and repenting for lying to her about what we knew."

"You love Marti, don't you?"

"Yes."

"Come on. You need to let us feed you. Then you need to get some sleep before trying drive all the way back up there. I'll take care of the deposition so you can concentrate on your end. I'll see if I can get Clay to fly me up there. That way you'll have the original to present to the court."

"Thanks, Mitch. You have no idea what a load you're taking off my mind."

"We always were a good team."

"Yes we were...you know, I was thinking: Clay is some kind of electronics guy, right?"

"Yeah."

"Well, the gas cans, the Pyrodex; that was obviously the stuff Greg was carrying out to the boat the morning he went missing. But how did he get it to blow up all the way out by the south buoy when he wasn't even on the boat? The question is, how difficult would it be? Would he have to have an electronics background? I'm wondering if Clay would be able to shed some light on how it might be done."

"Good question. I'll give him a call when we get home. I can also try to run down where Greg went to school—see if he had any electronics background."

"WELL I'VE NEVER TRIED IT, but I'm confident I could make a bomb out of just the Pyrodex and the light bulb," Clay said. "I think the twenty gallons of gasoline was just to ensure the complete destruction of the boat. Assuming the bomb went off in a fume-rich environment, it would have created a horrific explosion and fire."

Harry nodded. "We know the boat had a small dinghy that was later found in the marina. So, assuming he didn't have another means of escape, how could he make the boat blow up all the way out by the south buoy when he wasn't on it? I mean, I've heard of using a cell phone to detonate a bomb, but how would he know when to do it?"

"First of all, I don't think I'd rely on a cell phone. There are no towers out in the middle of the lake so it would be an iffy proposition at best. The simplest way to do it would be with a couple of timers. The first thing I would do is make the trip to see how long it takes to get from the marina to the buoy at a given speed. Once you know that, you lash the helm to the correct compass heading and let the timers do the work: the first one would both key the microphone on the radio and turn on a cassette player to play the mayday; the second one would detonate the bomb. The lake is really deep out there and a few miles one way or the other of the buoy wouldn't make any difference—blow a good big hole in the hull and, in a matter of minutes, the boat will be down where virtually no diver can go."

"Yeah, but would he have to have a technical background to pull it off?"

"Not necessarily. The most difficult part would be keying the microphone—he'd have to have some electronics knowledge to pull it off. But I don't think he'd even have to do that. I mean, if you tape down the push-to-talk button on the microphone and then tape the microphone near the speaker of the cassette player, all you have to do is make sure the radio is tuned to the distress frequency and use the timer to turn both it and the cassette player on. The second timer would trigger the bomb a minute or two later. It would require some basic knowledge so not just anybody could do it, but you wouldn't need a degree in electronics."

"So, get the boat headed in the right direction and swim back to shore," Harry said.

"Exactly."

"If we need to set up a demonstration for the court—"

"Jo and I will be up there with bells on."

IT WAS AFTER TEN P.M. when Harry arrived at home. It had been a long and productive day. He was dead tired and the thought of sleeping in his own bed, inviting as it was, made his heart hurt with the knowledge that Marti was spending the night on a jailhouse bunk. He got down on the floor and prostrated himself before God, crying out to Him in prayer to protect and comfort her and for help in finding the evidence that would set her free.

Chapter 36

RETURNING TO THE U.P, Harry drove directly to Don's house and reported the good news about Vicki Thomas and the deposition. However, he was disappointed to learn that, though he could enter Greg's house it wouldn't be until the following week when a deputy could be detailed to accompany him. *That's just unacceptable,* he thought as he drove away.

He carded his hotel room open at about 3:15 p.m., pulling a sticky note to call room 317 off the door. The room had been cleaned and the bed was made, but Marti's jeans were still hanging from the drapery rod. He looked at the note and was heading for the phone when a knock came at the door. He went back and opened it and was startled to see an auburn-haired woman standing there.

She proffered her right hand. "Harry? I'm Cam—Camille Beyers."

"You...you look like your mother," he said, shaking her hand. "Oh my goodness, for a second I thought it was she, standing there. Come in, come in," he said stepping aside so she could enter. "What are you doing here?"

"You need help. You may not agree with that, but from talking with you on the phone I know that you can use some help. Besides, I felt like I should meet you."

"You don't let any grass grow under your feet, do you?"

"Nope."

"Well, I guess you come by it honestly. Why is it so important to meet me?"

"Are those my mom's jeans hanging there?"

"Yeah."

"Whoa," she said, looking around the room.

"Whoa, yourself. It's not what you think, Cam. Being in jail was really horrible for your mom. She didn't want to be alone, so I let her stay with me. *But,* she slept in the bed, I slept in the chair—period. That's all there was to it. And I think you know your mom well enough to know that she's an honorable woman."

Cam laughed out loud.

"What?"

"She's head-over-heels for you. And you're head-over-heels for her, aren't you?"

"I love your mom...but we did not sleep together."

"Oh, I believe you. She wouldn't do anything like that, no matter how dreamy she thinks you are...I want to see her, Harry."

"I'm sorry, Cam, but we won't be able to get in there until tomorrow afternoon. Visiting hours are on Tuesdays and Fridays."

"Well, then, what were you going to do?"

He held up the note. "The first thing I have to do is make a call."

"No, that note is from me. I checked-in about noon. I'm across the hall and two doors down. It was as close as I could get. I just happened to see you get here."

"Well, I had hoped to have permission to go into Greg's house, but I checked with your mom's attorney and the sheriff's department can't arrange it until next week."

"So we just sit around and twiddle our thumbs?"

"No. Have you eaten yet?"

She shook her head.

"Come on, I'll buy you some lunch."

CAM TOOK A SIP of her cola. "I think we should go out there anyway and see what we can find."

"We? Boy, you Stafford women are an ardent bunch."

"You just finding that out? Look, Harry; you need help and you know it—and I need to help you. My mom is in jail, charged with murder, and I just can't sit around and let you do all the work. I knew that miserable excuse for a human being, and how much he hurt my mom, so I'm coming. You can either take me or I'll follow you over there in my rental car."

Harry threw up his hands. *"Fine,* come along. Did I also mention that you're scrappy and obstinate?"

"It's part of my charm...well, not really, but—"

"I know," he said. "Come on, we'd better get going."

He drove back to the hotel and they headed for their respective rooms to change clothes. Harry pulled on the same blue jeans he'd worn on Tuesday night—the only pair he had with him—and a flannel shirt. He checked his flashlight and was putting it in his jacket pocket when Cam knocked on his door.

"You ready to go," she said when he opened the door. She was wearing blue jeans and a silver and blue ski jacket and had a backpack slung over her shoulder.

"Ready," he said, letting the door go closed and placing the key card in his shirt pocket.

It was dusk when they turned off M-28 onto Strongs Road and Harry slowed significantly as they approached the house, looking carefully in every direction for any indication that someone else may be around. Once again he backed the car into the small clearing and shut it off.

"Do you have a gun?" Cam said.

"Yeah," he said, reaching for it in the console. "You're okay with this?"

"Of course. Don't you think we should have some protection?"

"Yeah, *I* do, but your mom was—"

"Afraid. I know. My illustrious father threatened her with a gun when she tried to get him to help her, before I was born. Of course, that was before he departed for places unknown."

"Well, I've looked down the barrel of a gun a few times myself, and I never quite got adjusted to it either. You know, your mom is a very special lady, and she loves you very much. She told me how much she misses you."

"I know she is, and I love her right back. That's why I'm here."

"Well, come on, we'd better get going," Harry said, opening the door.

He locked the car doors with the remote and together they set out to scout the area, following roughly the same route Harry had taken alone, two nights before.

"Hey," Cam whispered loudly.

Harry turned to see her beckoning to him, and walked back to where she stood.

"What is this thing?" she said, touching something attached to one of the trees.

It was a plastic box, about the size of a hardcover book and something less than three inches thick. Four rows of LEDs were in the top third, what appeared to be a lens was in the middle, and a small rectangular object was centered in the bottom third. The color of the box tended to blend with the tree trunk.

Harry knew he'd seen something like it before. He rubbed his forehead. "It's a...game camera. Hunters often set them up in an area they plan to hunt to spot deer or other game. This thing on the bottom is a passive infrared sensor. When the game gets in front of it, it triggers these infrared LEDs on the top and it takes a digital picture of whatever set it off."

Cam stepped in front of the device, with her back to it, and looked straight ahead. "It's aimed right at the front of the house."

She stepped aside and Harry released the two latches that held it closed, opening the front of the box on its hinges. "It's got a plug-in memory card, just like my digital camera...and a USB port. Boy, I wish I had something I could download this thing to."

"Why don't we just take the memory card out of it?"

"Because it may contain evidence, and we want to leave it pristine for the police to find. If our fingerprints are on it, it would raise a question about whether we planted it."

"Well, I've got my laptop in my backpack. Why don't we just download it?"

"Are you kidding? You've got a laptop with you?"

"Well, yeah. Doesn't everybody?"

"Everybody your age. Did I also mention that you're smart...and resourceful?"

"Well, *Mister Brannan,* I believe yo' tryin' to turn my head," she said in a good southern belle accent as they set out for the car.

Harry held the open laptop in his hands while Cam turned it on and allowed it to boot. "I wonder if there are more of these cameras around the perimeter of the house."

"Yeah, good question," she said. "I'll make a folder called 'front' for these pictures and, if we find more cameras, I can make additional folders so we can keep the pictures separate."

"Good idea," he said as she plugged the USB cable into the camera.

It took a moment for the computer to recognize the camera as a USB storage device, but when it did Cam copied all the pictures into the folder she'd made.

She electronically disconnected the computer from the camera before pulling the USB cable. "Okay, we're good to go," she said, folding down the screen of the laptop.

Harry closed the camera door and refastened the two snap-latches. "Okay, let's get going. Keep your eyes open for more cameras."

They paused when they came to the driveway, carefully checking the area for any sign that someone else may be present, and then continued on around the garage and to the back of the house.

"Here's another one," she said, standing in front of the camera. "It looks like the target area is the breezeway door and maybe the patio."

Harry released the latches and they downloaded the pictures to a separate folder she'd made and entitled 'back.'

They checked for additional cameras on the way back to the car, but found none.

Chapter 37

"IS THERE LOTS OF GAME up here?" Cam said when they were once again seated in the car.

Harry started the engine to keep the passenger compartment warm. "My guess is he wasn't looking for game. I suspect a certain degree of paranoia goes along with being a blackmailer. Greg probably was more interested in people than game, and maybe seeing who was here when he wasn't. Those infrared cameras will take pretty good pictures, even in the dark."

"Here we go," she said as the first picture came up on the screen. "This is the front camera and we're going from newest to oldest." The camera was situated such that the shots covered an area from the right edge of the garage door to the right edge of the main entry door of the house, and included a small corner of the driveway and the breezeway entrance.

"Hey, that's me," she said.

Harry looked at the picture. "Yeah, just a few minutes ago. You were the last one to get in front of the camera."

She continued to cycle through the pictures, revealing a photo of Harry, sneaking through the woods two nights before. Other photos were of sheriff's deputies, police cars, actual game and...

"Stop," Harry said. "That's your mom." The picture was of Marti bursting out of the house, one hand on the storm door and a terrified look on her face. "What's the time stamp say?"

Cam looked closely at the picture. "November fourteenth at 3:49 p.m."

"That was last Friday. How about the next one?"

Cam brought the next picture onto the screen. In this shot, Marti was standing on the stoop, apparently knocking on the storm door. "Time stamp on this one is 3:46 p.m."

"Next one."

Again it was Marti. She was walking on the sidewalk from the driveway toward the stoop.

"Time on this one is also 3:46 p.m."

"Keep going."

Cam cycled through the remaining pictures, but none of them seemed relevant.

"Let's look at the back door," Harry said.

Cam opened the folder containing those pictures and brought up the first one. The view here covered an area from just to the left of the patio to the corner of the garage. The photo was of the foot and leg of a person mostly out of view of the camera passing the corner of the garage.

"Try the next one."

In this shot a man was standing at the breezeway door, with his back to the camera. "Time stamp on this one is 10:13 p.m., last night," Cam said. "Can you make anything out of it?"

"No. Let's try the next one."

The next photo was also of the man at the door, with his back to the camera. The one following showed the man striding from behind the garage toward the door, with his face turned toward the breezeway. "The time stamp on both of those was last night at 7:51 p.m. He's not being very cooperative, is he?" she said.

"No, he's not. Let's keep going."

"That's mom...and you. Is she hurt? Where's your jacket?"

"I'll explain later. Let's keep going."

"There he is again...I can see his face this time." She turned the laptop a little so Harry could see it better. "He's got a familiar look. I think I've—"

"*Whoa*, it's Scott Jacoby!"

"Yeah, yeah, Greg's *business* partner. I *knew* I'd seen him before."

"When was this?"

"The eighteenth, uh...Tuesday night at 8:39 p.m."

Other pictures showed both Harry and Marti fleeing the house, Scott Jacoby arriving at the house, sheriff's deputies, deer, and...

"Stop," Harry said. "There's Jacoby again. Looks like he's running away."

"Yeah. Time stamp is November fourteenth at 3:46 p.m. Is that a gun he has in his hand?"

"Sure looks like it. Keep going."

"There he is again, coming out the door, and he definitely has a gun in his hand."

"Yeah, he does. What's the time?"

"Same time, 3:46. There he is again—getting there. The time is 3:35."

She cycled through the remaining pictures, but none appeared to be relevant.

"I wish we could drill down a little more on those times," Harry said. "Why don't you make another folder and copy the November fourteenth photos of your mom and Jacoby into it."

Cam complied with the request and once again turned the laptop a little so Harry could see it better.

He pointed at the photo of Jacoby arriving. "Right-click on that and open the properties."

"The time is 3:35:02."

"Okay, now the one of him leaving."

"It's 3:46:25."

"Now the one of your mom knocking on the door."

"The time is 3:46:17."

"Okay," Harry said. "Your mom knocks on the door at 3:46:17. Eight seconds later we see Jacoby charging out the back breezeway door with a gun in his hand. Remember, he had to get out the kitchen door, into the breezeway and out the breezeway door for the camera to see him. She got there right after it happened. I mean, she was probably driving up the driveway when Jacoby pulled the trigger."

"Well, now we know who really did it, we can take the pictures to the police."

"Yeah, that's great news, and hopefully, enough to get your mom released."

"You don't think they'll drop the charges."

"I don't know—maybe. I'd feel a lot better if I knew *why* he killed Greg. That way I could eliminate any possibility of Marti, uh...your mom being tied to it. I mean, obviously he didn't get what he wanted from Greg or he wouldn't still be looking for it."

"Well, why don't we just go in and see if we can find it."

"You're up for that?"

"In for a penny, in for a pound. I want her out of that jail for good."

"Me too. Let's go," he said, shutting off the engine.

Cam shut down her laptop, returned it to her backpack and stowed it on the back seat. She walked with him to the breezeway and stood beside him as he defeated the lock on the door to the kitchen. "That's pretty slick, how you did that."

"Yeah, if you don't have deadbolts on your doors you should get them installed," Harry said, closing the kitchen door behind them.

"Where do we start?"

"Let's go upstairs. That's where your mom and I were working when we had to bug out."

They climbed the stairs and stopped in the hallway. "I think we can cover more ground if we split up," Cam said. "What are we looking for, do you know?"

"I'm not sure: papers, pictures, anything that looks like evidence. That room down there is an office," he said pointing to the right. "We already searched it. This room here is a bedroom. I'll take that. The other room is a bathroom. You can take a look in there if you want to, but there are not a lot of places to hide something. That thing next to it is a linen closet."

"There's probably lots of places to hide something in there. I'll check out the bathroom first and then start on the closet."

"Sounds good. Keep your ears peeled, though, and if you hear *anything* let me know."

"Okay," she said, heading for the bathroom.

Harry went into the bedroom and pulled the upper drawer out of the bureau. He set it on the top and began to search through it.

"Harry," Cam said from the hallway.

He walked out of the bedroom door into the hallway to see Cam standing in front of the linen closet. Scott Jacoby had his right arm around her waist, holding her tightly to himself. His left hand held a revolver, pressed against her temple.

"Keep your hands where I can see them," he said.

I'm sorry, Harry," Cam said. "He was behind the bathroom door."

"Nice to see you again, Brannan. This time I got here a little before you instead of a little after you, and, as you can see, it makes all the difference."

"Let her go Scott," Harry said, taking a step toward them. "I'm the one—"

"You take another step and I'll blow her pretty little head off."

"All right," Harry said, holding up his hands.

"That's better. Now, keep your hands where I can see them and start down the stairs—slowly. And we're going to be right behind you, so if you even so much as slip on a step, she gets it."

Harry kept his hands up and started slowly down the steps. He heard them start down behind him. "Scott, keep me and let her go. She's got a husband and two little kids. She's got all the motivation in the world to keep her mouth shut."

"Nice try, Brannan—and so noble, but I wasn't born yesterday."

"Look, let her go. You can keep me and I'll help you find whatever it is you're looking for."

"Save it, Brannan, I'm getting tired of listening to you. Now walk into the kitchen."

"Let her go. It's one thing to shoot Greg. He probably had it coming, but it's a whole other thing—"

"I told you to shut up so do it, or I'll drop her right here. Now, open that door."

Harry opened the door, revealing set of stairs leading into the basement.

"Get in there."

He stepped onto the landing and switched on the basement light.

Scott took a couple of steps forward and pushed Cam onto the landing, knocking Harry down the steps. He caught himself on the handrail as the door slammed shut behind them.

Chapter 38

"COME ON," HARRY SAID, grabbing Cam's hand and rushing down the stairs with her. He pulled her off the bottom step and yanked her out of the line of fire and out of sight of the landing. "Are you okay?"

"I think so," she said. Her face was ashen as she leaned against the concrete wall. "I've never been so frightened in all my life."

Harry looked around. The room was much smaller than the house, maybe twelve by 24 feet. Its basic function appeared to be a place for the furnace and water heater to reside. Although it also contained a small workbench with a toolbox sitting on it, and a wooden shelf unit, about six feet wide and going from the floor to near the ceiling, against the back wall. Paint cans, roller pans, and miscellaneous junk populated the shelves.

"What do we do now," Cam said.

"Good question. There's not even a window down here."

"Do you think he's still up there?"

"I don't know—probably. He obviously hasn't found what he's looking for yet. That's a hollow-core door up there, and I hesitate to run up and give it a try because a bullet—"

A loud crash hit the kitchen floor above them and Cam screamed. *"What was that?"*

"Shh, I don't know. It was something big. Sounds like maybe he tipped the refrigerator over."

They heard scraping and, eventually, the sound of something heavy hitting the basement door. Then footsteps and a different sound of something heavy being moved in the kitchen.

"It sounds like he's blocking the door so we can't get out," Harry said.

They heard him walking above and then the kitchen door slammed. Harry hurried up the stairs and, turning the doorknob, tried to push the door open. It wouldn't budge. He slammed into the door with his left shoulder and pushed as hard as he could, but to no avail.

Cam raced up onto the landing, lending her shoulder to the attempt, but it was no good, the door was solidly blocked.

They heard the kitchen door come back open and they quietly went back into the basement, listening as his footsteps went back and forth in the kitchen and dining room above them.

"What is he *doing* up there," she said in a loud whisper.

Harry shook his head. "I don't know, but we're definitely trapped down here. Let's take a look at that toolbox; maybe there's something in it we can use to get out of here once he leaves."

He opened the box and found two screwdrivers, a hammer, a flat pry bar, and some nuts and bolts. "Well, the door's hollow so we can probably beat a hole in with this hammer and pry bar."

Cam turned her head and started sniffing the air. She walked over to the stairway. "Do you smell something?"

Harry stood next to her and sniffed the air. "Yeah, it smells like gasoline. For it to be that strong it must be right at the door."

He went to the foot of the stairs and began to tiptoe slowly up the steps. The *whump* of the gasoline igniting sent him hurrying back down. *"He's set the house on fire!"*

"We've got to get out of here," Cam screamed, jumping onto the steps.

Harry caught her hand. "Look, the door's already on fire, we don't stand a chance."

Burning gasoline had run under the door, setting the landing and one of the floor joists on fire, as burning drops dripped from the landing onto the concrete floor.

Cam looked up the stairs and melted into his arms. "We're going to *die* down here."

"I'm sorry, Cam," he said, helping her back down into the basement.

He held her close and she looked up into his face. "Oh, Harry, we're going to *die* down here." She began to cry.

"Don't look," he said, turning with her so she was facing away from the flames. He stroked her hair. "Shh, shh."

"Harry, I'm sorry I got after you on the phone and that I was rude to you. Please forgive me," she said through her tears.

"There's nothing to forgive, Cam. I'm so sorry I got you involved in this."

"It's all right, Harry, I made you bring me."

"Father in heaven, I know we've sinned against you in ways we don't even realize, but not because our hearts were against you. Please forgive us and cleanse us from all unrighteousness. And, for Christ's sake, receive us into your presence. In Jesus' name, amen."

"Amen," she said, clinging to him.

An explosion somewhere upstairs put the lights out as a piece of burning wood from the landing fell to the basement floor. Harry looked up into the gaping hole as the door disintegrated. The place was an inferno. He moved with Cam to the back wall, next to the shelves.

"Oh, my kids, my babies!" She wept as she slumped up against him.

Chapter 39

HARRY LET CAM GO and pulled out his flashlight, switching it on as he sank to his knees next to the shelves.

"What are you doing?" she yelled to be heard above the noise of the fire.

"I felt air on my legs," he yelled back. "There's air moving through here, lots of air. The fire is pulling a draft from behind these shelves."

There was a loud crack and the landing dropped about a foot as Harry shone his light where the shelf unit met the wall. He put the light in his pocket and dug his fingertips behind the edge of the unit. "Help me pull this thing out," he yelled.

Cam hunched down to get her torso underneath him as she, too, dug her fingers behind the shelf unit and pulled. *"It won't budge,"* she screamed, letting go and falling to a sitting position on the floor.

Harry grabbed her hands and pulled her to her feet. "Come on—let's get this junk off the shelves."

Together, they jerked the items from the shelves, throwing them haphazardly toward the other end of the basement. When the shelves were empty, Harry dug his fingertips behind the unit again and tried to pull it away from the wall. Nothing.

He gave the flashlight to Cam. "Try to see behind this thing as I pull."

Harry dug the fingertips of his left hand behind the shelf unit and put his right foot against the wall as he dug the fingertips of his right hand behind the unit and pulled as hard as he could, pushing against the wall with his foot.

Cam laid the side of her face against the wall as she shone the light into the small gap. "Something's holding it," she yelled. "Looks like metal."

He let go of the shelf unit, took the flashlight from her and looked into the gap. Something was there, but he couldn't make out what it was.

Cam screamed as the landing crashed onto the basement floor in a shower of sparks, and a loud creaking noise came from somewhere above them.

Harry rushed to the workbench and grabbed the hammer and pry bar from the toolbox. The room was aglow in an eerie yellow radiance as he knelt in front of the shelf unit and began to beat on the next to the bottom shelf with the hammer.

Cam knelt beside him, picked up the pry bar and began to beat on the shelf as Harry stopped and pulled the flashlight out of his pocket, training its beam on a piece of metal, about the size of a cell phone, in the back right-hand corner of the bottom shelf. "What is it?" she yelled.

"I don't know," he yelled back. "It looks like it goes through the back. Give me the pry bar."

She handed it over and took the light from him, training it on the metal object as he struggled to get the edge of the pry bar under it.

There was another loud creak as a second floor joist, just feet behind them, burst into flames. Harry picked up the hammer and beat on the back of the pry bar until it slid under the metal object. He pushed down on the back of the bar, trying in vain to move it.

The burning stairway crashed onto the basement floor and Cam screamed again as Harry pulled himself to his feet. He put his foot on the back of the pry bar and pushed down. Nothing.

"Help me push this thing against the wall," he yelled.

She stood, putting her back against the shelves and pushed with her feet as Harry pushed against the side with his hands. Once again he put his left foot on the back of the pry bar and pressed down. The object lifted.

"Okay," he yelled. "See if you can budge this thing."

He stepped to the side, continuing to hold the bar down with his foot as Cam rushed around him to the side of the shelf unit. She dug in her fingertips and they both pulled. The shelf unit came away from the wall about two inches and cold air blasted against their faces.

Harry let his foot off the bar and looked behind the unit with his flashlight. It was hinged on the left-hand side with a large continuous hinge. He put his back against the wall and pushed on the edge of the unit. It began to move, and together they walked it out into the room, revealing a concrete culvert pipe about three feet in diameter in the back wall.

Cam ran to the entrance of the pipe and he put his hand on her shoulder, stopping her as he stooped and trained his light down the long concrete tunnel. "Okay," he yelled.

Stooping, she crawled a few feet into the dark tunnel and turned toward him. Harry was beginning to stoop when a glint caught his eye. He reached above the culvert pipe and extracted a small glass jar with a screw-on metal lid. The label said 'cinnamon.' He stuffed it in his jacket pocket and went in after her.

Harry trained his flashlight beam down the tunnel and crawled in, working his way in front of Cam, as they made their way toward freedom. It was impossible to hurry, having to crawl, and it seemed to take a long time to go the distance to the end, which was maybe 250 feet away. They came out into a thick stand of spruce trees, planted so close to the culvert pipe that they had to go through them rather than around them.

"Where are we?" Cam said.

"Someplace behind the house, I think."

"Greg must have been awfully paranoid to bury that thing—not that I'm complaining."

"I guess if you're constantly worried about somebody coming after you, you take whatever precautions you think are warranted."

"It must have cost him a fortune."

"I'm sure it wasn't cheap," Harry said, bending down and rubbing his knee. "He must have been bleeding Jacoby for quite a bit."

"However much it cost, I thank God it was there."

"Yeah, me, too," he said, digging in his jacket pocket. He handed her the little cinnamon jar. "Here, I found this right at the entrance to the tunnel."

"What is it?"

"I didn't take a lot of time to look, but I think it's a USB memory stick—a thumb drive."

She examined the jar. "Yup. That's what it is, all right. I'll check it out when we get back to the car."

"Speaking of which, we'd better get out of here."

Cam followed as he turned to the right and began to pace with deliberate speed. They were part way down a hill and he led her at an angle, going up at the same time as they were going south, toward the car. Light from the fire reflected in ghostly convolutions off the snow on the pine boughs and, once they crested the hill, the crackling sound was loud enough to make talking in normal tones difficult so they hurried on in silence to the car.

Harry unlocked the doors with his remote and they both got in. Cam reached back for her laptop as he started the engine. It had begun to snow while they were inside and he turned the defroster on full-blast before getting out to brush off the car. "How are we doing?" he said as he resumed his seat.

"I am *so* ready to get out of here."

"Me, too," he said, putting the car in gear and starting forward.

"Somebody's coming," Cam said.

Harry stopped the car and looked to the right. Headlight beams, yellow against the new fallen snow, were approaching from the direction of the house.

"It's *him*," she exclaimed as the large SUV passed by their location.

"Are you sure?"

"I will never forget that face."

"You think he saw us?"

"I don't think so. He was looking straight ahead."

Chapter 40

HARRY PULLED OUT ONTO Strongs Road, turning right to go north. He turned on the headlights as they passed the burning house and simultaneously pressed down hard on the accelerator. "Jacoby must have parked up in there," he said, pointing to the road that led back to the camp that was closed for the season.

"Why did he wait so long to leave?"

"My guess is he watched the house burn for a while to be sure he'd done a good job destroying the evidence. But it wasn't really that long; it's not even seven o'clock yet."

"Boy, it seemed like we were in there for hours."

"I know. I didn't think we'd ever get that shelf thing to move. I suppose, if we knew what we were doing we could have walked right out."

"Yeah, if it was Greg's escape route, you'd think he'd want to be able to get out of there in a hurry. But, we made it, and that's the important thing. I'm just surprised it wasn't smokier."

"Well, the fire was above us, and we were in the air path," Harry said, turning into the driveway of the house on the corner of Strongs and M-28.

"Why are we stopping here?"

"Because I think Jacoby will be coming by any minute," he said, shutting off the lights.

"But he was going the other way."

"I know, but one twenty-three is two-lanes all the way to St. Ignace. My guess is he'll come back up this way so he can catch I-75. As far as he knows, we're dead, so he doesn't have to be in a hurry. He probably wanted to get one last look at his handiwork. But we're not dead, and the way we went is shorter."

"You can't possibly want to tangle with—oh-my-goodness, there he goes."

Harry switched on the lights, backed out of the driveway and drove to the stop sign, turning right on M-28. He kept several hundred feet back from the SUV as they followed it east, toward the Soo.

Cam plugged the memory stick into her laptop and waited a moment for the computer to recognize it. "Here we go," she said as a box opened on the screen.

"What's on it?"

"More pictures. Just a second," she said, moving her finger over the touch-pad. "First one is of a building under construction—no time stamp, though."

"We can probably get that from the properties," Harry replied.

"Yeah. Next one is of Scott Jacoby digging a hole with some kind of machine." She turned the screen toward Harry and he quickly glanced at it. "It's a backhoe."

She turned the unit back and moved her finger on the touch-pad again. *"Holy..."*

"What is it?"

"He's putting a woman's body in the hole."

Harry glanced quickly at the picture before turning his eyes back on the road. "It's probably his wife. She went missing a few months before Greg did."

"Oh, I remember that."

"Are there more pictures?"

"Uh, yeah, hold on a sec."

She manipulated the touch pad some more. "There's three more; in one he's filling in the hole with that back...thing, then he's driving over it, and the last one is of him walking away."

"Well, now we know what this whole thing was about...Humph, your mom's friend, Gary Hammond, said those two guys were ruthless, and—"

"He was right," Cam said shutting down her computer.

They passed the blinker for the Brimley cutoff and continued on, following the SUV onto the northbound ramp of I-75.

"I thought sure he would go south and head for the Mackinaw Bridge," she said.

"He's been up here most of the week. He's probably checked in at some hotel. We'll just hang back here and let him lead the way."

"I kind of wish he'd gone south. I really don't want to meet up with him again."

"It's all right to be afraid, Cam, but you can't let it rule your life. Don't worry, though, you're not going to have to get any where near him."

"Thanks, Harry, and thanks for offering yourself in my place back there. I know what Mom sees in you."

They exited I-75 onto the business spur and followed Jacoby until he turned into the parking lot of the Viceroy hotel. Harry continued on slowly past the hotel and pulled into the parking lot of the restaurant next door, maneuvering the car around the building and back out onto the spur. He drove to the hotel and parked several spaces away from the SUV.

Cam took a breath and blew it out as she unbuckled her seatbelt. "I'm coming with you."

"Thanks, Cam," Harry said. "Stay behind me, though, at least until we make sure he's not in the lobby."

They walked under the canopy and paused at the glass doors while Harry scanned what he could see of the lobby. Continuing through the door, he stopped again for a better look and then turned to Cam. "I want you to go up to the desk and ask for Scott Jacoby's room number. Be happy, be nonchalant, act like his girlfriend, whatever; just don't let on why we're here."

As she walked away, Harry found an upholstered chair near a fireplace on the other side of the room and sat in it. He massaged his right leg, above the knee, with his fingertips—trying to ease the pain, which had increased significantly since they left the house.

"It's seven-sixteen," Cam said, startling him as she plopped into the seat beside him.

"Seven-sixteen, okay. Now, I'm going up there, and I want you—"

"*No,* Harry, let's just—"

"It's okay, I'm not going to knock on the door or anything. I just want to make sure he doesn't leave before you can get the police over here. You have your cell phone on you?"

She nodded.

"Okay. I'm going up there. You call 9-1-1 and tell them you need the police at the Viceroy hotel, room seven-sixteen—that there is a man in there that has murdered two people. Give them whatever other information they ask for and wait for the police to arrive. But hang back over here so Jacoby won't see you, if he makes a run for it."

She nodded, reaching into her pocket for her phone as Harry started for the elevator.

He pressed the button to go up and stepped in when the doors opened, pressing the button for the seventh floor. Finding himself alone, he unzipped his jacket and removed his pistol from its holster. He pulled the slide back to chamber a round and cock it, making sure the safety was on before placing it back in the holster.

The doors slid open and he stepped out, scanning the corridor in both directions. There was no one around. The even-numbered rooms were on the side opposite the elevator doors and the numbering indicated that seven-sixteen was to the right. Harry turned right, walking slowly until he came to the room. He approached the door carefully and ducked under the peep-sight. The hinges were on the left-hand side of the door so he flattened himself, back first, against the wall to the right of the door, removing his pistol from its holster and slipping it off safety with his forefinger. Listening carefully, he lowered the pistol and laid it gently against the side of his leg.

The toilet flushed. Then he heard water running in the sink. An unidentifiable sound, then the bathroom door hitting against the stop. The sound of drawers opening and closing. Then a snap...another snap. Footsteps. Harry took two steps back and raised his pistol.

Jacoby pulled the door open, catching the knob on the corridor side and holding it with his left hand as he stepped around the door, turning to pull it closed, his suitcase in his right hand.

"You make one false move and I'll kill you where you stand," Harry said calmly.

Jacoby jumped, dropping his suitcase. "B-*Brannan?*"

"Yeah, surprise, Put your hands behind your head and interlace your fingers...slowly."

Jacoby complied, slowly raising his arms.

"Now back in the room...slowly—or I'll put a hole in you big enough for a cat to jump through."

Jacoby side-stepped into the room, holding the door open with his back. When he cleared the door he turned to walk forward and Harry caught the door with his left shoulder.

"That's far enough. Now stop and do not move a muscle," Harry said, sliding the suitcase into the door path and letting the door go closed against it. He stepped from the entry foyer into the room.

"What are you going to do?" Jacoby said, fear dripping off his voice.

"Keep your mouth shut. Now, turn toward me and get down on your face on the floor."

Jacoby was standing in front of the bureau as he began to slowly turn counter-clockwise, lowering his hands.

The ice bucket flew from the top of the bureau, bouncing off the opposite wall as he charged toward Harry with his head down.

Harry side-stepped and quarter-turned, knocking him hard on the back of the head with the butt of his pistol.

Jacoby collapsed, facedown on the floor, his hands immediately flying to spot where he's been hit. "My head, my head—"

"Shut-up and Spread eagle," Harry commanded.

"My *head.*"

"Yeah, yeah, you're wasting the springtime of your youth repeating that. Now, shut-up and spread eagle. Or would you like some more?"

Slowly he complied, spreading his legs apart and stretching his arms out in front of him.

Harry heard the sirens first. He waited for what seemed like a long time after they stopped until he heard the sound of footsteps in the corridor and the police arriving at the door. "Come in," he said. "My name is Harry Brannan. I'm a retired police officer. I have a weapon—"

"Harry, is that you?" came a woman's voice.

"Pat? Pat Kavanaugh?"

"It's me, Harry."

"Do you have your weapon drawn?"

"We do," came back a man's voice.

"I'm going to safety my pistol and throw it on the bed," he said, throwing the gun on the bed. "I have my hands up and in plain sight."

The door eased open, and when the deputies saw Harry with his hands in the air they came in. "What's going on here, Harry?" Pat said.

He put his hands down. "This is the man who really murdered Wayne McCarthy, a.k.a. Greg Forrester. He also murdered his wife about five years ago, and he just burned down a house in the village of Strongs, out near the county line."

The male deputy removed the handcuffs from his belt and looked at Pat. Receiving a nod, he began to put the cuffs on Jacoby.

"Pat, May I pick up my weapon?"

"I'm assuming you're licensed to carry it."

"I am."

"Go ahead."

Harry retrieved his pistol from the bed and holstered it. "I have a lot of evidence against this guy and I'd like to accompany you to the station."

"Oh, we wouldn't have it any other way, Harry," Pat said.

Chapter 41

The next day

CAM WATCHED THROUGH the windshield as someone unlocked the doors to the courthouse and went back inside. She continued to wait in Harry's car until she saw Don Ripley arrive some minutes later. *He's a nice man,* she thought as she exited and ran to catch up with him.

Don led her to the proper room and showed her where to sit before going off to meet with her mother. She yawned as she took her seat. What a night it had been: *That Mr. Bostwick was not happy to be called to the sheriff's department from home, but he calmed down some when he saw the evidence Harry and I got. And that Stark guy—whew. He took it as a personal affront that we had been at the scene and found the evidence he missed. Boy, his face got red when Harry told him we had the permission of the owner of the property to be there, and I thought he'd burst a blood vessel when Bostwick told him to be quiet and go out there and impound those game cameras. Well, he's a bona-fide jerk so he probably deserved it.*

That Don—the way he talks, he should have been a senator or something. I'll bet he was a force to be reckoned with when he was younger. I absolutely loved it when he insisted, in his senatorial voice, that mom's case be first on the docket today. And what a great idea to check on whether Greg had a bank account and whether there was insurance on the house.

I wish Harry were here. He worked so hard for this. Come to think of it, though, his face looked a little pasty even last night. Oh, here she comes.

Don took his seat at the defense table as Marti entered the courtroom from the front, accompanied by a female deputy. She wasn't handcuffed and she was wearing black jeans and a green sweater. She smiled radiantly when she saw Cam standing behind the table and, limping quickly to where she waited, threw her arms around her as they stood on opposite sides of the half dividing wall.

"Oh, *sweetie,* I never *dreamed* you'd be here. It's *so* good to see you."

Cam blinked back tears. "Oh, Mom, I love you so much. I just couldn't stay away."

"Oh, honey, I love you. Don't cry, or you'll get me started," she said, wiping Cam's tears with her fingertips. "Ummm," she said, pulling Cam tight again and cuddling her face next to hers.

Suddenly she let Cam go and looked around. "Where's Harry?"

"All rise!...The 91st District Court of Chippewa County, Michigan is now in session; the honorable Jefferson Rhodes presiding."

The judge stepped up onto the dais. "Be seated," he said taking his own seat.

Marti quickly turned and took her seat next to Don.

The judge perused something on his desk. "Regarding R-0-9-5-6-2-8-F-Y, the people versus Forrester, I understand, Mr. Bostwick, that the prosecutor's office has dropped the charges.

Bostwick stood. "That's correct, your honor. If it please the court, the prosecutor's office has obtained new evidence that completely exonerates Ms. Forrester. Therefore, the charges against her have been dropped and we join with the defense in requesting her release."

"So ordered," the judge said, banging his gavel. "Ms. Forrester, you are free to go with the apologies of the court."

Marti stood. "Thank you, your honor."

"Next case," the judge said.

Marti hugged Don. "Thank you. I hope I never need a lawyer again, but if I do you'd be my first choice."

Don smiled and led her around the half wall, giving her into her daughter's arms as he made his way toward the back of the room and out the door.

"Oh, Mom, it's so good to have you back."

"It's so good to *be* back, honey, but where's Harry?"

"Come on, I'll take you to him," she said, leading her mother out of the courtroom.

They walked out of the building and got into Harry's car. Cam started it and backed out of her parking spot. "I guess he injured his knee a few days ago, and having to crawl through a concrete tunnel last night didn't help it. Anyway, he was in a lot of pain and couldn't bend it, this morning so I took him to the hospital."

"*Ohhh,*" Marti groaned. "He hurt it Tuesday night when we were trying to get away from Scott...*Yuck.*"

"What?"

"Oh Scott called me up a couple of weeks ago and asked me out to dinner, and I went. And he kissed me—it was on the cheek, but he kissed me. Yuck!"

"Oh, *yuuck!*"

"Oh-my-goodness, we talked about Greg. That's how he knew he was alive."

"Do you think?"

"I don't know, but it makes sense," Marti said as they turned into the hospital parking lot.

The two women walked into the hospital emergency entrance and headed across the waiting room for the registration desk.

"Marti," Harry said, using crutches to pull himself up out of a chair.

She walked to him. "*Ohh,* Harry, is it bad?"

"They injected steroids around my knee. I have to stay off from it, for the time being, and see my own doctor when we get home."

"Let's get you out of here," she said, reaching out for him.

"Just a minute," he said, putting his arms around her. "It's so good to have you back."

One of his crutches fell and Cam picked it up. "Come on, Harry, there's plenty of time for that later. Let's get out of here."

When they arrived at the hotel, Cam checked on possible flight connections, then rushed to her room to collect her belongings and check out, hoping to make a noon flight home, via Minneapolis. After tears, hugs and kisses, Harry and Marti went to their room to collect their belongings.

Harry sat on the end of the bed and Marti walked over to him, putting her hands on his shoulders. "Harry, are you okay? You've been kind of reticent since we picked you up and I...well—"

"We need to talk," he said softly.

"Are we all right?"

"Well, things just kind of suddenly happened between us and I feel like I haven't been totally honest with you."

"Is there someone else?"

"Oh, no, Marti, there could never be anyone else. But having to go to the hospital, this morning, was kind of a reality check for me." He reached down and pulled up his right trouser leg. "I want you to look at this," he said, waiting while she looked at his knee. "Pretty ugly, huh? I have an artificial knee. It's one of the outcomes I got from being shot. It keeps me awake sometimes and gives me trouble, especially when I bump hard it or when I've been on it a long time. That's one reason why I can't work and that's why I was in the hospital today."

"And you think I won't want you because of that?"

"Well, I think you have the right to know. Actually, you had the right to know before you said that you loved me."

She knelt down, carefully placing her hands on either side of his knee as she gently kissed the scar. "I can see that it's swollen, and I'm so sorry that it hurts you, Harry, but it looks a lot better today than it did right after the surgery."

"What?"

"I'm sorry, Darling...but I haven't been totally honest with you, either. I visited you when you were in the hospital. Actually, I'd been praying for you because Mitch had asked all of us to pray. And on the day you had your surgery, I came to the hospital with Liz to sit with Mitch while they were operating on you. I know you were out of it so you didn't know I was there, but I was. And I prayed for you, every day, for over a year.

Harry's eyes had a strange look and he was shaking his head in small movements.

"Listen, Harry, that first night, when you came to my house and I cried because of Jenny, you held me in your arms, and I let you because something was there—I knew you, I felt a bond with you. And she wouldn't admit it, but I know you called Liz and asked her to come over and comfort me. I knew then what kind of a man you are. And then, last Saturday, when you came to me in jail, I tried to apologize for hurting you, but you just acted like nothing ever happened. And you held me and kissed my forehead, and I could feel it all the way down to my feet. And you paid my bond, and Tuesday, when I broke through the ice, you gave me your shirt and coat and put my needs ahead of your own. And I realized that's what you've been doing all along. So I know everything I need to know about you, Harry. I'm not in love with your knee...or with your shoulder. I'm in love with *you*—with the man that lives inside."

"Come up here," Harry said.

Marti half stood as his arms went around her. "I love you," he said, pulling her toward him.

They fell back onto the bed as her arms went around him and their lips met in a long and passionate kiss.

"Ummm," she said as their kiss broke. "I don't think I'm ever going to get tired of that...so you just better get used to it, Henry Allen Brannan, 'cause I'm planning to love you for the rest of my life."

"Ummm," he said, pulling her close. "And I'm planning to love you right back."

"Let's go home."

Epilogue

Christmas Eve

MARTI PULLED INTO THE driveway and stopped, turning off the engine. She slid the strap of her purse onto her forearm and slipped her hand through the handles of the two plastic bags of groceries and started for the house, holding her coat closed against the wind and blowing snow.

Cam heard her mother drive in and held the storm door open as she stepped up onto the stoop, placing her finger up to her lips as Marti side-stepped past her into the house.

"What's going on?" Marti whispered.

Cam put her mouth near her mother's ear. "Callie took her favorite book to Harry. She's sitting on his lap and he's reading it to her."

Marti took off her coat and hung it over the back of a chair as both women stole quietly to the entrance of the living room. They could see the back of Harry's head and Callie, sitting on his lap, engrossed in the story:

"...the prince knelt down and kissed her on the lips and the princess awoke. He took her by the hand and she arose, and they rode away together on his white horse. The end."

"And they lived happily ever after," Callie said.

"I think they did," Harry replied.

"I liked that story."

"I did, too, Callie."

"Daddy says I'm his princess."

"Well you *are* a princess. Does he come and kiss you and wake you up in the morning."

"Sometimes," she said, nodding her head. "But most of time he kisses Mommy."

"Well, Mommy's a princess, too."

"And Grandma's a princess, too."

"Well, I think Grandma's a queen."

"*Nooo*," she scolded, shaking her head. "The queen is wicked."

"Ohhh, that's right. I forgot," Harry said, suitably chastised. "Grandma's not wicked, so Grandma must be a princess, too."

"That's what I said."

"That *is* what you said, isn't it, and you were right. Grandma's a beautiful princess."

She raised her eyebrows and tilted her head down, taking him into her confidence. "Daddy kisses Mommy *all* the *time*."

Harry smiled big. "Well, honey, Daddy loves Mommy. See, when a man and woman love each other, they like to kiss. It's kind of like saying, 'I love you' without using words. Then they get married so they can kiss all the time."

"Is that why you kiss Grandma?"

"That's the reason why—because I love your grandma very much."

"Are you going to be my grandpa?"

He pulled her close and cuddled his face next to hers. "Oh, Sweetie, I would love to be your grandpa."

"Are you going to get married to my grandma?"

"I would love to get married to your grandma."

"When?"

"Yeah, when?" Marti chimed in, walking into the room.

"Yeah, when?" Cam chimed in, putting her arm around her mother's shoulders.

"Yeah, when?" Callie chimed in, jumping off his lap and running over to stand next to her mother."

Harry stood and turned, facing the women. "I think I detect collusion going on in this room."

"Hey, we girls have to stick together, you know," Cam said, laying her hand on Callie's shoulder.

Harry put his hand into his pocket and smiled. "Well, I was going to save this until tomorrow," he said. "But..." He approached Marti as he removed his hand from his pocket and Cam backed away, taking Callie with her.

Harry opened the box, revealing the ring, and held it out to her. "Martha Celeste Stafford, You are wonderful and I love you with all my heart. I can't even imagine trying to live a life without you. So, if you will have me, I would consider it the highest of honors if you would be my princess—my wife."

Marti's was smiling as she lifted the ring from the box. She nodded her head and Harry took the ring from her, placing it on the third finger of her trembling left hand. "Yes," she said, flinging herself into his arms. "Yes, yes, yes. And I will make you happy, Harry."

"You already make me happy—just being who you are. I love you, Marti."

"Oh, Harry...I love you."

About the Author

Andy Van Loenen, after a career in technology, now devotes his time to writing. To date, he has authored three books and numerous articles. A Christian for over thirty years, Andy has a keen interest in Biblical doctrine and has written broadly on the subject—as evidenced in his non-fiction book, *What in the World is God up To?*

Andy loves to hear from readers and can be contacted via his web site, www.andyvl.com.

O Love That Wilt Not Let Me Go

George Matheson 1842 – 1906

O Love that wilt not let me go,
I rest my weary soul in thee;
I give thee back the life I owe,
that in thine ocean depths its flow,
may richer, fuller be.

O Light that followest all my way,
I yield my flickering torch to thee;
my heart restores its borrowed ray,
that in thy sunshine's blaze its day,
may brighter, fairer be.

O Joy that seekest me through pain,
I cannot close my heart to thee;
I trace the rainbow thru the rain,
and feel the promise is not vain,
that morn shall tearless be.

O Cross that liftest up my head,
I dare not ask to fly from thee;
I lay in dust life's glory dead,
and from the ground there blossoms red,
life that shall endless be.